"Great clothes, great mystery, great fun!"
—*New York Times* bestselling author
Jennifer Crusie

**Praise for Nancy Martin's**
***How to Murder a Millionaire***

"A Main Line Philadelphia backdrop, a self-deprecatingly funny former debutante, and a cast of wonderfully quirky characters combine for a thoroughly entertaining mystery that also provides some red-hot sexual tension between the heroine and her tough-guy protector. Can't wait for the next installment in this smart and sophisticated new series."
—Jane Heller, bestselling author of
*The Secret Ingredient*

"Nancy Martin has a rich, engaging, and funny hit in *How to Murder a Millionaire*. With a scandalous mystery, hot romance, and the delightful to-the-manor-born Blackbird sisters, Martin also treats us to a rare peek into Philadelphia's exclusive high society where all is not Grace Kelly. It's a book to curl up with and savor. You won't want it to end!"
—Sarah Strohmeyer, author of *Bubbles in Trouble*

"Sing a song of suspense, a pocket full of wry, Nora's funny Blackbirds make you laugh until you die."
—Mary Daheim, author of *The Alpine Obituary*

"Martin has a way with quirky characters and this first in the Blackbird Sisters series promises treats for readers." —*Amarillo Globe-News*

*continued . . .*

"If you're not hooked by the end of the third paragraph of the first mystery by this well-known romance writer from Pittsburgh, you have neither a sense of whimsy nor humor. . . . And if you're not smiling when you finish the book, you are no true fan of cozies. . . . What scandal for high society, but what fun watching Nora figure it out."

—*Pittsburgh Post-Gazette*

"Fans of cozy mysteries will be excited to discover Nancy Martin's new Blackbird Sisters series. *How to Murder a Millionaire* is an intriguing tale with a mystery that's far from predictable. This lively story is fast paced, with dynamic characters, a vibrant setting, and just enough romance to leave you wanting more." —*Romantic Times* (Top Pick, 4½ Stars)

"Murder with Style: My definition of escapism is 'well-dressed, well-spoken people misbehaving.' Throw in a fast-paced whodunit, and you have a perfect page-turner, *How to Murder a Millionaire* by Nancy Martin. The Highland Park romance writer has turned her talents to creating a Philadelphia former debutante who dresses in Grandmama's couture classics to cover Society events and uncover a Society murder while dealing with her parents' delinquent tax bill, her eccentric sisters, and an Italian stallion who is as gallant as he is studly. Grab your cozy slippers and another hot chocolate." —*Pittsburgh Magazine*

"Welcome the Blackbird sisters, Philadelphia aristocracy, born to money, now widowed and strapped. . . . *How to Murder a Millionaire* is clever, good-humored, and sharply observed. It ain't Edith Wharton, but it works." —*The Philadelphia Inquirer*

Previous Books in the
Blackbird Sisters Mystery Series
by Nancy Martin

HOW TO MURDER A MILLIONAIRE

# Dead Girls Don't Wear Diamonds

A BLACKBIRD SISTERS MYSTERY

*Nancy Martin*

SIGNET
Published by New American Library, a division of
Penguin Group (USA) Inc., 375 Hudson Street,
New York, New York 10014, U.S.A.
Penguin Books Ltd, 80 Strand,
London WC2R 0RL, England
Penguin Books Australia Ltd, 250 Camberwell Road,
Camberwell, Victoria 3124, Australia
Penguin Books Canada Ltd, 10 Alcorn Avenue,
Toronto, Ontario, Canada M4V 3B2
Penguin Books (N.Z.) Ltd, Cnr Rosedale and Airborne Roads,
Albany, Auckland 1310, New Zealand

Penguin Books Ltd, Registered Offices:
80 Strand, London WC2R 0RL, England

Published by Signet, an imprint of New American Library,
a division of Penguin Group (USA) Inc.

First Printing, July 2003
10 9 8 7 6 5 4



Printed in the United States of America



PUBLISHER'S NOTE
This is a work of fiction. Names, characters, places, and incidents either are the product of the author's imagination or are used fictitiously, and any resemblance to actual persons, living or dead, business establishments, events, or locales is entirely coincidental.

*This book is dedicated to my daughter Sarah Martin.*
*I love you very much.*

**Grateful thanks**

To Mary Alice Gorman and Richard Goldman, proprietors of Mystery Lovers Bookshop in Oakmont, PA, and at www.mysterylovers.com.

Many thanks also to Rosemary Stevens for contributing the Double C, to Becky Mertz and Ramona Long for timely reads, and to Jack Hillman for weaponry advice. Of course, undying thanks to Meg Ruley, whom I'm very lucky to have in my corner. Jeff Martin and Cassie Martin have my love and appreciation for their patience and good humor.

# Chapter 1

In the final weeks of her pregnancy, my sister Libby inexplicably took to wearing an enormous tie-dyed shirt that magnified her belly with a nauseating swirl of pink and green that seemed to depict a pair of lovesick whales.

When she waddled into my kitchen at Blackbird Farm one crisp afternoon in October, I said, "Paint a peace sign on your stomach, and you'd pass for the Partridge family bus."

"How about if I just give you half a peace sign?" she asked, plunking a plastic bag from The Home Depot on my kitchen counter and making a beeline for the pantry. She returned with the box of assorted Godivas I'd been saving for a crisis. "When we're pregnant, the Blackbird women all get as big as Guernsey cows. Is there any danger of that, by the way? Does the gangster have you hanging on to the headboard for dear life yet?"

"Not that it's any of your business," I said. "But no."

"Darn. I don't even get vicarious sex anymore."

She sat down at the kitchen table and tore the gold cord off the candy box, and I opened her plastic bag to see what she'd brought. Over my shoulder, I said, "And Michael is not a gangster."

She put both her Birkenstocks on an adjacent chair.

"I thought the two of you had broken up. Now I see he's back—and with reinforcements, no less. What are all those men doing out at the barn?"

"Working on an idea."

That got her attention, and she looked up from the Godiva box with wide eyes. "Dear heaven," she said. "What is it this time? Another tattoo parlor? A motorcycle shop? Or maybe something classy like a strip joint?"

"He doesn't run any strip joints. He thinks there's a way for Blackbird Farm to make some income by growing grass."

Libby looked shocked. "Oh, Nora!"

"Not marijuana! Lawn grass, for heaven's sake! God knows I could use the money."

I was still scraping every penny to pay the bill left to me by our tax-evading parents, who were currently avoiding extradition while traipsing around Brazil in search of the ultimate piña colada. Meanwhile, I struggled to keep the ancestral homestead out of the hands of land developers eager to turn two hundred years of family history into an outlet mall.

But of course Libby didn't want to discuss anything as mundane as financial matters. My dear sister could easily be mistaken for a complete ninny, if she didn't love her family to excess and prove it by way of an occasional selfless act and frequent butting into business other than her own. She frowned prettily over the selection of chocolate truffles. "Well, I was much happier when you weren't seeing Sonny Corleone."

"I'm not 'seeing' him," I said, which was true for the most part, since Michael Abruzzo and I had agreed to disagree over the summer and he'd just turned up again last week to propose his latest business venture.

"Your association with him is doing damage to our family reputation."

I laughed out loud. "First our parents blew our inheritance and fled the country to avoid paying their taxes. Now we've learned they stole money from their best friends to make their escape in style. How much worse can our reputation get?"

"Well, you know what I mean," Libby said, unapologetic. "At least they're not connected to organized crime."

"What will it take to terminate this discussion right now? And why are you bringing me plaster of paris?"

She popped a truffle into her mouth. "I need your help."

I watched my sister lean back, close her eyes and savor the chocolate with bliss. Okay, maybe she deserved a break. Libby had buried her second husband just a few months earlier. But true to form, Libby managed to put all that unpleasantness out of her mind—at least, that's the appearance she worked at keeping up—and seemed to be enjoying her pregnancy even if the father of the baby had been shot dead at a high-society wedding. Of course, some of us secretly suspected that Ralph's death was the result of his own suicide mission after he learned he was going to be a father to one of Libby's demonic offspring.

So it was with the foreknowledge that my sister might require some service I was going to find highly unpleasant that I asked uneasily, "What kind of help do you need?"

"I want to do a belly cast."

"A what?"

"We're going to take the plaster and make a cast of my stomach."

We both looked at her stomach, and I said, "I don't think you brought enough plaster."

"Nonsense. It'll be a work of art. Or I can use it as a fruit bowl."

Her sixteen-year-old son, Rawlins, chose that moment to come out of the downstairs powder room. He'd been using the mirror to examine his new nose ring, which nearly got lost among the eyebrow studs, lip post and the multiple hoops in both his large ears. He slouched into the kitchen chair farthest from his mother and proceeded to sulk on general principal.

I said, "Rawlins, would you like some hot chocolate? I'm going to make some for your mother in the hope that it will bring her back to sanity."

"May the Force be with you," he said.

"Rawlins," Libby said, "tell your aunt Nora what you're doing in school these days."

Rawlins didn't answer. He picked at the tablecloth.

"What's going on in school?" I asked. "Are you playing basketball this year?"

"Nu-huh," he mumbled, and began to gnaw at his thumbnail.

Libby gave me a helpless look. Libby liked the idea of having lots of children, but she didn't cope terribly well with the houseful she already had. Her baby would make five children by at least three different fathers, who were either dead or missing in action. Like all Blackbird women, she had bad luck with husbands.

She said to me, "Do you have a plastic bucket?"

"Under the sink."

"Great. I'll mix the plaster."

She began rummaging under the sink while I got a quart of milk from the refrigerator and some cocoa from the pantry. Then we heard a truck in the loop of driveway behind the house, and an instant later the door slammed. Our younger sister, Emma, strode into the kitchen in boots and riding breeches. The three of us were tall with auburn hair and very pale skin, but Emma looked like Barbarella with a punk haircut.

She said, "I love the smell of testosterone in the morning!"

"Go wipe your feet," I said automatically. "You've been riding horses."

"No, I haven't," she said, and plunked a large, filthy puppy on the counter. "There. I brought you a present."

"This is a joke, right?"

It was either a very large puppy or a young water buffalo. It had matted black hair and slightly crossed blue eyes, a blunt Newfoundland's nose and white toes on his enormous front paws. Emma pinned the squirming beast firmly on the counter. "You need a dog, Nora. You shouldn't be living out here all alone."

"I don't want a dog. I don't need a dog. I certainly don't want a dog on my kitchen counter!"

"Try him out. You'll get to like him."

"It's not a question of liking," I said, trying to keep the hysteria out of my voice. "I'm too busy to take care of a dog properly. Take him back where you got him."

"Look at this face!"

I looked at the puppy's face. I'll admit he was cute. He had floppy ears that reminded me of my mother's cousin Cuss. But I didn't need a dog to make myself feel safe. Certainly not one that looked like he might grow into a marauding grizzly that overturned garbage cans and minivans for sport. I said, "Take him out of here immediately."

With a sigh Emma handed the puppy to Rawlins

and plucked a pickle from the array of sandwich ingredients I had spread out on the counter. I guessed she'd given up smoking again. "Why are all those men out in the barn? Is Mick planning some sort of assault on your virtue with those troops?"

"We were just discussing that," said Libby, pouring white powder into the bucket of water. "Rawlins, dear, wouldn't you like to go play with the puppy outside?"

"No," he said, tussling with the delighted dog. "I'm old enough to hear about Aunt Nora's sex life."

"I have no sex life," I assured him.

Emma looked into Libby's bucket. "What are you doing?"

"You're going to help me make a belly cast. Where have you been this morning?"

Emma pulled a beer from the refrigerator despite the clock clearly stating the time was not quite noon. "Shopping."

"In those clothes?"

"For horses," she said, twisting off the cap with a practiced yank. She always managed to look stunning, even with a smear of mud across one of her perfect cheekbones. Emma wore dirt with as much aplomb as an eighteenth-century French courtesan displayed her beauty spots, and men fell at her feet even when she had manure on her boots. She said, "I've decided to go into the training business for myself. I bought a jumper this morning. Can I rent some space in your barn?"

"You'll have to get in line," said Libby, already elbow deep in plaster. "She's letting Mr. Abruzzo do something out there."

"Yeah, I know all about that." Emma dug into her pocket and came up with a grubby business card.

She tossed it onto the counter. "Look what I found down at the gas station yesterday."

She drank her beer while Libby leaned over and peered at the card.

"Oh, my God," said Libby. She read aloud, "The Marquis de Sod."

"You're going into the sod business?" Emma asked me.

I snatched the card off the counter and read it for myself. "He said he was only going to grow grass!"

"And sell it to rich people who want instant lawns."

"That man!" Libby said. "He has no sense of propriety, no sense of—of—"

"It's not a bad idea, if you ask me. But that name, Nora," Emma said, cocking an eyebrow at me, "isn't exactly your style."

"Catchy, though," Libby admitted before going back to the plaster.

I threw the card onto the table. "I'm not a part of that business. It's his idea. He's just leasing fields from me!"

"Well, everybody is town assumes you're partners."

"We're not!"

Emma's grin broadened. "Everybody thinks you own the used-car lot, too."

Libby moaned. "A Blackbird reduced to selling old cars!"

I'd found myself entangled with Michael "The Mick" Abruzzo for a short while about five months earlier, when he and Rory Pendergast conspired to buy some of Blackbird Farm to start one of Michael's dubious businesses. Despite his building Mick's Muscle Cars just a stone's throw from my front porch, we'd hit it off, if I could put it so mildly, except on the subject of his wheeling and dealing. Not to mention the shadier aspects of his life, which I admit I found both frightening and annoyingly magnetic.

Safe to say I didn't care for the various ways he made his living. Michael argued that I was being unnecessarily righteous about finances when I really should have been searching for every possible source of income to hang on to my admittedly ramshackle inheritance. If I wanted to keep Blackbird Farm, he said, I ought to be ready to make sacrifices. My job as a society columnist for the *Philadelphia Intelligencer* barely paid me enough to live on, let alone help with my tax problem. But most of Michael's ideas seemed to involve the sacrifice of too much dignity for me.

This grass-growing venture was business as usual for Michael. He didn't care if he looked ridiculous as long as he made money. Except he wanted to use Blackbird Farm to make it happen.

The Marquis de Sod, indeed.

The man in question appeared at the kitchen door just then. He was six-foot-four with a well-used face and incendiary blue eyes, not to mention the kind of shoulders most women dream about clawing during the throes of passion. "Lunch ready yet?"

I picked up a knife and sent him a look.

"What?" he asked. "What did I do?"

"We'll talk later," I vowed. "Lunch will be ready in fifteen minutes."

"She's a terrible cook, you know," Libby volunteered, laboring over the bucket. "Usually she eats only food that microwaves in plastic."

"Careful," I said. "I'll find another use for that plaster."

Michael grinned at my other sister. "Hey, Emma."

"Hey, yourself, Mick," she said back, and they

shared a look that communicated something amusing in the secret language Emma had with men.

"That your dog?"

"I tried to give him to Nora, but she's stubborn. You want him?"

He laughed. He'd been the first to bring a puppy around for me, and I assumed he was still trying to find a home for the gangling Great Dane he'd procured somewhere in New Jersey. "No, thanks," he said.

"You gonna take me for a ride on your motorcycle later?"

"Nope," he said. "You're too scary for me."

"Nora scared you off, too, I notice, but that didn't last."

"Not for long," he agreed, and turned his grin back on me. I felt as if he'd trained the guidance system of a nuclear missile in my direction.

It surprised me that any man would pass up Emma, who oozed willing sex appeal from every pore, in favor of anyone else. She was thinner, bolder, and more available than I would ever be. I'd been widowed two years ago, and I still hadn't found a way to understand what had happened to my life, let alone trust any member of the male persuasion. But Michael had made his choice, and from the look of things, it was going to be very difficult to steer him off course.

The wobbly sensation in my knees every time I got close to him was pretty hard to ignore, too.

He said, "We need somebody to sit behind the wheel of the tractor while we tinker with the engine. Any takers?"

"Not us," said Emma. "We are about to hear Nora's side of your breakup. Take Rawlins."

"Okay," he said peaceably. Then, to Rawlins, "That hardware in your face help you communicate with aliens or something?"

"No," Rawlins said.

"Can you drive?"

"Yes."

Michael jerked his head towards the barn. "Then hustle."

To his mother's amazement, Rawlins obeyed with alacrity, hitching up his loose jeans and trailing Michael out of the house at a trot, puppy in his arms.

"Okay," said Emma when the three of us were alone. "Tell us everything."

"There's nothing to tell," I said, going back to stacking kaiser rolls with layers of capicola, provolone and other Italian delights, as instructed.

"They're not sleeping together," Libby reported. "I got that much out of her."

Emma grimaced. "How can you resist, Nora? That man is so hot for you!"

"There are other issues," I replied.

"Yeah," Libby chimed in. "In addition to his very tacky businesses, there's his family. And of course the little matter of his jail record." She held up a handful of wet plaster for me to see. "Think this is ready?"

"It's still lumpy. He was a kid at the time. Younger than Rawlins." I was determined to avoid discussing the complexities of the Abruzzo crime family and my almost rock-solid conviction that Michael had no contact with them. "He grew up differently than we did."

"Uh-huh," said Emma, the youngest and therefore the sister who hadn't been raised during the luxury years. "He knows how to make a buck when he needs it."

Libby sighed and went back to mixing. "Filthy lucre. It's too bad we're poor now, isn't it?"

"Get you," I said, glad to change the subject. "How was Disney World?"

She didn't take offense. "The children were having a hard time getting over Ralph's death. For that matter, so was I. And in another month, I'll have this baby to take care of, so we need to be well rested." Typical for Libby, she avoided further discussion of unpleasant business by throwing up a diversion. She said, "You'll understand when you're a mother. Emma, don't you think it's time Nora had a baby, too?"

I dropped my knife. "Now wait a damn minute—"

Emma said, "Does my opinion count?"

Libby said, "Open that jar of Vaseline while I take off my shirt. Nora, you told me just a few months ago how much you regretted not having children with Todd."

"I said that in a weak moment."

"That's usually when instinct kicks in. Hormones cause a chemical reaction in your brain to come up with the idea just in the knick of time, you know." She began rinsing the plaster from her hands under the tap. "You're not getting any younger. Just think, if you got pregnant soon, we could raise the children together. I could baby-sit while you go to your parties. I think I should do this without the bra, don't you?"

Emma said, "God help the next generation."

"We know you, Nora." Libby dried her hands on a tea towel. "You aren't as calm and reasonable as you pretend. You're just as likely to be impetuous as any of us. I'm only afraid you're going to suddenly make up your mind to have a baby, and Mr. Abruzzo will be too convenient to resist."

Emma muttered, "I can't believe she's resisting at all."

"Well, I'm genuinely worried," Libby concluded, and began wrestling out of her shirt. "Do we really want a union with the Abruzzo family?"

"She can't marry him, if that's what you're blathering about." Emma looked into the extra-large jar of Vaseline and warily sniffed the contents. "She's a Blackbird. If she marries him, he'll die."

It was true. Family legend had it that all Blackbird women married rogues who died young. My sisters and I were just the latest in a long line of Blackbird widows who sent regular flower deliveries to gravesides. And although Libby's late husband Ralph appeared to have contributed to his own demise, there were some opinions that he'd still be alive if he hadn't married a Blackbird.

Emma said to Libby, "I like Mick. I don't want him dead. But if she wants a kid, I think he'd be a good choice."

"Well, he's obviously got sturdy genes," Libby agreed, as if I had suddenly disappeared in a puff of smoke. "And I suppose she could give her children nose jobs for their sixteenth birthdays. But if she needs a father, why not consider somebody else? What about that Jamie Scaithe? Or Hadley Pinkham? They'd make darling babies."

"Can I get a word in edgewise?" I asked.

"Hadley Pinkham is gay," Emma said. "And Jamie lives on cocaine."

Libby finally got her T-shirt off and stood in my kitchen wearing nothing more than an enormous brassiere, a pair of drawstring pants and her Birkenstocks. "Hadley's gay? How astonishing. I'm not good at figuring out that sort of thing. But I'll get better with practice." She peered into the box of chocolates again, letting her last remark float suggestively in the air.

Over her head, Emma and I exchanged glances.

I said, "What do you mean you'll get better with practice?"

"Nothing serious." Libby waved her hand. "Sometimes you need a man, that's all."

"Oh, God. Are you looking for another husband?" Emma demanded.

"I'd rather catch pneumonia than another husband. No, I need a Lamaze coach."

"I told you I'd do it," I said. "I'll be your coach."

Libby shook her head. "A sister isn't right."

"Why not, for crying out loud?"

"It takes a man. I know these things. Can you help me unsnap? I have a lifetime of childbearing knowledge stored up. I know what kind of coach I need." Libby struggled to reach her bra hooks. "I'm determined to do everything right this time. After all, this might be my last child, so—"

"Might be?" Emma repeated.

"—so I want everything to be perfect. The whole family will be there. Well, except for Ralph, of course. And we're videotaping this time. The twins are recording the birth for a class project."

"What class?" Emma demanded. "Who encourages thirteen-year-old boys to videotape their own mother in childbirth?"

"Well, they won't actually see much," Libby went on. "I'll be underwater."

I dropped the wooden spoon.

"Underwater with incense. It's very relaxing. Next week I'm having the incense specially mixed to match my pheromones. And, see? I've already started wearing my magnets and crystals." From inside the depths of her bra, she pulled a packet filled with colorful stones.

"Where," I demanded, "are you getting these crazy ideas?"

"I've been seeing this wonderful duenna. She's not exactly a midwife yet, but she's hoping to get certification soon. She's got a lovely Jacuzzi in her backyard."

"Oh, my God," Emma said.

"What's wrong with a nice, sterile hospital?" I asked. "And lots of drugs? Remember all those drugs you took when you had Lucy?"

"You don't understand," Libby cried. "Giving birth can be a magical experience wherein the mother bonds not just with the newly born, but with her entire family."

I put my hands on her shoulders and turned her around to face me. "Libby, your hormones have made you certifiable. Let me go with you to Lamaze class. You need somebody sensible by your side."

"No, you should experience childbirth for yourself first." Libby took my hands in hers and peered earnestly into my eyes. "Dear Nora. Trust me on this. Besides, I'd feel peculiar with a woman coaching me. I like panting with a man."

The hot chocolate boiled over.

"Now," said Libby, "who's going to smear me with Vaseline?"

"Speaking of unpleasant," said Emma with admirable self-control, "have you heard about Flan Cooper?"

"What about him?"

"You won't believe it." Emma drank another slug of beer.

I began mopping up the puddles on the stove, and

Emma said, "Last night his wife, Laura, drowned herself in the family pool. He had to pull her out himself. She's dead."

All the sisterly squabbling evaporated in an instant, and some force of nature sucked all the air out of the room. I sat down hard on a kitchen chair.

Death has a way of overcoming me. I'm not physically fragile, or even especially squeamish. But terrible emotion can seize my heart and drain all the blood out of my brain. The doctors tell me it's all psychological, and it wouldn't happen anymore if I'd just start seeing a nice, calm therapist. But therapists cost money, which was in short supply for a person living in a two-hundred-year-old farmhouse with a slate roof and plumbing installed in a previous century. So I faint a lot.

"Laura Cooper is dead?" Libby repeated, sounding far away.

"A shocker, huh?" said Emma. "Suicide. I heard she tied one of those concrete garden gnomes to her ankles and jumped into the pool."

Libby said, "Isn't her hubby an old boyfriend of yours, Nora? I can't believe he'd have a gnome in his garden."

I put my head between my knees. "Yes. Flan."

Emma instantly sounded contrite. "Oh, God, I forgot about that. I'm sorry, Nora. You okay?"

The gushing wave of blackness threatened to swirl up and overwhelm me. I couldn't gather my breath.

"Flanders Cooper." Libby's voice sounded about six miles away. "Now, there's a man with good genes."

"Shut up, Lib." Emma ran cold water into a glass and brought it to me. "Nora?"

I sat up unsteadily, accepted the glass and tried to sip. But I couldn't get my throat to function, and I choked on the water. Emma patted my back until I stopped coughing. When I finally managed a swallow, she eased the drinking glass out of my shaking hands.

In a moment, I croaked, "I saw them last night. She was fine. Laura was just fine."

"You were at their house?" Libby asked.

Emma remembered. "They were having a party for Oliver, weren't they? To celebrate his nomination for something or other? Were you there?"

I nodded.

Oliver Cooper was a millionaire several times over, thanks to his long ownership of Cooper Aviation, the aircraft-manufacturing company most famous for the Cooper Wolverine fighter jet. Oliver had been nominated by the president to serve as the next secretary of transportation. His family, pleased and proud, had thrown a party in his honor before the confirmation hearings began. It had been a joyous occasion. The hard-drinking, fun-loving Coopers threw open the doors of their family estate and blasted rock-and-roll music loud enough to make William Penn dance atop city hall in Philadelphia.

Emma sat down beside me. "You talked to Laura?"

"Yes, around nine o'clock. She was—she was—"

"It's okay." Emma hugged me around the shoulders.

Libby shoveled around in her handbag and came up with her handkerchief.

When I could speak again, I said, "She can't possibly have killed herself."

# Chapter 2

Of course, my boss had not been invited to the Cooper bash. And Kitty Keough had chewed hard on her pride when she phoned me about the assignment that afternoon.

"Have you been asked to the Coopers' tonight?" she had barked in my ear with all the charm of an enraged Pekinese.

Rory Pendergast, billionaire industrialist, international philanthropist and owner of the less-than-respectable daily newspaper the *Intelligencer,* had hired me to write for the society column shortly before his death. Bless him, he found me a job despite my complete lack of employment history. I was better suited to hosting social events than writing about them, but I was learning fast, and some of my best lessons had come from Kitty herself, despite her dislike of me. The ironclad contract he created had so far prevented Kitty from getting me fired after my first fumbling attempts at journalism and encroachment on her territory. But I knew Kitty was still looking for a loophole to get me canned.

"Yes, I've been invited." I had endeavored to sound polite even though Kitty still treated me with less respect than she did the panhandler who hung around outside the newspaper office building. "Oliver Cooper's son Flan is an old friend of mine."

"Spare me the details of your teenage romances," she had snapped. "I just want to know if you're going."

"I am. But I've been invited as a friend, not a representative of the press."

"I'm not asking you to snoop in their bedsheets. Just get a couple of good quotes. If the old man gets rejected at his confirmation hearing, we'll need something juicy. See if you can handle that."

She hung up without allowing me to decline. That was Kitty's style. She'd been the poison pen of the *Intelligencer*'s society page for more than a decade, and readers loved her switchblade prose.

I couldn't imitate Kitty's style—not when my friends, the oldest and most distinguished families of Philadelphia, were often the targets of her cruel copy. As I saw it, our job was to cover the activities of the so-called high society as they helped and promoted various charities. But Kitty wrote an old-fashioned gossip column full of innuendo and character assassination. She was very popular with readers.

Some of our colleagues assumed I'd been hired to learn the ropes and replace Kitty when the newspaper's ownership finally managed to ease her into retirement. I believed, however, that Kitty was going to die at her keyboard, blood pressure exploding off the chart as she pounded out one last lambasting column. I toiled in her shadow and tried to keep my friends at the same time. I had bills to pay, after all.

So I had gone to the Cooper party with a notebook and pen in my beaded clutch.

More parties were thrown in Philadelphia from September through November than even Kitty could keep up with. The Coopers were lucky to find a night that wasn't already booked with two benefits and a dozen private cocktail parties, not to mention a noisy political fund-raiser or two. By luck, my calendar was free, so Reed Shakespeare, my driver, took me out to the Cooper estate just as a glorious Indian summer sunset began to blaze in the sky.

"Whoa," said Reed when we hove into view of the house. "You visiting Bill Gates tonight, or what?"

We both stared out the windshield at the new Cooper mansion. When Oliver Cooper divorced his first wife, he gave back her ancestral home on the Main Line and moved his new wife, the former Doe Slansky of Scranton, out into the county where they constructed a replica of the Vanderbilts' Biltmore at astronomical expense, mimicking every detail up to the chimney pots. Except alongside the driveway to the Cooper mansion was, as befitting an aviation king, a private airstrip.

As his four sons finished their MBAs at Wharton and joined the family business, Oliver built nearby homes for each of them in turn, along with more amenities than a luxury resort. The rambling houses were surrounded by pools, tennis and basketball courts, a nine-hole golf course, a stable for the Cooper granddaughters' ponies and lush gardens that Doe reportedly expanded every spring.

I had counted eight private aircraft parked on the grass near the family hangar that evening. One of the planes was a corporate jet with the name of an Atlantic City casino emblazoned on its tail. In addition to big military contracts, Cooper Aviation built custom aircraft for wealthy clients who sometimes stayed at the Cooper compound while perfecting the mechanics of flying their new acquisitions. You never knew who you might bump into if you visited Oliver. Movie stars, professional athletes, even teenybopper boy bands with money to burn all the jet fuel they wanted.

A cluster of security men stopped me on the driveway, asking to see my invitation, and told Reed to take the car about a mile away to a secured location. Obviously, Washington had already made some changes around the Cooper compound.

"Nora!" Oliver Cooper greeted me himself when I'd passed through the security checkpoint. Proud patriarch, he stood in the open doorway of the main house. His voice roared out at me over the thump of rock and roll behind him. "Nora Blackbird, how come you didn't marry one of my sons?"

"Hello, Oliver." I kissed his ruddy cheek and allowed the burly captain of the aviation industry to gather me up in a bone-crushing hug. I gasped, "Congratulations on your nomination."

"Thank you. Thank you." He nuzzled my ear before planting a hearty kiss on my cheek and setting me on my feet. "So nice of you to help me celebrate!"

He looked me up and down with the womanizing gleam that never seemed to leave his gaze. He was dressed casually in khaki trousers and a well-worn leather aviator's jacket, clearly a favorite item from his closet brought out to celebrate his latest career success. It suited his image—still the rough-and-ready pilot despite his stratospheric position in the corporate world.

I smiled, but stepped back to a safe distance. "How does it feel to be the next secretary of transportation?"

"I'm officially honored and humbled, if you're asking as a member of the press," he said with a laugh. "But if it's just you, Nora, I'm also pleased as punch. There's no guarantee I'll make it through the confirmation process, of course, but I'm going to give those bastards in Congress a piece of my mind if they start hinting I'm unfit for the job. By God, you look ravishing this evening. Your mama was a bombshell in her day, and I must say you're giving her a run for her money."

"Thank you, Oliver." I had the advantage of spotting his young wife coming towards us from inside the house, so I kept my voice light and cool. "Coming from you, that's high praise. Good evening, Doe."

"Nora," she breathed, as she double-kissed the air beside my jaw. She was careful not to touch me, however. Doe rarely made physical contact with another person, except her husband. "How delightful to see you."

She sounded convincing, but I could see her struggle to decide if I were there as a potential rival for her man or as a representative of the *Intelligencer*'s society column. She must have decided the latter, because she smiled at last.

As blond and tanned as Malibu Barbie, Doe kept her eye-popping figure taut and her hair perfectly flipped up at her shoulders. Her silk sweater with its deeply cut neckline and the matching snakeskin pants were exactly the color of an Afghan hound. A diamond necklace as tight as a dog collar gleamed on her neck, heightening my impression that she was Oliver's sleek pet. Her toes peeked seductively from very pointed spike-heeled sandals.

The only flaw in her appearance was the condition of her hands. A gardener, Doe proudly wore her stubby nails as merit badges to her prowess with flowers. Otherwise, she was stunningly turned out.

Beautiful, slightly jealous second wives were not necessarily bitches, I reminded myself sternly. Doe did good work on the city's landscape board, and I'd recently heard she was helping organize a hospital fund drive. Unfortunately, she was as dull as a dial tone in social situations.

I knew Oliver's first wife, Annabelle, very well indeed. It was still jarring not to see tall, elegant Annabelle by Oliver's side—her distinctive white hair cut no-nonsense short around her aristocratic face, and her raspy, smoker's laugh ringing out with ironic amusement. The daughter of a prominent old family and a woman of exquisite taste and impeccable social grace, Annabelle had held her head high through her husband's many dalliances, worked hard for several unglamorous charities and nursed her father through colon cancer. She had been a wonderful mother to four rambunctious sons, too, raising them with a sense of humor as well as a firm hand. She was well read, down to earth and called 'em like she saw 'em. If you sat near smart, vivacious Annabelle at a dinner party, you undoubtedly had a great time. When I dated her son Flan, she'd welcomed me warmly despite rumors that my parents were fiddling while Rome burned. She was a class act. Oliver had earned every penny of his fortune, but he had needed Annabelle's polish to be accepted in the city.

She did not deserve the treatment she got when Oliver finally roamed too far. Because I loved Annabelle, it was hard for me to like Doe, who had all the bad taste her husband's money could buy.

I mustered a smile, though. "Your garden looks fantastic tonight, Doe. I love the cornstalks and Halloween decorations."

"Thank you very much. Gardening is my passion. Well, after Oliver, of course." She picked an invisible bit of lint off her husband's sleeve and tipped her face adoringly up at his. "I wanted the grounds to look spectacular in case a special occasion came along, and look what happened!"

"She's always ready to throw a party," Oliver said on a laugh.

Doe tried to look modest. "Oh, Nora goes to oodles of parties better than this. Are you here officially, Nora? I thought about inviting Kitty, but—well, Oliver is still angry about what she said the last time we asked her."

I remembered Kitty had chewed up Doe Cooper's party-throwing skills and spat them out for all Philadelphia to despise. Poor Doe had been unprepared for entertaining the people her husband enjoyed, and Kitty spotted every shortcoming.

"Oliver felt that since you were invited, we could safely leave Kitty off our guest list."

I could see her anxiety. "Kitty did ask me to write something about tonight, but I wasn't sure you'd want me to."

"Of course we would!" Doe cried, relieved. "We trust you, Nora. Don't we, Oliver?"

"Well, I hate to look like a publicity hound."

Most of the city's Old Money liked to keep their names out of print, whereas New Money worked hard to get themselves splashed around the newspapers. Oliver's reluctance almost rang true.

Doe pouted. "Darling, don't be silly!"

"I'll take it easy on you," I promised Oliver with a grin. To Doe, I said, "Do you suppose you'll move to Washington?"

"Oh, yes," she said quickly. "As soon as Ollie is confirmed, we'll start house hunting. It's going to be our primary residence."

Doe had never been embraced in certain circles of the city. Starting all over in Washington was probably exactly what she wanted—a fresh start towards becoming a respected member of a community in her own right.

"That sounds exciting," I said. "But you just built this wonderful new home."

"Oh, we might build the same house again. With my allergies, I need a home with absolutely no synthetic materials whatsoever."

"You should see her swell up around polyester," Oliver added. "It's not a pretty sight."

"Ollie!" Doe punched his arm affectionately.

"Well, you certainly did a bang-up job here." I indicated the enormous house.

"It's our dream home," Doe assured me. "I'll build it all over again if we can find enough ground. And I'd want all the same amenities. It's amazing what you can't give up once you have certain things—the home theater, the caterer's kitchen, the safe room, the wine closet—well, all of it! We want everything to be perfect for our friends."

Oliver groaned. "I'm going to have to ask the president for a raise!"

We laughed.

"But what about your family?" I asked Oliver. "They're going to miss having you right next door."

I must have said something wrong, because immediately both Oliver and Doe looked as if I'd just brought up a bodily function.

Oliver recovered first. "Oh, they'll get along fine, I'm sure."

All was not peace and harmony with the Cooper clan, I gathered.

"Oliver?" asked a male voice behind me. "May I beg an introduction?"

If Doe was Barbie, the newcomer was a Ken doll. He was fortyish and L.L. Bean–catalog perfect, with ex-military posture, wearing a snappy blazer, tailored trousers and a golf shirt. His dark brown hair looked as if it had been shellacked in place. He was Barbie's boyfriend, all right—handsome, but . . . well, plastic. He put out his hand to me. "I'm Jack Priestly."

Oliver said, "Jack, this is Nora Blackbird."

"She's the one I told you about," Doe added.

Both men pretended not to hear her, and Oliver said quickly, "Jack's here to ride herd on me until the confirmation hearings start. He's from the White House. Jack, Nora's an old friend of the family."

"Hello," I said, accepting Jack's handshake.

"I'm delighted, Nora." He had a slightly Appalachian lilt in his voice. Tennessee, maybe. "Any woman who wears Chanel is a woman worth getting to know."

Doe looked confused. "Are you talking about perfume?"

"Clothes," Jack said, continuing to hold my hand. "Am I right? Your suit is vintage Chanel."

In my role as a society reporter, I needed a wardrobe that matched the expensive clothes worn by the people in my social circle. My own closet had a few good pieces left from the flush years, but nothing formal enough for the constant string of posh events I attended. Because of my severely reduced financial situation, I had taken to raiding my grandmother's stored collection of vintage couture dresses. Fortunately, Grandmama's excellent taste managed to transcend the decades . . . and fit me, too. The somewhat shabby-chic style had become my signature "look." For the Cooper party, I had pulled out a favorite pink pencil-skirted Chanel.

I smiled at Jack Priestly. "You have a good eye."

"No, just a sister who works for a fashion magazine. A few things have rubbed off." He indicated his own rather pedestrian attire. "But not too much."

Oliver said, "Nora always looks great."

"Unique," Doe agreed, although halfheartedly.

Behind us, more people had been checked by the security team and were approaching the front door, so it was time for me to move along and allow our host to greet the arriving guests.

I wished Oliver and Doe the best of luck and eased past them as the new arrivals approached. Jack and I went inside.

Jack said, "Nora, can I get you a drink?"

"Thank you. A glass of white wine, please."

"Coming right up."

Alone for a moment, I gauged the party. All my life I'd been trained to listen to party noise and make instant judgements.

This one felt forced. I could see young men of the cigar and martini set talking football in the middle of the action while a few older gents demonstrated their putting technique in corners. Overdressed young women displayed their toned abs center stage, and the older women . . . were absent. Several Sixers basketball players and their hangers-on sprawled gangsta style on the couches and watched a gargantuan television set.

I knew at once it was the wrong crowd. No old pals had been called to celebrate Oliver's rise to national political stature. Instead, young scavengers seemed to sniff the wind as the old lion prepared to leave his long-held territory. The Old Money crowd, loyal to Oliver's first wife, perhaps, had stayed home.

The Cooper house might have been the Biltmore on the outside, but inside it was another story. Ponyskin upholstery was my first clue that Doe had done the decorating herself instead of hiring someone who would have known how to spend generously but with taste. Saddle blankets adorned the second-floor railings. A chandelier made of elk antlers shone light onto a Native American–style carpet. Paintings of Appaloosa horses hung over cases of Pueblo Indian pottery and kachina dolls. Nothing was synthetic, yet it looked unnatural in eastern Pennsylvania. It all looked expensive, but trendy and a little tacky. Like Doe.

The place was the kind of playground that might have been built by a college fraternity that had just won the lottery. It was hardly, I thought, the home of an up-and-coming statesman. I wondered if Oliver was relieved to be leaving his shiny new home behind.

Once again I mused that Annabelle Cooper should have been standing proudly beside her husband in his moment of triumph. Instead, Doe seemed to be presiding over a disco for denizens of the Playboy mansion.

In the crowd, I spotted my friend Jill Mascione, whose family owned Main Events, the catering company. Her family had been throwing parties for my family since the two of us were old enough to switch car keys in the pockets of the coats tossed across my bed. Rather than tending the bar in her usual tuxedo, my childhood partner in crime balanced a tray of empty glasses as she wove through the throng in a miniskirt. She grinned as I looked askance at her outfit and raised my brows.

"I borrowed it from my sister. What are you doing here? Hardly your crowd."

"Working, of course. Give me the short version."

"On the party? Well, Yale Bailey wants to know if we have Jell-O shots." Jill rolled her eyes.

"At least the food looks good." I noted that cocktails, canapés and dinner seemed to be circulating at the same time, with the waitstaff encouraging guests to take small plates to various chairs and small tables around the room.

"Doe's trying to pull off a *dinatoire,*" Jill reported, which I knew was a hostess's tactic to avoid the agony of a seating chart. Especially in a crowd that mixed so many walks of life and levels of the social strata, someone was certain to be offended by the hierarchy of arranged seating. The *dinatoire* should have solved that dilemma, but it also risked irritating even more people if they perceived the social slight of inadequate deference by the hostess.

"But Doe also wanted roasted meats, to make things more difficult," Jill continued. "Ever try to carve a rib roast, standing up?"

Just as the words were out of Jill's mouth, I saw a young waitress bobble a spit of meat as she braced it on a dish she'd set down on a coffee table. The slab of greasy beef slipped and landed in the lap of a very drunk professional basketball player. For an instant I thought he was going to slap her.

Jill sped off in that direction, and I saw her send the waitress back to the kitchen while she devoted herself to apologies.

"Hey, Nora! Lookin' good!"

I turned. "Hello, Yale."

Yale, the general manager of an Atlantic City casino, had one arm draped around a woman I knew from my Junior League days and his other arm around a very young girl I didn't recognize. They roadblocked me, the two women smirking. Yale had a Donald Trump lip curl, too—womanizing and arrogant. He said, "Where's your sister Emma? I haven't laid eyes on her in months."

"Busy," I reported, immediately put off by his implied lust for my sister. "How about you?"

He unwound his arm from the Junior Leaguer and reached for my hand. "Never too busy to party."

His grip was part handshake, part hand kiss, but it hurt me. Men who squeeze a woman's hand until the bones crunch always make my antenna go up. But I was damned if I'd let him see me wince. I said, "Nice to see you," and as soon as he released me, I turned away as if distracted by the rest of the party.

I heard him laugh. "Guess she's got a touch of PMS."

"Someone you know?" Jack asked, reappearing in record time with a glass of wine for me and a bottle of beer for himself, which he used to indicate Yale's departure.

"Mostly by reputation," I replied, glad to distance myself from Yale. "Thank you for the drink."

"That was the casino manager, right? What's his reputation?"

I smiled. "That he gambles with women."

Yale had more fiancées than most men have tennis shoes, but I didn't share the details with Jack.

"Doe says you're a reporter."

"You've been warned about me?"

He managed to smile and look pained at the same time. "I'm sorry Doe couldn't have been a little more subtle."

"So you've been assigned to 'ride herd' on me for the evening, too?"

"Only until I get a handle on what you're going to say about Oliver."

It seemed silly to play games with a man who had such an intelligent gaze. I said, "Let me be honest, too. I'm a society reporter caught between the proverbial rock and the receiving line. If I write rude things about these people, they'll never invite me back. And how can I do my job if I'm not invited? I'm here only to spread the buzz about Oliver."

"Like we say in Kentucky, just so the buzz isn't a chainsaw."

I laughed. "Only the good stuff, I promise."

"I'm sorry to hear that," Jack replied, broadening his smile. "It means I technically don't have to spend any more time with you."

"On the other hand," I said, charmed by his gentlemanly flirtation, "I suppose I could look around for some dirt."

His turn to laugh. "That's more like it. Shall we find some place quieter to talk? Have you been out to the landing strip yet?"

We headed through one of the arches and passed down a cavernous hall where a bar had been set up. Around it, a crowd jostled for drinks and advantageous conversation partners. I recognized a Delaware congressman as he spoke with a very pretty local interior designer, and a mayoral staffer chatting up a fickle campaign contributor.

Jack and I passed the bar and wound our way along a corridor to stained-glass French doors that opened onto the terraced patio. Outside, it was quiet. The summer awning had been removed for the season, but the framework remained overhead. Teak armchairs were still grouped around a handsome matching table with lighted candles flickering inside glass chimneys. Wide stone steps led down to the airstrip, and we strolled down to the planes parked along the grass. Another plane was coming in for a landing. We watched it touch down in the gathering dusk.

I said, "More guests arriving the Cooper way. Did you fly up from Washington?"

Jack strolled beside me. "Yes, I came with Oliver after his meeting with the president."

"Are you one of the Red Barons?"

He looked politely curious. "Who?"

"With your own plane. The Red Baron Supper Club—well, it's not really a club. Just friends of the Cooper boys, all private pilots. They meet for dinner one night a month."

"Ah, yes." He nodded. "I have heard about those guys. They fly their own planes to airport restaurants for dinner, right? I just didn't know they had a name."

"Last month I believe they all flew to a restaurant at an airport near Memphis. Nothing fancy. They say flying is the fun part."

"I believe Yale Bailey, the casino manager, is a member."

"Yes, I think so."

The roar of the taxiing plane cut off our conversation, so Jack pointed at one of the parked jets ahead of us. We could see the logo of Yale's casino painted on the tail. We walked over to it together. The narrow gangway had been left down, and the plane's interior lights were turned on.

Jack raised his voice over the engine noise of the plane that taxied closer. "We can't seem to get away from the noise. Want to take a look inside?"

"Think Yale would mind?"

Jack grinned. "He left it open. Let's go."

I climbed up the steps and ducked my head to enter the corporate plane. It was smaller than the charter jets I had flown in when invited on vacations with some of my old friends. I expected the usual in aircraft luxury—lacquered paneling, plush upholstery and all the amenities of a sumptuous hotel suite. I'd endured endless discussions on the subject of private jet décor and knew interior decoration was part of the cache.

But Yale Bailey's jet looked like none other I'd ever seen. Poisonous green shag carpet was underfoot, and a full bar glittered with glassware and bottles. One of the luxurious couches was opened into a bed as if ready for Agent 007 to seduce the latest Bond girl. The sheets were black satin and untidy. An airborne bachelor pad.

"Who is he kidding?" I asked.

Jack glanced around the cabin. "Looks like the Red Barons know how to enjoy themselves."

"Trust me. This isn't what the other planes look like."

He tried out one of the armchairs, politely putting his back to the unmade bed. "You've attended their dinners?"

"I was someone's date a few times."

"Flan's?"

I shouldn't have been surprised. No doubt Jack Priestly had done a lot of research on Oliver and his family. I sat down opposite him in another armchair. "No. Flan and I haven't been an item for many years. It was a friend of his—Jamie Scaithe. We dated after I was with Flan but before I was married."

"Jamie Scaithe . . ." Jack said, frowning.

It was a prompt for me to say more, and I noted again how sneaky he was at prying information from me. I changed the subject by saying, "Tell me why you're here instead of enjoying the bright lights of Washington this evening. Or is that top secret?"

"The lights aren't very bright these days because everybody goes to bed before ten." He crossed one leg over the other and glanced out the cabin window as the other plane shut down its engines. "I'm here to prep Oliver for the hearings. And to meet his friends, get to know his family a little better."

"'Fess up," I teased. "You've read background checks on all of us, haven't you?"

He turned away from the window and looked at me with a smile. "I read a few reports on the plane coming up, yes. It's not the most interesting way to meet people. I'd much rather have a native guide. If you're an old friend of the family, for instance, I suppose you already know everybody."

"You make me feel like Pocahontas."

"So tell me." He nodded in the direction of the new plane. "Is that Cher climbing down from that private jet? Or a drag queen?"

It didn't take even a glance for me to understand whom he was asking about. Stepping out of her plane was a tall, gaunt woman elaborately swathed in several Hermes scarves. She lugged an expensive cosmetics case and wore very large sunglasses.

I said, "That's Tempeste, Oliver's half sister—or maybe a cousin. I'm not sure. Tempeste Juarez is her name. Pretty terrifying, don't you think?"

The daunting woman in question finished her cigarette with one sucking pull and flicked away the butt with her long fingernails as she descended the gangway steps. Tempeste's long, youthful legs were encased in tight black trousers, her upper body enfolded in a black-and-white zebra-print scarf. She had wrapped another flowing scarf around her neck, perhaps to hide a few wrinkles but also to give the impression of a dashing aviatrix dropping in for cocktails with Denys Finch-Hatten. As far as I knew, however, Tempeste never went closer to a cockpit than first-class seating. Her black hair, worn Veronica Lake style, screened half her pale, hatchet-shaped face. Her mouth, stained Jungle Red, was going a mile a minute as she lectured her pilot.

"She's a world traveler," I told Jack. "She's lived in Paris, Istanbul, Argentina, Johannesburg—and she's had at least one husband in every port. Last I heard she was marrying a Portuguese polo team. See that red Vuitton cosmetics case?"

"Yes."

"That's not makeup she's carrying. She never travels without the ashes of her first husband, Benito Juarez, the famous stunt pilot."

"That's some ring she's wearing, too," Jack observed. "I can see it from here."

Even at our distance, we could see the flash of diamonds on her skinny fingers.

"Tempeste loves jewels. She collects all kinds. And because she's nearsighted, they have to be big enough for her to see."

Jack raised his eyebrows at me. "Is that the sort of thing you write in the newspaper?"

"No, no. I'll probably write about what Tempeste is wearing—especially her jewelry—and where she's having dinner tomorrow night."

"Which is?"

"Hmm." I considered the question. "She's a big supporter of animal rights. I'll bet she's going to a fund-raiser for the zoo tomorrow evening."

"Will you make a catty remark about her zebra-skin ensemble?"

"That's not my style," I assured him, getting to my feet with a plan of getting back to the party before he wooed me into an indiscretion. "I told you. I'm here to make people look good."

He looked as though he wanted to linger for further gossip in the quiet plane but was too much of a gentleman to propose the idea. He stood up also, and we went to the open cabin door to see guests come spilling out onto the patio to greet Tempeste. He asked, "Who's the lady in the wheelchair?"

"You haven't met Alice Cooper yet?"

"Alice Cooper?" Jack laughed. "You're kidding, right?"

"Cross my heart. She's Oliver's mother. You haven't met her?"

"We haven't been introduced yet. I get the idea someone's keeping us apart. What's her story?"

"She's harmless. Maybe a bit colorful for Washington these days." I watched the small knot of people surge forward as Tempeste went up the stone steps. "Don't be fooled by her grandmotherly appearance. She is every bit as intimidating as Tempeste. She's from Texas originally. Story goes, she lassoed Oliver's father at a debutante ball in Dallas. With a real rope. While riding a horse. Shall we?"

We left the airstrip and went up the grass towards the house. Ahead of us, the family reunion began.

Alice Cooper, nearly ninety and wheelchair-bound for reasons not discussed by anyone in the family, approached the top of the patio steps with a stiff drink clutched in one clawlike hand. Her other hand, covered in rings and weighted down by a sparkling bracelet, was free to gesture to her companion, a young woman dressed in a white nursing uniform that was ever so slightly too snug to be the genuine article.

"Mama!" Tempeste bellowed when she was close enough to see the wheelchair blocking her path. She took off her dark glasses and peered myopically at the woman before her. We could hear her voice clearly. "Gawd, you look like death warmed over."

"You look like something the cat dragged in," warbled Alice Cooper right back. "Didn't I say you shoulda had your eyelids done last Christmas, honey?"

"I decided to go on safari instead. The wildebeests were magnificent!"

Tempeste bent and wrapped her long arms around fragile Alice, whose improbably yellow Eva Gabor wig went askew during the embrace. Alice made a grab to save her hair at the last second and said, "Well, I hope you got all the right shots. We don't want any of those African diseases here, you know. Remember Elizabeth Taylor sweating like a pig in *Elephant Walk*?"

"That was India, Mama."

"Well, it was very unattractive."

"Hell's bells, where is everybody? Is Oliver in Washington already? And where's my favorite nephew, Flan? Come out, come out wherever you are!"

Jack and I watched the mother-daughter reunion until the nurse pushed the wheelchair into the house, leaving us alone on the patio.

Then Jack said casually, "Looks like Alice has some pretty pricey jewelry on tonight, too."

I sipped my wine and noted Jack's bland expression. "You're intrigued by the family jewels, I notice. Does that interest come from your fashion-editor sister, too?"

Our eyes met. He said, "You want to know what my background information said about the Blackbird sisters? That you were the brainy one."

"I'm stunned that we rated a report. But thank you. Are you putting all your cards on the table now?"

"That depends on how discreet you can be."

"If something's off the record, it's off the record."

He sighed like a man who knew his way around

the fourth estate. "Word is, you can be trusted, so here goes. My job is to make sure Oliver passes the congressional hearings with flying colors. So far, we don't foresee any problems."

"Except?"

"There's the little matter of Oliver's daughter-in-law."

"Laura," I said, guessing which of the four Cooper daughters-in-law had the White House concerned.

"There are rumors," Jack said.

"A family without rumors is a pretty boring family."

"This rumor says Laura Cooper is a kleptomaniac," Jack said bluntly. "We hear she steals jewelry."

I took a deep breath and let it out slowly. This, I realized, was the information Jack Priestly had hoped to charm out of me from the moment he'd sought his introduction. I said, "That's a very ugly rumor."

"Any truth to it?"

"Surely you have some kind of federal agency that can find out."

Jack looked uncomfortable. "If Laura becomes the target of an official investigation, we're obliged to reveal the results."

"Ooh," I said, "what a tangled web."

"Right." Jack unconsciously lowered his voice. "Look, I can housebreak Oliver Cooper in a few days. We think he's a clean-cut guy, except for his romantic inclinations, which everyone is willing to overlook. He's the best man for a very tough job. But if there's trouble in this henhouse, you can imagine what the media will do. We don't want to be undermined by family problems."

"Families can be chaotic. Sometimes you can't control the way people behave."

Jack shook his head. "Failure is not an option in this case."

For the first time, I sensed the unyielding soldier behind Jack's gentlemanly facade. "Why would it matter? Oliver can't be held responsible for Laura. Unless—no, it can't be possible. Unless he helped cover up her stealing?"

Jack did not respond.

A cabinet post was no place for a man with a tainted background, and paying off his daughter-in-law's crimes was damning indeed. The press would have a field day, and Oliver's moment in the sun would turn very black.

"So?" Jack asked. "What do you know about Laura?"

I weighed my options. Of course, I could tell Jack Priestly everything I had heard about Laura Cooper over the years. But Laura had never stolen from me, and I couldn't spread rumors about her, no matter how attractively I was asked.

And I owed something to Laura Cooper.

She had always seemed a little desperate to me. Desperate to be accepted by a society that didn't care if she came from a good Charleston family, the famous Hayfoots. Desperate to have a career despite the Cooper family's tradition of putting the wives in charge of philanthropic and entertainment matters. I'd heard she'd gotten a part-time job with a prominent construction company, but her architectural degree had been ignored and she'd been reduced to choosing bathroom fixtures for spec houses.

She'd chosen the wrong Cooper, too. Flan hadn't quite grown out of his college-boy exploits. The other brothers worked hard for the family business while Flan appeared only for the golf games and Christmas bonuses. Flan was least likely to follow his father's footsteps to glory and the financial stratosphere.

And Laura avoided me. I sensed that she feared

my relationship with her husband. Or maybe she figured I was the only person who knew she'd made a mistake.

I understood Laura's desperation. I knew how difficult it was for wives to truly see into their husband's hearts.

So I said to Jack Priestly, "I'm not in the best position to know. Laura and I are not exactly friends. Before she married, her husband and I—"

"Yes, I know. You and Flan Cooper were college sweethearts. Does Laura hold that against you?"

"I have no idea," I said calmly. "Our paths rarely cross."

"Has she ever—?"

"Has she stolen from me? No. I don't wear jewelry."

His gaze traveled to my grandmother Blackbird's sapphire ring on my right hand.

I said, "I don't have any jewelry except this."

If he knew the whole saga of the Blackbird family and my parents' recent fall from grace, Jack had the good manners not to bring it up while our flirtation was going so swimmingly.

"I see," he said, studying my face for a moment for signs of weakening. Then he smiled. "Well, this dog has obviously barked up the wrong tree."

I suddenly wondered if I hadn't convinced him of my discretion at all. Maybe I'd just made myself look secretive instead.

# Chapter 3

But there was no time to correct the impression I might have communicated to Jack Priestly. At that moment we were interrupted by Flan himself.

I saw him shouldering his way through the French doors like a rampant bull in Pamplona. He headed in our direction with a grin on his wide and friendly face.

"Nora! You've been hiding from me!"

He gathered me up in a hug, clumsily bobbling his drink in the process.

"Flan," I squeaked.

"Sorry." He cheerfully released me from his powerful embrace and stepped back from the puddle of bourbon he'd left on the flagstone. He laughed at his own ham-handedness.

"Flan, have you met—?"

"Jack!" Flan wobbled on his feet and tried to focus. "They're asking for you at the front door. The governor just arrived, and Dad thinks you ought to be there."

Jack turned to me. "Duty calls. It's been a pleasure, Miss Blackbird. I hope to see you again later."

"I'll look for you," I promised.

He departed and left me with Flan.

Flanders Cooper, the object of my most passionate twenty-year-old affections, had been a handsome devil with an instinct for finding the best parties. The ringleader when it came to playing prep-school pranks, he'd always conned the right student to crib from and allowed his father to pay when he "borrowed" someone's sports car and inflicted some damage. He'd grown up burly like his father, but not as smart as his mother. Now, in his early thirties, he looked like a well-fed aristocrat. His rosy skin had that steam-bath shine to it, and from the strength in his upper body, I guessed he still rowed, although probably in an expensive health club instead of on the Schuylkill.

He'd been fun to date. But he'd been lousy as a partner in a real relationship, full of games when substance was in order.

"Pretty in pink." Flan gave me a once-over that made me feel like filet mignon. "But then, you'd look good in any color. How're you doing, Nora? Where'e've you been keeping yourself?"

"I don't know how you can miss me. I go to half a dozen parties every week. And you never miss a party, Flan."

He laughed and slugged back the remains of his drink, then tossed the ice cubes to the flagstones. He ignored the mess. "Yeah, I heard you were working with Kitty Keough. What's with that?"

"Some of us have to make a living," I said lightly. "Congratulations are in order for more than just your father, I suppose. Which of you Cooper brothers is taking over as keeper of the family store?"

He grinned sheepishly. "It won't be me, that's for sure. Life's too short to work hard. Live fast, die young and leave a good-lookin' corpse, right?"

It was a thoughtless remark, considering what had happened to my life, but I didn't wince. "How's CanDo Airline?"

Flan might have been a dilettante from the time he could hold a bottle, but he had his noble side, too. The son of an aircraft mogul, he'd found a way to make use of all the planes that his family collected the way old bicycles gathered in other people's garages. Flan had organized his pilot friends into a cadre of volunteers capable of flying cancer patients to treatment hospitals around the nation. They flew youngsters from small towns and rural communities to the finest urban cancer centers, taking no money for their efforts and allowing Cooper Aviation to buy the fuel and pay expenses.

Of course, I'd always wondered if the whole idea for CanDo Airlines had been Flan's or that of his mother.

Flan shrugged off his accomplishment. "It's doing okay. We're busy."

"Your father spoke about CanDo on television the other day. I saw him on the *Today Show*."

"I heard about that," said Flan.

"He's very proud of you, Flan," I began, but there was no use getting past his determination to make light of his charitable side. So I said, "I'm glad your father is getting this wonderful opportunity."

"Yeah," Flan joked, "we're just hoping he passes the multiple-choice exam."

I smiled. "Think he'll get through the confirmation process without throwing one of his famous temper tantrums?"

"Probably. Hey, I need another drink. C'mon."

Grabbing my already-sore hand, Flan led me off the patio and into the house. He turned left and pulled me past the kitchen and away from the party. I bumped into a waitress in the shadows, but Flan only laughed and didn't release his grip. I tossed an apology over my shoulder.

Moments later, he shouldered open a door and flicked on a light. Then I found myself being dragged into an unoccupied powder room.

"Flan, no. Hold on—"

"I'm tryin'." He pulled me inside and kicked the door closed behind us.

In another instant, I was wrestling to get out of his embrace and trying not to breathe the bourbon fumes on his breath. "Flan, stop. I'm not going to do this!"

He was laughing and only halfheartedly trying to kiss me, but I was still angry, and that penetrated his drunken brain. "What's the matter, Nora? Don't you want to see what it's like on memory lane?"

"We've both moved to other streets." I backed up against a sink that had been fabricated into the shape of a monstrous blue sea shell. "Now, keep your distance." Less severely, I said, "Think of your wife."

"You're afraid of little Laura?" He leaned against the door to prevent my escape. "What about your new boyfriend? I hear he's the biggest badass in town."

"I don't have a boyfriend," I said.

"That's not what everybody's saying."

"Flan, let's go back to the party. I truly don't want anyone to get the wrong idea."

He blocked me again, standing very close. "Stop worrying. Laura doesn't care what I do."

"I'm sure that's not true."

He glanced away. This was a Flan I knew, too. Mercurial with caring qualities tamped down under the frat-boy persona. I realized he was truly upset about his wife.

"What's going on?" I asked. "You and Laura having a bad time?"

He didn't answer, but looked back at me, measuringly. "You ever think about us?" He tried to summon a smile. "About what might have happened if the good times kept rolling?"

"Are you okay?" I asked. I reached out and put my hand on his forearm. "Forget this pickup patter for a minute. It's me you're talking to."

He passed one hand down his face as if to wipe away the things he might be revealing there. "It's nothing," he said. "Just weird stuff that's been happening. Hell, sometimes I want to punch her lights out."

"What's going on, Flan?"

"Let's just say my marriage probably won't last the weekend."

The news surprised me. "I'm so sorry."

"You know, we're living in this house while we have some work done on ours. New wing, bigger kitchen. It's a mess. We're supposed to be sharing a suite here. But Laura moved out on me. Took all her junk across the hall, paraded everything past my father. You know how that makes me look?"

"It takes work to fix a marriage," I began.

"Oh, we've done plenty of work. You want to guess how many therapists I've paid? The woman is nuts."

"You don't really believe that."

"Oh, yes, I do."

I took a shot and said, "You must still love her."

He glared up at the ceiling and admitted, "I used to. But I don't even know who the hell she is anymore."

"I wish I could help, Flan."

He shook his head. Then he seemed to brush off the whole subject the way a big dog shook off pond water. He looked at me and pasted his bleary grin back in place. "I thought I'd cuddle up with the real thing for once, that's all. You gonna let me kiss you, or not?"

"Not," I said just as lightly, wishing I could be helpful to my friend. Obviously, though, he was determined to play the role of the party boy, and I wasn't going to get through to him. I'd call him later in the week, perhaps. I said, "Now, let me out of here."

He bowed and obeyed, opening the door with a flourish.

And revealing us both to Laura Cooper, who stood in the passageway.

It was bad enough to be surprised by his wife.

But there was something drastically different about Laura Cooper. Something everyone in the world must have seen but me until that very moment.

I stared at her.

She'd done something to herself. She looked . . . different.

Her hair was cut to shoulder length and layered away from her face, the way I wore mine. And she'd colored it. Auburn—exactly my shade. She balanced on a pair of very high heels to stand to nearly my height. Her suit was pink—my color. All the details came together before me like a computerized picture morphing into a portrait . . . of myself.

Laura Cooper had turned herself into a copy of me.

"Laura," I said.

Her expression twisted with rage, and then she threw her drink in my face.

"Screw you," she snapped in her tiny Carolina-accented voice. "Or did he do that already?"

"Oh, hell," said Flan. "Don't make a scene over nothing, you bitch. Not tonight."

She spun around and catapulted down the passageway.

"Laura!" Flan shouted. But he didn't move to go after her. All we saw was her auburn hair swinging as she stormed away.

"This is ridiculous," I said, dashing the wine from my face and taking off in her direction.

Laura was as quick as a deer. She headed straight back to the party, elbowed her way through startled guests and headed up the curving staircase as if shot from a circus cannon. She took the steps two at a time, drawing attention from the people gathered below. I didn't have a choice but to match her speed, and I knew heads turned to watch as I followed Flan's wife up the stairs.

"Laura," I said when I reached the landing. "Wait, please."

"Shove it," she snapped over her shoulder, clear enough to be heard below. "You're the one he's always wanted. Well, you can have him!"

I made it up the last run of stairs and nearly caught up with her in the hallway. But she thrust open a bedroom door and disappeared. I managed to reach the doorway in time to prevent the door from slamming in my face.

"Get out," she said, spinning away from me into the room. "I don't speak to my husband's girlfriends."

"I'm not anything to your husband, Laura," I said to her stiff back. "We were friends ten years ago. That's it."

"I'm not an idiot!"

"Of course you're not. That's why I came up here to explain."

She faced me, her absurdly made-up features pained beneath the cosmetics she'd used to make herself look like someone she wasn't. Her blue eyes overflowed with tears of anger and sorrow. With less fury than before, she said with a much more ladylike Southern drawl, "I don't want to hear any lies."

"I'm not lying. I want you to know the truth. It was stupid for us to go into the bathroom like that. I didn't mean to embarrass you."

The fire went out of her, and her lower lip began to tremble.

I said, "I'm very sorry."

She bit her lip and hooked the loose strands of her dyed hair behind her ears in a gesture I suddenly wondered if she'd copied from me.

"I hope you can forgive Flan," I said. "He wasn't thinking straight. I should have done the thinking for both of us."

She blinked her huge eyes at me. She had the voice of a little girl under the best of circumstances, but just then she sounded like an eight-year-old. "He's a lousy excuse for a husband."

I decided there was no tactful response to that remark and kept quiet.

Laura went to the bed and sat down. With her head bent, she began to cry with a kittenish noise and no tears.

I glanced around the bedroom. A large, cheap vase of long-stemmed roses stood in the middle of the dresser, surrounded by the usual detritus of a cluttered female life—rolled-up pantyhose, makeup, handbags. Every inch of floor space around the furniture was packed with boxes, clothing and books. Mostly self-help books, I guessed, noticing the pile on the desk. She had set up a drafting table in one corner, and I could see architectural drawings under a T square. It looked like Flan was right. She'd moved all of her possessions into a room for herself alone.

Laura continued to weep. Either she knew how to

play a role, or she was in genuine pain. I took a deep breath, then went to the bed and sat down beside her. Awkwardly, I patted her hand.

My touch drew her sleeve back slightly. I couldn't help noticing a huge purple bruise on her wrist. I found myself staring. The imprint of someone's fingers were clearly visible on her slim wrist. I knew Flan could get out of control and throw his weight around, but this bruise was more than accidental. I looked more closely at Laura and realized the thick makeup had been applied to conceal a blue bruise beneath her right eye. Had Flan done this? I felt a wave of revulsion.

Inadequately, I said, "I'm so sorry."

She shook her head. "Flan hates me and I hate him." She caught my hand in both of hers and squeezed me so hard I almost yelped. She said, "I wish I'd never married him in the first place."

I was hazy on Laura's circumstances, but I dimly remembered she had been at Penn while he was in college there. I had attended Barnard and come to Penn on occasional weekends to be with him. She'd been in the background somewhere—a Southern girl out of place in Philadelphia. Had she been the coxswain on his crew team, perhaps? I couldn't remember. For all I knew, she had set her cap for him while Flan and I dated.

I flushed, thinking how I'd ignored her back then. She's been a face in the crowd to me. I'd obviously made a much different impression on her.

Miserably, she said, "It's you he always wanted."

"Laura, I'm sure that's not true."

"He loves everything about you. The way you look, the way you talk. You're Old Philadelphia, and I'm not."

"That's not important."

She ignored me. "My family is a big deal, too, in Charleston. But here, I can't—I'm not important enough."

"Laura, that's silly."

"When your husband got killed, he couldn't stop talking about you. For ages, all he could blab about was how pretty you looked at the funeral. A tragic beauty; that's what he said. And how brave you were. How nice you were to everyone even while you were so sad. All those rich people making a fuss over you. You were like a heroine in a book or something. When I—well, Flan thinks I'm crazy."

"I'm sure he doesn't think that at all."

She became aware of her appearance and tugged her sleeve down over the bruise on her wrist. "I can't get through to him. I try so hard to make him happy, but he shuts me out. Even in bed, he won't touch me no matter what I do to encourage him."

Cautiously, I ventured, "Have you spoken with anyone? A therapist? A minister? I think you could use some professional help, Laura."

She heaved a gigantic sigh. "I'll be okay. Thanks, Nora." She tried to smile. "I'm sorry I exploded like I did. I know I can get pretty upset."

"Please leave the apologies to me."

She smiled at last. "You're really nice. I didn't expect that."

I cleared my throat. "Thank you."

She reached out and touched my hair. "Maybe we could be friends."

I could see she was lying. She didn't trust me in the slightest.

# Chapter 4

"That's it?" Emma asked. "That's all she said after you made whoopee in the bathroom with her husband?"

"Weren't you listening?" I asked.

"I wonder how long she was obsessed with you." Libby nibbled on a slice of provolone. "I mean, was she studying you back in college?"

"I doubt it," I said. "Surely somebody would have mentioned it to me earlier if this had been going on very long."

"Is it flattering?" Libby asked.

"My God, no! It's very weird."

"Laura was jealous. But why you, of all people? You're broke, your husband was an addict, and you've got more baggage than American Airlines."

"Thanks, Lib," I said tartly.

"I remember her at Rory Pendergast's funeral," Emma said thoughtfully. "And she did watch you, Nora. Flan carried a torch for you once, so maybe she's still taking it seriously. She may have been planning her makeover then."

"Those Southern girls can get very peculiar once they're sexually awakened."

"Anyway," I said, heading off Libby's next conversational train wreck, "that's not the end of the story."

"What happened after that?" Emma asked. "Did the White House guy escort you off the property at gunpoint? Did Flan take you back to the loo and have his wicked way with you?"

"No," I said. "I left the party, and Reed brought me home. But when I got ready for bed, I discovered Laura had stolen Grandmama's sapphire right off my finger."

Both my sisters gaped at my naked hand.

"Grandmama's ring!" Libby cried.

"How did she manage that?" Emma demanded.

"I can't figure it out. She must have slipped it off when we were sitting on the bed."

"The little sneak!"

"The little dead sneak," Emma reminded us.

My sisters and I allowed an uneasy moment of silence to pass in memory of Laura Cooper.

Then Libby said, "So all those rumors about her were true. She really was a kleptomaniac."

"How will you get it back, Nora?"

"I can't exactly go to the poor woman's funeral asking for my jewelry. After all, the whole family either knew about her behavior and hushed it up, or they genuinely didn't realize what she was doing and would be—oh, dear, and there's Flan."

"Yeah." Emma looked at me speculatively. "There's Flan."

"What about Flan?" Libby asked. "You wondering if he's the one who bruised Laura's arm?"

"No, of course not," I said without much conviction. "She must have fallen or something."

"But you said the bruise looked like fingers," Emma said. "When you and Flan broke up, wasn't it over his temper?"

"He was a kid then. He never hit me."

"But he was rough."

"Yes," I admitted. "We split up for many reasons, though. Basically, he was immature."

"Some people never grow up."

Libby ate more cheese. "She must have been pretty distraught to kill herself."

"Did she look distraught?" Emma asked. "I mean, it sounded like she was angry, not despondent."

"She was very upset," I conceded after a moment.

Emma put her hand on my shoulder. "You gonna be okay?"

"Yes," I said.

"Her death isn't your responsibility, Nora."

"I know that."

"I can see the look in your eye," Emma said. "You're taking this to heart."

"Nora takes everything to heart."

"Laura obviously had some issues with me, and I was too arrogant to notice."

Emma snapped, "You are the least arrogant person I know. She was crazy, that's all, and she picked you to focus all her crazy energy on. Now she's dead, but it's not your fault."

"If you say so."

But I felt as though something was my fault. Laura had chosen me. Did that mean I had to choose her, too? What did I owe her now that she was dead?

I didn't want to dither about it with my sisters, though. Libby and Emma had stepped out of line when the guilt gene was distributed, and I must have been given their quotient. They weren't going to understand how I felt.

Emma noted the time and professed a need to get going but wanted some lunch first. Libby put her T-shirt back on after extracting our promise that we'd do her belly cast another time. My sisters pitched in and helped finish the sandwiches.

We carried the food outside along with a plastic bucket loaded with ice and bottled beer—to the barn where Michael and his associates were fixing the old farm tractor. We arrived just in time to see Rawlins with an ear-to-ear grin drive the smoking, thundering machine out of the barn and into the crisp sunlight, where it promptly gave a tremendous backfire and stopped running. The men cheered, the puppy barked, and everyone fell on the food like a starving army.

We pulled the old picnic table out from inside the barn, and the afternoon took on some of the elements of a summer picnic, except we were all dressed in layers and the breeze blew colorful leaves around our feet.

I saw Michael casually hand a beer to Rawlins, who nearly dropped the bottle in astonishment before following the example of the other menfolk and twisting off the cap. He took his first drink while his mother's back was turned, and I realized Michael had just made an adoring friend for life.

When the sandwiches were gone, Emma, Michael and Rawlins played basketball under the rusted hoop over the barn door while I found an old lawn chair for Libby and made pleasantries with the posse that tended to follow Michael wherever he went. That loyal crew of motley buccaneers drank beer and muttered among themselves in a language I wasn't always sure was English, perhaps plotting a bank heist or debating world-peace initiatives, for all I could decipher. But they were exceedingly respectful to me.

I tried to be sociable, but my thoughts kept wandering back to Laura Cooper. Then Libby suggested charades, for crying out loud, whereupon everyone hastily departed. Rawlins took the puppy, thank heaven.

When everyone had gone, Michael helped me finish the cleanup and then lingered on the porch. "You going to tell me why there's a bucket of whipped cream in your kitchen sink?"

"It's plaster," I corrected, knowing full well he'd guessed what the glop was. "And it's one of Libby's artistic ventures, not a home-improvement project."

"Okay." He leaned one shoulder against a pillar and looked down at me with a lazy-lidded smile. "Since you probably won't let me smear you with something delicious, how about a ride on my bike? It feels like spring."

"Michael," I began, not trusting myself to be alone with him.

"Just a ride," he promised. "Although some women consider motorcycles a kind of foreplay."

Although we'd been apart for many weeks, I appreciated him for this—grabbing me by the scruff of my neck when I wandered too close to the dark side. He forced me into the moment, demanded my full participation. Made me laugh.

I tried to rise to the occasion. "Since when do you need help with foreplay?"

"Never. But don't worry. I've sworn to use my powers only for good."

"I'm impressed by your self-control."

Softer, he said, "I stayed away all summer like you asked. Which took more self-control than I thought I had, by the way. Did you miss me?"

I raised one eyebrow. "The Marquis de Sod?"

He threw back his head and laughed, rocking on his heels. "Pretty good name, huh? I thought of it myself. I've got six orders for next spring already.

Seriously, I really appreciate you letting me use Blackbird Farm. I can't fill the orders without you."

His eyes were such a vivid Irish blue that he was called "The Mick" by his underworld acquaintances, and he sometimes used that blasted gaze of his to beguile the less discerning. I recognized his technique, and I wanted to ask him if he truly had more orders than he could fill or if he was just using one of his business ventures as an excuse to come hang around the farm on an occasional autumn afternoon. Or worse yet, was he committed to finding more embarrassing ways for me to get out of debt?

But I chickened out.

He must have seen my hesitation because he put out his hand and touched my face. His grin evaporated. "Come on," he said, in a tone that told me I definitely hadn't kept any secrets from him. "My new bike can cure whatever ails you."

"Nothing is ailing me."

But I took his hand anyway, and we walked across the lawn together. He gave me a helmet and helped me fasten it under my chin. He'd left his leather jacket hanging on the handlebars, and he put it on me. The motorcycle was a lot bigger than those things looked in traffic, and I climbed on clumsily. Then I discovered myself sliding forward until my thighs were locked around his. He revved up the earsplitting engine, and there wasn't anything I could do but grab on to him tight. When we hit the main road and accelerated on the smooth, dry pavement, I didn't let go.

We roared northward with the wind whipping the engine noise into our wake. Autumn leaves scattered behind us. The river ran in a silver wash to our right, and the sunlight dashed between the tree limbs overhead. I felt the powerful quiver of the machine beneath us, and my heartbeat sped up to match the rhythm of the engine. The tail of Michael's flannel shirt flapped in the wind beside me.

I don't know how many miles we traveled or how long it took. I felt as if we were flying, breathing sharp October air and letting the real world slip away behind us.

It was the kind of glorious day that brought everyone outside for one last grab at summer. We passed several vehicles that were parked alongside the road. When I looked up, I could see weekenders climbing the cliffs above us. Farther up the road, I glimpsed a hot-air balloon in the sky. A gaggle of small children chased it across a field. I felt as if I could be in that balloon—going fast and leaving my troubles behind.

At last Michael pulled off the highway into a sandy spot and guided the motorcycle down into a roadside turnaround near a railroad bed. Below us, a cluster of old men played bocce on the smoothly raked gravel between the set of tracks. Beyond them, the Delaware's white water eddied around large, flat rocks.

Michael stopped the bike and killed the engine. We took off our helmets, and I shook out my hair. I could hear the men talking below us and smelled their cigarette smoke. One of them looked up and raised his hand at Michael.

He waved back. "Feel better?" he asked over his shoulder.

"I was fine to begin with."

"Good," he said, hooking his helmet strap over the handlebars. "But Emma said something about a friend of yours dying."

Blast Emma.

I sat back on the seat. "She wasn't a friend, just

someone I knew. The wife of a friend, I guess you could say."

"Old boyfriend."

"Yes."

He climbed off the motorcycle and helped me stand. "How did she die?"

"She supposedly drowned herself in the family swimming pool."

Michael was a practicing Catholic who had firm opinions about the church's rules. We had sparred a few times about issues we disagreed on. I braced myself for a discussion of the church's stand on suicide.

Instead he said, "Supposedly."

I led the way down to the river's edge. "She was found drowned in a swimming pool with a garden statue tied to her ankles."

He strolled behind me. "What do you think?"

I realized I was absentmindedly frowning. "I just—well, I had spoken to Laura just hours before she supposedly killed herself."

"There's that word again. Supposedly." He crouched on the riverbank at my feet and picked up a couple of small stones. "You aren't saying she died by something other than her own hand, are you?"

"Of course not."

He stood up, hefting a stone in his palm. "Nobody in the Social Register would end up swimming with the fishes? On my side of the tracks, however—"

"Now, don't start that business again. We may be from different worlds, but I never said anything disparaging about your side of the tracks—which is your turn of phrase, not mine."

"Okay." With an easy motion, he skimmed the stone out across the surface of the water. "Forget I mentioned it. What about your old boyfriend?"

"What about him?"

Michael turned to me. "Emma suggested he used to manhandle you."

"He never hurt me," I said calmly. "He didn't know his own strength."

"And now?"

"He's a physical person, but not abusive. He's big."

"So am I. That doesn't mean I go around hurting people."

"Neither does he. Actually, he's very sensitive and—"

"Okay, okay. Forgive me for not wanting to hear the details. So maybe your boyfriend didn't kill his wife."

"Who said anything about Flan killing anyone?"

Michael laughed. "His name is Flan? Like the dessert?"

"His name is Flanders," I snapped, "and he didn't kill his wife."

"You sure about that?"

"Of course I am. It's Laura who was strange last night."

"Strange how?"

"She—well, it's too embarrassing, really."

Michael waited.

"I hardly knew Laura," I said at last. "But . . . she had a thing about me."

"About you? What kind of thing?"

I avoided his inquiring gaze by looking out at the river again. "Laura had changed her appearance lately. She cut and dyed her hair. She wore different clothes. She wanted to look like—well, like me."

His interest sharpened. "Spooky."

"And there's this other element." I don't know why I felt I could tell Michael, after keeping this information from Jack Priestly. But I said, "For years, people have whispered that Laura Cooper stole things. Jewelry."

"You mean from stores? Shoplifting?"

"No, from her friends. A kind of high-society jewel thief."

"Wait a minute. You mean, like Cary Grant in that Hitchcock movie?"

"In a way, yes. Among other things, I think she stole my grandmother's ring last night."

He immediately took my hand and held it up to see. "You're kidding. How'd she get it off your finger?"

"I don't know. I was sitting on the bed and talking with her when she grabbed my hand. She had a strong grip. That's when I noticed how badly bruised she was, too, so I was doubly distracted. When I got home, I realized my ring was gone."

"Have you told the police yet?"

"Of course not. I don't want to embarrass anyone."

"Your ring is missing," Michael said, "and you're worried about embarrassing people?"

I pulled away from him. "It's hard to understand, I know, but the Cooper family is special to me. I've known them since I was a child. And Oliver Cooper is on the brink of a national political appointment. I can't go running to the police with wild ideas—especially if the ring turns up in Reed's car later."

"Do you think it's in the car?"

"Well, no."

"Then you've got to tell someone."

"I'm not going to the police, Michael."

"Don't worry," he said. "They'll come to you."

We were quiet for a time, looking at the river and sharing the same thought.

Finally, I said it aloud. "I don't want to go through this again."

"I know," he said.

"First Todd, and then Rory. And now this."

He was quiet, and the river slipped past us. When I'd first met Michael, he had already perfected an expect-the-worst-of-life sense of humor that was engaging but also kept people at bay. But I'd seen past that to the wary light at the back of his eyes. I'd been drawn by an emotional vulnerability, maybe, and he'd seen the same in me. I'd let him take care of me when Rory died. But I'd gotten too close for comfort, too entangled with this man who was very different from anyone else I knew. He kept a roll of bills in his pocket instead of carrying credit cards, and he slipped off late at night to meet men with nicknames like Mad Dog. He ran businesses he wouldn't talk about and he had appetites for food and wine that made me think his other hungers must be just as daunting.

Half the time, I didn't understand where he was coming from. So I'd ended things with him. Trouble was, he hadn't gotten the message. Or maybe I wasn't delivering it clearly enough.

I said, "I heard what you did to the Tacketts."

"What?"

"You bought Harold and Eloise Tackett's estate."

"Yeah, I did. Twenty-two acres."

"And the house. That house is one hundred and fifty years old."

He nodded. "Yeah, it's a wreck. We're probably going to have to knock it down."

I faced him. "Sometimes I think you're from another planet."

He looked genuinely surprised. "What?"

"You told Harold Tackett you would put his family's home to good use. You promised him. That house was designed by his great-grandfather and built by stonemasons brought over from Italy—

probably relatives of yours. Craftsmen, artists. Plus, Franklin Roosevelt stayed there once. And now you're talking about bulldozing it."

"I'll do something nice with the ground. I've got a couple ideas cooking and they're both—"

"I don't understand you!" I cried. "Harold has been forced into an assisted-living facility and Eloise is going along just to take care of him, and you are so blind that you can't—"

"They sold it to me!" Michael's voice rose to match mine. "They didn't want it anymore!"

"You took advantage of two sweet, trusting, generous old people!"

"Took advantage? I paid them exactly what they asked, Nora. They would have sold it to somebody eventually. Why not me?"

"Because you have no respect for the history or—or the sensibility of a wonderful old family. What are you going to do with that property? Open another used-car lot?"

"Are you still mad about that? All of Blackbird Farm would be gone if I hadn't come along."

He was right, of course, but hearing him say it just made me angrier. "What are you going to do with the Tacketts' home?"

"I don't know yet," he said. "We might put some houses up there."

"A housing development? You mean a bunch of plastic buildings with above-ground swimming pools and—"

"What is with you?" he demanded. "Nobody's allowed to have a nice home but you and your crazy family?"

"My crazy family?" I repeated. "Who do you think you are? I read about your brother in last week's paper!"

"Yeah, well, he's in jail now, so society is safe."

"From him, maybe."

His brows snapped down. "Wait a minute. Are you saying that me buying an old house is the same as illegal gambling? Which has no victims, I would like to point out, so—"

"You're kidding, right?"

"You're upset about my brother? I haven't seen him in years! Him or my father."

Which was as disturbing to me as anything the New Jersey Abruzzos had been caught doing in recent months. How did anyone stop communicating with his family? He might as well have amputated his arm. All right, so my own parents had run off to faraway lands, but at least they telephoned regularly.

Destroying a family's history was bad enough. But the fact that Michael hadn't laid eyes on his own father in a decade still stunned me.

It made me wonder what other kinds of emotional cruelty he could be capable of.

And I'd had my share of that already.

# Chapter 5

That evening I hoped to put my troubles on hold by going to a party. Before I went out, I put on one of my grandmother's oldest Madeleine Vionnet crepe dresses. It had been designed in the thirties with a fish-scale motif done in fringe that scalloped all the way down the back like the tail of a slim and sexy mermaid. Its original emerald-green color had faded to a subtler shade of sage that set off my auburn hair quite nicely. Even so, I wasn't exactly feeling festive.

But I tucked my notepad into a shell-shaped handbag and attended a dinner at a Center City hotel to honor people who supported the zoo. Zoo employees dressed in safari duds greeted guests at the ballroom door. Inside, I chatted with a smattering of young socialites who liked the low ticket price and the chance to wear animal-print items from their wardrobes. A crowd of corporate representatives also seemed to be in attendance thanks to donations given by their companies.

The real zoo enthusiasts were the people with pizzazz, however. I directed an *Intelligencer* photographer to snap a few shots of the big players amid the imaginative decorations, then mingled during the cocktail hour to gather some quotes for my piece.

Unfortunately, everyone wanted to talk about Laura Cooper's death, and rumors ran rampant. I overheard one young man asking whether it was true Laura had slit her own throat, for heaven's sake, and in the center of one large group of bankers, I heard a woman loudly describing how she'd spoken with Laura at a nail salon only two weeks ago.

Thankfully, I soon came upon Marian Jefferson, a poet who wore stunning African headdresses and championed a neighborhood literacy program that was the first cause to get me out of the house after Todd died. Her droll husband, Ezekiel, a specialist in kidney transplants at Children's Hospital, favored purple ties and Democratic politics. He often wore a stickpin with the word "muse" inscribed on it. Also at the table were their friends the Hilliards—both doctors—and the Smythe-Rhines, who brought along their nine-year-old daughter who declared she wanted to be a veterinarian when she grew up. Because of the uneven number at the table, I joined them. The presence of the child caused us all to avoid discussing Laura Cooper, and after many compliments about my fish tail, we had a lively conversation about pets. Daneesha Smythe-Rhines was very sad to hear I was pet-free.

During the after-dinner speeches, however, Ezekiel fell asleep beside me, and I admit my mind wandered, too.

Laura had been dead less than forty-eight hours. Had she really drowned herself? It seemed impossible to me. Almost as impossible as her compulsion to transform her appearance. And why me? If someone killed her, was there a connection to me I wasn't understanding?

I also wondered how the Washington people had reacted to Laura's death. Was Jack Priestly in charge of damage control?

And what about the family? What was Flan feeling?

I glanced around the ballroom. I had expected to see Tempeste Juarez among tonight's guests, but even she was not bizarre enough to attend a party after a family loss.

As the master of ceremonies got up to drone, the Hilliards both claimed to have been paged by their respective hospitals and ducked out early. The Smythe-Rhines slipped away, too, citing the need to get their daughter home to bed. As soon as the child was gone, Marian leaned over her husband and whispered to me, "It's a damn shame about Laura Cooper."

"Yes, just dreadful."

"Bullshit." Ezekiel's deep voice rumbled in his chest.

"Hush, now," said Marian. "Don't speak ill of the poor girl."

"Poor girl? What are you talking about?" Ezekiel opened his eyes. "That girl stole your Kikuyu necklace, and you said you'd never forgive her."

"I said no such thing."

"Did, too."

"Well," Marian said, looking flustered, "I can't be sure she stole it."

"You said there was nobody else in the bathroom when you took it off," Ezekiel said. To me, he added, "Marian loved that necklace, but she always took it off to brush her teeth. In case she dribbled. She's got a thing about her teeth, you know. Always brushes after a meal, even one like this. You wait. In ten minutes, she'll run off to the ladies' room and get out her toothbrush."

"Hush, now," Marian whispered, although less fiercely than before.

Ezekiel grinned. "It's why she's got such a nice smile."

Marian poked him to be quiet, but she was gentle.

After the master of ceremonies finished introducing the next speaker, we politely applauded. Marian leaned across the table as she clapped her hands. "We built a new house last year. Laura Cooper designed our closets."

Her husband said, "You said you'd never fill 'em up, but you did."

"She did a good job for us even though she was only a part-time employee for the contractor." Marian good-naturedly ignored her husband. "I told her she ought to be doing more than closets. Like kitchens, maybe."

"Don't get started on kitchens," Ezekiel moaned. "I never want to hear about marble countertops again."

"That's why I was so hurt," Marian said. "That she could take something from me after we'd worked so well together."

The three of us pretended to listen to the speaker for several minutes, but my mind began to whir. When the speech concluded, I leaned toward Marian once more. "Did you get to know Laura very well?"

"Not really. She worked hard, though. She's an expert in the extras—wine cupboards and safe rooms and Jacuzzis—things the contractor wants to tack on to the project."

"All that junk's ridiculous," her husband added. "What do we need a wine cupboard for? I just keep a few beers in the icebox alongside the mustard."

"She kept telling us that all our neighbors had the extras, and we should, too," Marian recalled. "She seemed genuinely concerned—not just that we could increase the value of our property by adding things, but as if we were doing ourselves a disservice by skipping the status symbols. She was very concerned about appearances, I think."

The evening's keynote speaker got up to talk, so I didn't have another opportunity to ask my companions for further insight into Laura's character.

When I got home that night, I filed the zoo story with my editor via e-mail. Stan Rosenstatz, the features editor and therefore my boss, always fired back a quick thanks when I filed on-line. I think he felt guilty for encouraging me to stay out of the office and away from Kitty.

Afterwards, I found myself worried about Flan. I didn't want to intrude on the family and decided it was too late to telephone his mother, Annabelle Cooper, for information.

Unable to sleep, I spent another hour working on the details of a Big Sister/Little Sister outing I had volunteered to organize when my friend Lexie Paine had been forced to step aside due to business commitments. But my heart wasn't in the project that night. I kept thinking about the Coopers.

On Sunday morning, I tried phoning Annabelle. No answer, but that was no surprise. She was a loyal churchgoer. I told myself I'd try again later.

Sunday's newspapers were plastered with stories about Oliver Cooper's nomination and Laura Cooper's death. I read in the car on the way to a brunch while Reed Shakespeare drove.

Before Rory Pendergast's death just a few months earlier, when he had hired me to work for the *Intelligencer,* he had also arranged for a car and driver to take me to the social engagements that I covered. Since I didn't drive—due to my unfortunate tendency to faint at inopportune moments—Rory's kindness was a godsend. The company he contracted was owned by Michael Abruzzo, not surprisingly, considering the two of them had quite a conspiracy going, but the driver turned out to be Reed, a young student who was working his way through college. It had taken months to get Reed to speak more than monosyllables to me.

So I was triumphant when he held the car door open for me and actually said, "Are you really going to wear that?"

Reed didn't grasp the concept of vintage couture dressing. That morning I had dug out of my grandmother's collection a really wonderful St. Laurent Mondrian-inspired dress and short matching coat. Blocks of red, blue and yellow on a white background were crisp and surprisingly contemporary. I was stretching the season a little, maybe, but the weather was still warm and sunny. By his expression, however, Reed indicated he'd rather be seen with a shedding llama.

"What's wrong with it?"

"Nuthin," he said at once. Then, clearly losing the struggle to keep his thoughts to himself, he burst out, "Just—can't you wear something normal once in a while?"

"What's normal?"

"You know. Plain. Not all this weird stuff."

Reed never put on anything but neat-as-a-pin blue trousers and a white dress shirt with a tie, unusual for a young man whose contemporaries wore baggy shorts and Fubu basketball shirts, so I wasn't sure what he considered weird. I said, "I'm going to a party, Reed. Don't you get dressed up to go to parties with your friends?"

"I don't go to parties." He closed the door and walked stiffly around the car to get behind the wheel.

He didn't mention whether or not he had any friends, I noticed. If he continued to be so tight with personal information, I might be forced to break down his defenses with my ultimate weapon.

"Have you met my sisters yet, Reed?" I asked from the backseat.

"No," he said without glancing into the rearview mirror.

"Does it bother you to be seen with me when I look this way?"

"You can wear whatever you like, I guess. Forget I mentioned it, okay?"

"Actually, I'm thinking about somebody else."

He did look at me in the rearview mirror then. "Who?"

"Someone very concerned about appearances."

"Does she dress like you?"

"She was trying, yes."

"Why?"

"That's what I'm trying to figure out."

"Maybe she's just weird. Which way you want to go this morning? Interstate or back roads?"

"You decide," I said.

It took a mere twenty-five minutes to reach our destination that morning—a brunch at the Philadelphia Museum of Art.

My job might look frivolous to many people, but I had come to take my social engagements very seriously. Sure, I made note of what people wore and what food was served, but I felt my real purpose in covering various philanthropic events was to highlight fund-raising for worthy causes like the arts, social services and other good works—like the zoo—that required private funding to survive. With proper publicity, I knew generous donations begot even more donations. I felt the *Intelligencer*'s society column did a public service in the guise of shallow parties and events.

But the museum brunch didn't suit my taste. I walked through the lobby and up the stairs past the statue of Diana with her bow—modeled after Evelyn Nesbit, the girl in the red velvet swing, whose husband shot Stanford White—and went into one of the galleries where a light brunch had been set up. As soon as I saw the crowd, I knew the party invitation hadn't been completely truthful.

The party wasn't a fund-raiser to acquire a painting for the museum gallery. It was an opportunity for the hostess to show off the work of art her ex-husband had been forced—by divorce decree—to give up to the museum in her name. And even though the first Bloody Marys were just being served, there was a good bit of gloating going on. I made a polite appearance but ignored the buckets of caviar—which might as well have been publicly rubbed in the ex-husband's face. I made my excuses to the hostess and tried to slip out unnoticed.

"Nora! Hi!"

I found my route blocked by Blane and April Mae, two of the ex-wife's snide friends. They had just come out of the ladies' room, decked out in nearly identical Manolo Blahniks and Prada outfits. Not for the first time, I thought to myself that Prada often looks like someone's home economics project gone woefully awry.

"We were just powdering our noses," said April Mae, snapping shut her Chanel compact and pointing to the logo on the lid with one enameled forefinger. "We needed a shot of the Double C."

"This whole thing is too tawdry," said Blane, tucking her own compact into an expensively ugly handbag. "I mean, how many ways can she stick it to her husband?"

April Mae snorted. "Maybe you ought to stick it with her husband, Blaney. Now that you're single and sassy yourself."

Blane, a known sexual predator among the Young Money crowd, laughed breezily. "Oh, I definitely plan to add him to my list."

"But first you have to finish with Yale."

I couldn't help myself. "Yale Bailey?"

Both April Mae and Blane looked at me with blank faces, and it took me a moment to realize they had both been Botoxed into complete facial immobility and couldn't make appropriately surprised expressions.

"You, too?" Blane sounded startled.

"No, I only meant—"

"Listen, I was finished with Yale a couple of months ago, so don't worry about a catfight over him."

"Did he give you a bracelet, Nora?" April Mae began to giggle. "Or did you just get roses?"

My confusion must have been obvious, because Blane explained. "You get a dozen roses from Yale if things get a little too rough. He really doesn't like to leave marks. But you get roses *and* a tennis bracelet if you have to pay a visit to the doctor."

"The doctor?"

"You know. If you need the pill." When I still didn't respond, she added helpfully, "RU-486. The do-it-yourself abortion."

"We don't want any little Baileys running around, do we?" April Mae laughed. "God knows, bracelets are cheaper than child-support payments! You didn't have to get rid of anything, did you, Nora?"

"Oh, no," I said hastily. "I'm not seeing Yale. I never did."

"You must be the only woman in Philly who hasn't been to bed with him, then," April Mae said. "What a slut he is."

"But worth it." Blane let out an appreciative moan. "Once, at least. I am proud to say that I was the one to send *him* roses, though. I mean, I can kick it up a notch, too, if I feel like it."

April Mae trained her expressionless gaze on me again. "I thought you were dating somebody else, Nora. Someone scary from Jersey."

"I'm not dating anyone." I tried to be polite. "What about you, April Mae?"

"Me?" She laughed and waved off the suggestion. "I'm an old married lady. Who can manage it all? I get the kids off to day care, go to my yoga class, take the Escalade for a tune-up, and run a charity meeting all before lunch. Time for love in the afternoon with a schedule like that? I don't think so. Besides, who wants to end up like that Laura Cooper?"

"You mean dead?" Blane asked.

"Not just dead," April Mae replied. "I mean *dead.*"

"Hold it," Blane snapped. "You think Yale killed her?"

"Well, you said yourself . . ." April Mae allowed her voice to trail off suggestively.

Blane shook her head disdainfully. "It was fun and games, that's all. He's not a psychopath, Ape, just a little twisted. In a good way, of course."

"Hey, Nora, are you okay?"

I said, "I'm sorry. I don't feel very well."

"Shit, were you friends with Laura?"

"Not really, no."

"Oh, okay. Because I thought maybe you were

upset for a minute. You knew she was sleeping with Yale Bailey, right?"

"Well, I—"

"That girl was busy," Blane declared. "I haven't seen her in months. I'd like to get a glimpse of her Palm Pilot, though. Working a job, all those Cooper family commitments, plus a guy like Yale three afternoons a week, if I know anything about him."

I said, "Will you excuse me? I need some air."

"Sure." Blane called after me, "Hey, get us a mention in Kitty's column, huh, Nora?"

I fled outside in search of fresh air to clear my head, pushing through the front doors and staggering out onto the museum steps where Rocky did his victory dance. I didn't feel remotely victorious. The roses in Laura's bedroom, I thought. I'd assumed they'd come from her husband.

My head cleared when I saw who was waiting for me outside.

"Hey," said Detective Benjamin Bloom. "Are you all right?"

"Detective Bloom." I stepped into the sunshine and breathed deeply.

"What's wrong?"

"I'm okay. Just light-headed for a second."

He started to touch my arm, but thought better of it and shoved his hands into the deep pockets of his black trench coat instead. "Do you have a few minutes? Can we take a walk?"

Reed wasn't due to return for an hour, so I agreed. I was glad to put some distance between myself and the Botox Babes. A brisk breeze snatched at our coats as we strolled down the museum's back steps towards the stretch of the river where the famous boathouses stood. A pair of Rollerbladers flew past us, heading for Fairmount Park. A couple with a baby carriage sat on one of the benches, sharing a bagel and a coffee. A happy couple with no bruises, just a beautiful child.

"Take it easy," Bloom said when my strides lengthened. "This isn't a race."

"Sorry."

"You really okay?"

"Yes, fine. I suppose I can figure out why you're here." We slowed to a meander along the sidewalk. "How did you know where to find me?"

"I phoned the newspaper."

"You can call my home, you know."

He hadn't changed since the investigation of Rory Pendergast's murder when I'd first met him in the line of duty. He had a young, elongated face and old, soulful eyes. With a lanky build and a dark shock of *Leave it to Beaver* hair that fell boyishly across his forehead, his Joe Friday seriousness seemed incongruous. It didn't help that he always wore very large white sneakers and acted like he had never learned how to talk to girls.

Okay, maybe Michael Abruzzo was too much for me. Too big, too demanding, too overtly the sexual animal. Detective Ben Bloom seemed . . . manageable. I sometimes found myself wishing he would come throw pebbles at my bedroom window late at night.

During the investigation of Rory Pendergast's murder, I'd learned that underneath his mild manners, Bloom was actually an ambitious cop who was willing to bend as many rules as necessary to get his career out of a sleepy suburban police department and into the excitement of a big-city homicide division.

"Am I going to be interrogated?" I asked lightly.

"I thought we could have a conversation. You know, just friends."

I sent him a look.

"Okay," he amended. "Let's talk about Laura Cooper."

I said, "I heard about Laura's death yesterday. And I read this morning's papers. I can't believe such a vital woman would kill herself."

"I can't believe it, either," he said.

I glanced at his face. "You're serious, aren't you?"

"I'm always serious about murder."

"The papers say it was suicide."

"It's not open and shut." He walked a few more yards before adding, "Because of Oliver Cooper's connection to the White House, our department's been cut out by the FBI. I'm just asking around a little. You know, to make sure all the bases are covered."

He had learned to put a better spin on his Lone Ranger activities, I noticed. "You're on your own, is that it?"

"Right. Nothing official. We heard you had a little scene at the Cooper party Friday night."

"A little scene was exactly that—little. It was a misunderstanding," I said. "I had been talking with her husband. We're old friends and we were—"

"—in the bathroom together," he finished for me. "Yes, we heard about that, too."

I felt myself flush. "It was perfectly innocent, Detective. Laura and I had a conversation afterwards, and I apologized. She understood that what happened was completely innocent."

"Okay," he said.

I decided that further defense of my honor was going to sound fishy, so I said, "Laura was angry, but she was hardly suicidal that night. I thought she was more in a mood to murder someone else, in fact, not hurt herself."

"Who did she want to murder?"

"It was a figure of speech. I only meant—"

"Who was she angry with? Besides you, that is."

"Her husband," I said before thinking about how I was delivering my friend into the hands of the police. "I mean, she was angry with Flan, but not furious. Not really."

"Have you been seeing Mr. Cooper socially?"

I met his eye. "Flan and I were not having an affair, if that's what you're asking."

He shrugged. "Okay. Tell me what you know about Laura Cooper's life. What did she do with her time? Who were her friends?"

"I don't know."

Bloom shot me another look. "Did she have a reputation for doing anything in particular?"

"You mean her work? She was a part-time designer for a contractor, but that's all I know." I looked at him suspiciously when he didn't respond. "What are you asking? Which clubs she belonged to? Or something else?"

He shrugged. "There was a rumor."

I stopped walking and waited for him to face me. He did. His soulful eyes didn't look so soulful anymore. "A rumor about things she did."

I didn't respond. Maybe I was attracted to Bloom because he felt safe. But at that moment, he wasn't feeling safe in the least.

"Dammit, Nora," he said. "Do I have to pull your teeth?"

"I don't know what you're talking about."

"I talked to a friend in Philadelphia Vice. Apparently, there have been suspicions that Laura Cooper stole things. Jewelry. Trouble is, the people who complain suddenly get amnesia when the real investigation starts."

"Well, did you look inside Laura's jewelry box?"

"The FBI did. They didn't find anything. Of course, Laura Cooper probably knew better than to hide stolen goods with her personal jewelry. Look, if I could find somebody whose stuff had been stolen by Laura Cooper, it might prove that her murder doesn't involve Oliver's appointment. The case would become a local matter again."

And Bloom would get another shot at impressing his superiors. "Well, I guess you'll just have to start investigating."

He shook his head. "I can't. We don't have the jurisdiction. The FBI is supertwitchy on this. I need some evidence to get started."

"I don't know how I can help you."

He said, "I think you can."

He reached into the pocket of his raincoat and came up with a Ziplock plastic bag. He opened it and upturned the bag into his palm. Before I saw the glitter and flash of the blue stone, I knew what it was.

Grandmama Blackbird's sapphire ring.

I let out a shaky breath, suddenly feeling as if he'd backed me against a wall in preparation for throwing knives.

He said, "It's yours, isn't it? I recognized it."

"How did you get it?"

"Let's just say I found it in Laura Cooper's possession, only a few hours after you had a public argument with her, hours after she was found drowned in a swimming pool. Don't worry. At the moment, nobody else knows I have it."

At the moment. "You don't think I hurt her."

He tossed the sapphire up and down in his hand.

"You can't be serious," I snapped. "You're trying to coerce me. And you're probably interfering with the real investigation by withholding evidence."

"Is this your ring?"

"You know it is, but—"

He was very calm. "How many people do you think will tell the FBI about the scene between you and Laura Cooper? And how many people noticed that Laura Cooper bears an uncanny resemblance to her husband's old girlfriend? Yeah, I noticed. Maybe the FBI won't put the two of you together, but I saw it right away. She was pretty bad coming out of the pool, but she definitely had a familiar look. You're going to be the first suspect, Nora."

I felt breathless, clammy and dizzy, along with a few other flulike symptoms. "I didn't kill Laura Cooper."

"I know that," he said earnestly. "I'm just asking for your help. I want to know who else Laura Cooper stole from. Who's missing jewelry? Who would be angry with her?"

If the police became interested in Laura's career as a jewel thief, they couldn't be looking at Flan for her murder. Suddenly I liked the idea of steering the investigation away from Flan. "All right," I said cautiously. "I can ask around a little."

"Okay. I won't tell the FBI about this ring, and you'll find out what you can about Laura Cooper. Deal?"

Bloom might look like a kid with a stamp collection, but he had killer instincts.

I said, "What should I do first?"

"Find out about stolen jewelry."

# Chapter 6

Afterwards, I sat in the back of the car and tried to think like a detective. Except I was trembling so hard my brain wouldn't function. I put my head between my knees.

"My most creative inspirations often come from billboards," my mother used to say. The billboards Mama noticed usually advertised department stores, and her inspiration involved buying new sets of china we didn't need.

But an electronic billboard outside the car window swam into view when I sat up.

"Reed, can you park here?"

Puzzled but obedient, he pulled to the curb across from the Civic Center. Above us, on the marquee outside the Civic Center, large black letters welcomed the Mid-Atlantic Cat Fanciers to Philadelphia.

My sinuses began to swell just looking at the sign. But I had an idea.

"What do you want to do?" Reed asked.

I reached for the door handle. "I'm going inside."

"You like cats?"

It's not that I *don't* like cats. I think they're lovely, and I have an appreciation for their Greta Garbo kind of temperament.

But I'm allergic. Not the charming little sniffle kind

of allergic, either, but the purple eyes, hives and streaming nose kind of allergic.

On the other hand, I was either a prime suspect in Laura Cooper's unofficial murder, or I was being blackmailed into helping the local police grab a high-profile case away from the FBI. Either way, I needed to do something. And suddenly I knew just where to find a certain person on this particular day.

So I pulled a handkerchief out of my handbag, said good-bye to Reed and went into the cat show. The lobby was crowded with people. I followed the enthusiastic throng along a wide concourse to the ticket counter, then rode the escalator up to the exhibition hall, which had been converted into a cat lover's heaven.

I'd visited the Civic Center during the fabulous Philadelphia Flower Show. But that event didn't prepare me for the chaotic extravaganza inside the exhibition hall today. The cavernous space was a maddening mass of cat fanatics, who slowly wound their way up and down the lines of exhibit tables where every breed of cat known to man lolled in splendor for all to see. It was almost human gridlock.

I peeked over shoulders to glimpse a slinky Siamese sleeping on a velvet pillow but failed to see what all the fuss was about. In the judging area, a solemn woman prodded the unmentionable parts of a pug-faced Persian, then stretched the animal's body to examine it before tossing it into the air like a pizza and scrutinizing the way the poor cat landed on the table.

Constantly, people carrying cats brushed past me as amplified voices called various competitors to be judged. I tried not to breathe deeply. I could feel the cat dander making my face blotch.

One frowning gentleman who clearly took his sartorial theme from Prince Philip or Dame Edna wore a tweed jacket and flowered cap as he stood beside a cage and made *tch-tch* noises. He shook his head and made a note with a pencil in his program. "Mother," he finally said severely to the lavender-haired woman beside him, "you're absolutely right. That Maine coon has a loathsome nose."

On the next aisle over, a large black-and-white cat sat like a sultan on a tufted pink cushion, and I noticed his owner had propped a *Cat Fancy* magazine beside him. Yes, the same cat was pictured on the magazine cover. The cover boy sat motionless, accepting his due from passersby. When he yawned, the people oohed and applauded.

At last I spotted the man I'd come to see. Considering how much time he'd spent with my grandmother, I could recognize his toupee from any angle.

"Sidney?"

Sidney Gutnick turned. He was a short, portly man with a Hapsburg mouth and no eyelashes. A jeweler by profession, he wore two pendant necklaces over a nubby sweater, matching pajamalike trousers and nubuck clogs. His pudgy hands were decorated with antique rings, each with plenty of diamonds. In his arms he cradled a blue-gray cat with the same expression Sidney wore—as if he smelled something putrid. On the floor lay a cat carrier, a leather satchel and an industrial-sized bag of Doritos.

"Nora Blackbird," Sidney said in a nasal voice that always managed to sound accusatory. "I didn't know you were a cat person."

"I love cats," I said. "At least, I love looking at them. Unfortunately, I'm allergic."

He shook his head fiercely. "It's been proven that cat allergies are all psychological. I can recommend someone to help you."

"That's very kind of you. Who's this?" I indicated the cat in his arms. An enormous blue ribbon in Sidney's hand bespoke a recent victory.

Sidney cuddled the cat, and his voice turned childish. "Jean Pierre, say hi to Nora. Say 'I'm Jean Pierre, and I'm the grand champion Chartreux.' "

Belatedly, I realized what the proper response was and said, "Hi, Jean Pierre."

"Jean Pierre says hi, Nora." Sidney planted a kiss on the cat's head. The cat blinked and turned his face away from me.

I noticed Jean Pierre's fur was very woolly and almost iridescent. "I've never seen a cat like that."

"Exquisite, isn't he? Go ahead, touch him."

"Oh, I shouldn't."

"Go on. He doesn't scratch."

I prayed my allergies wouldn't kick in immediately and gave Jean Pierre a small pat. He didn't deign to notice my attention. "Lovely. And so soft."

Sidney looked shocked. "It's not soft. His coat is water-resistant."

"Well, he's very pretty."

"The judge thought he was beautiful," Sidney corrected.

I had forgotten that Sidney disagreed with nearly everything anyone said to him. Jean Pierre opened his mouth and—for all his royal appearance—let out a ridiculously high-pitched meow.

Sidney laughed affectionately. "You see? He likes you! How could you possibly be allergic to such a beautiful boy?"

I smiled, but I felt a telltale tickle building in my sinuses.

"Now that we've won the competition," Sidney announced, "we're finished here. Enjoy the show, Nora."

"You're leaving already?" I held back a sniffle. "I was hoping we could talk for a few minutes."

"Oh?"

Sidney Gutnick never had much time for my sisters or me, but he'd been my Grandmama Blackbird's dearest companion during her declining years. She purchased mountains of silver from him to add to the Blackbird collection, and some of her showiest jewelry had come out of his velvet-lined trays. Her early patronage had certainly started young Sidney on his way, and now he was a fixture among our social circle.

Sidney Gutnick called himself a dealer in jewelry and silver and kept a shop on Sansom Street, also known as Jeweler's Row. Perhaps he sold a retail necklace or two, but his real business came from families who found themselves in unfortunate circumstances that required the unloading of a few heirlooms to pay their expenses. With equal discretion, Sidney bought silver tea sets, tennis bracelets and even the wedding rings of deceased family members. He sold them quietly, and over the years had created a long list of steady clients on both sides of the equation.

Grandmama bought some Revolutionary War silver from Sidney, for instance, but years later when my mother needed an extended stay at her favorite Arizona spa, Sidney bought the silver back.

He must have had hope for the next generation of Blackbirds because he said, "You have an item for me to look at? Or perhaps you're in the market for something?"

"Nothing in particular, but I'm hoping to learn a little more."

"Ah," he said. "You've come to the right person, of course."

Shamelessly, I said, "Grandmama Blackbird thought the world of you, Sidney."

He nodded as if receiving his due. "Of course she did. And I'm grateful to you, by the way."

"To me?"

"For mentioning in the newspaper the necklace Lexie Paine wore at the polo matches last summer. It was kind of you to print where she bought the necklace. I had several new clients who remarked on the article."

"Well, the necklace was beautiful."

"It was stunning," Sidney corrected. "Nora, I'm dying for some mint tea. Usually I carry a supply, but I used it all today. Would you like to go back to my place to have some? We could discuss other ways you might mention my work in your column."

It hadn't occurred to me that Sidney might actually court the social column, but here he was, undoubtedly sucking up. I decided it might be wiser to conduct our discussion someplace private. "I have a car and driver outside, if you'd like a lift to your place."

"I accept. Would you be so kind as to carry my things? I can't possibly manage them with Jean Pierre, too."

I gathered up the cat carrier, slung the leather satchel over my shoulder and struggled to control the bag of Doritos without spilling any of the chips on the floor. Like an overloaded pack mule dressed in St. Laurent, I struggled through the crowd after Sidney.

Sidney loved the trappings of wealth. He swanned out of the Civic Center and with a royal nod to Reed, climbed into the backseat, carrying Jean Pierre as if he were the crown jewels. Disapprovingly, Reed stepped forward to relieve me of my burden.

I got into the car while Reed stashed Sidney's

things in the trunk. I suppressed a sneeze and wondered if it were true that a person could kill a thousand brain cells that way. If so, I'd be down a quart of IQ points by the time we reached Sidney's shop.

I gave Reed directions to Jeweler's Row, just a few minutes away. The city's best wholesale jewelers were all located around that single city block. The crowded buildings were all three-story Federal-style town houses with the street-level windows enlarged so that every shop could display an astonishing array of wristwatches, diamond rings and fine jewelry. When business was slow, the proprietors often stood outside together, talking on the sidewalk. Today, however, the street was nearly deserted.

Sidney's name was painted in gilt letters on a small door wedged between two flashier shops. He unlocked it and led me into a small foyer that contained a lift chair to help elderly clients avoid climbing the stairs to his second-floor atelier. Sidney scrambled onto the chair, fastened the seat belt around his paunch and pressed the button. He rose smoothly upwards, with the cat on his lap. I labored up the narrow steps behind him, lugging Sidney's bags.

His shop was barely more than a waiting room with three overstuffed chairs and a coffee table suitable for displaying his wares. Today, an exquisite silver sauceboat graced the table alongside a gracefully curving ladle, the handle shaped into the form of a deer antler. A stack of his distinctive mint-green shopping bags was within easy reach.

"This way," Sidney commanded, unlocking another door and leading me past the safety-deposit–style drawers where he kept his inventory. Finally we arrived in his private quarters.

Sidney's apartment was even more torture for me. The stench of litter box hung in the air like industrial waste over Bayonne. Cat hair floated everywhere. It lay on the antique furniture, the chintz draperies, the glass-topped tables. When Sidney opened the door, I could see large tufts blow across the floors like miniature tumbleweeds. I stepped inside and let out a tremendous sneeze.

Sidney stopped stock-still. "You're catching a cold. Good thing I have such a strong constitution or I'd throw you out right now. But germs don't bother me in the least. This way."

Like most cat owners, he breezed through the stinking apartment without a clue as to how the place smelled to anyone else. He put Jean Pierre down on the kitchen counter. The cat sat and waited for his supper like a dauphin patiently enduring the service of a slow valet. Sidney bustled around the kitchen and finally slit open a foil bag of tuna. He forked the fish out onto a glass plate and placed it in front of Jean Pierre. The cat sniffed the pungent dish, then turned up his nose.

"Oh, Jean Pierre!" Sidney looked distressed. "You're queasy, aren't you? He hates to ride in a car. He mopes for days. I wonder if I should call the vet?"

"Maybe he just needs time to relax," I suggested, resisting the urge to point out we'd hardly been in the car more than five minutes.

"He's already relaxed! He just dislikes cars." Sidney stroked the cat's head, but Jean Pierre swatted his hand away with irritation. Sidney sighed. "He's out of sorts. Well, let's have some tea and hope for the best."

Sidney's kitchen was done in stainless steel and shades of silver—all the better to show off the cat's blue-gray fur, not to mention Sidney's collection of cookware, which hung from a massive wrought-iron rack attached to the ceiling. Everything Sidney owned had been chosen for its aesthetic appeal. He filled an Alessi teapot with water, opened a Quimper jar filled with mint tea leaves, then sliced a loaf of crusty bread with a German knife and dropped the pieces of bread into a silver toaster shaped like a Volkswagen. All the while, he regaled me with descriptions of the silver he had acquired for my grandmother.

"There was one Irish wine ewer," he rhapsodized. "She wasn't one for ewers, frankly, because the handles often looked awkward to her, but I had a lovely one and convinced her to pick it up. She was so surprised! Of course, it had exquisite balance. Very cleverly decorated, too, without being undignified."

"You're a master, Sidney. Grandmama knew it."

"I had to convince her first!" he objected. "You don't know how many times I had to literally cajole her!"

"Do you still have time to give such individual attention?" I asked.

"God, no. People flock to buy whatever I choose to have around. Your grandmother was very special."

"My mother appreciated your help, too, Sidney. She was very grateful when you were able to sell the coffee service for her."

He sniffed. "I told her she shouldn't part with that service. It really was one of a kind. But sometimes we have to let beautiful things find new homes."

"You must see a lot of wonderful jewelry, too."

"Only the best." He spooned loose tea leaves.

Ever since walking into the cat show, I'd been debating how to draw information out of Sidney. He claimed he didn't gossip, so my challenge was to find just the right chink so the dam could burst.

I said, "You have excellent security, too, I notice."

I had seen the stickers for a well-known guardian firm on all the windows.

"I've never had an incident," he said. "I'm very careful about locks."

"Not everyone is so vigilant."

"What do you mean?"

"I know people who have had jewelry stolen."

He blinked at me. "From their homes?"

"Yes. Even at social events. Actually, I was at the Cooper estate on Friday, and I swear someone stole Grandmama's sapphire ring while I was there."

"No!"

I displayed my bare hand as evidence.

"Oh, God, what a tragedy!" His pasty skin turned whiter than before, but then the toast popped, and Sidney hastily turned to stack the slices onto a silver toast rack. "Well, you can't be frightened out of wearing your good things in public," he lectured. "Fine jewelry needs air and light."

"Of course," I said. "But I wonder what happens to things that are stolen?"

"Are you hoping to find your ring?"

"I hope to get it back," I said quite honestly. "Do you know where a thief might get rid of stolen jewelry?"

"Certainly not with me," he replied sharply. "I don't accept that sort of thing. Not ever. It's wrong, wrong, wrong."

"But where—?"

"At some cheap criminal's lair, I suppose," he went on quickly. "But not here. Never, never. I deal with reputable families, upstanding people who have legitimate reasons for disposing of their items."

"No one would question your integrity, Sidney. Not a soul."

"Not a *single* soul," he corrected.

The tea kettle began to whistle, and he turned to lift it from the stove. I felt a twinge in my conscience as I said, "I suppose you heard about Laura Cooper."

The kettle clattered back onto the burner, but he snatched it up again quickly. "Heard! I had phone calls half the night!"

"The police say it was suicide," I ventured.

"They'll soon learn otherwise," Sidney declared. "If ever a woman was the ideal murder victim, it was Laura Cooper."

"You're joking, of course."

"Not even slightly. Everyone hated that girl. Including me." He poured boiling water through the tea leaves into the teapot. "I've spent many a night contemplating her murder myself."

"Not you, Sidney," I said, smiling.

"I'm not kidding." He looked at me darkly.

He put the tea things onto a silver tray and carried them out to his dining room. I followed hastily, and we sat at the table. Sidney poured, then passed me toast and marmalade.

Slathering his own toast, he said, "Many of us disliked Laura Cooper. Do you know anyone who was a friend to her? Of course not! Because she had alienated everyone over the years. And you know how."

I noticed cat hair floating in my teacup and put it down gently. "How?"

"Don't play dumb," Sidney commanded. "She stole from people."

"Are you sure, Sidney?"

"Of course I'm sure. Some of the best pieces that ever came through my inventory disappeared because of her."

"How can you be certain Laura was the thief?"

He placed one plump elbow on the table and leaned towards me like a conspirator. "Did you hear what occurred in Palm Beach last winter?"

"No. What happened?"

"Oliver Cooper invited all his friends down to his winter house for a long weekend. And every single guest lost a piece of jewelry! I'd just sold an exquisite brooch to Mamie Hill, and it was gone in sixty seconds. Word has it that Oliver himself asked Flan to take his wife home before somebody called the police."

"Why didn't one of the guests confront Laura?"

"Confront her?" Sidney laughed coldly. "Who would accuse Oliver's daughter-in-law after he offered to take everyone on a shopping spree to replace their jewelry? I'm sure somebody finally decided to bump her off! And I congratulate whoever it was." He lifted his teacup in salute.

"Are you sure Oliver replaced the things people lost?"

"I have it on good authority. A Florida competitor. You see, not a single person came back here to buy from me! And if everyone starts worrying their things are going to be stolen, they're not inclined to buy more. I could be out of business in a snap!"

I made sympathetic noises. "Do you know who attended the Florida house party? What about Tempeste Juarez, for example?"

Sidney dropped his teacup into its saucer. The clatter made us both jump. Hastily, he began mopping up spilled tea with his napkin. "What about her?"

"Was she at the Palm Beach house?"

He concentrated hard on dabbing up the spill, but his hands shook and he managed to knock over the toast rack. "Well, perhaps. I think so. I can't be sure."

"I wonder if Laura ever stole from Tempeste?"

"At least once," Sidney said without forethought.

"Are you sure?"

"A few years ago Tempeste had a screaming fit when a ring went missing. She went on like a deflowered virgin in an old-fashioned talking picture. I'm surprised the newspapers didn't give her a review on the drama page." He dropped his napkin and took a healthy chomp into his toast and marmalade. A dribble of marmalade landed on his chin when he shook his head. "There's nobody with a worse temper than Tempeste when she's lost one of her sparklies."

"You know Tempeste?"

"I wish she'd never crossed my doorstep. But yes, I do know her. She was a good customer long ago. Not anymore, of course." Bitterly, he snapped, "She's found better places to buy her damned sparklies."

Just talking about Tempeste made his cheeks quiver. He soon had marmalade on his sweater as well as his chin. He grabbed another slice of toast, and I wondered what his history with Tempeste was. Carefully, I ventured, "Considering Tempeste's great jewelry collection, I assumed she was one of your most frequent customers."

"She used to be." Sidney took another vicious bite out of his toast. "I'd rather not discuss the circumstances of our parting. It's too painful."

"I'm sorry."

While he chewed, Sidney made a business of stirring more sugar into his mint tea. "If you're interested in Laura's death, you might consider her current lover."

I must have looked startled, because Sidney laughed.

He said, "You didn't know? You're out of the loop. Laura had another man on the side. Personally, I think she was an old-fashioned gold digger from the very start. Even after she was married, she was looking for a better deal. Her lover was—well, let's just say he's a very good customer of mine. I've sold him many tennis bracelets."

Sidney was playing coy. I felt uncomfortable pressing him for more gossip, but I wanted to be sure he was talking about Yale. I bought myself a few seconds of time by pretending to sip from my cup.

In a moment, Sidney leaned forward, unable to hold back. "In fact, he buys all kinds of jewelry from me. And quite frequently, too."

"He must have a busy love life, whoever he is."

"He does. You'd be surprised what men tell me while they're shopping for jewelry." He tapped his spoon on the cup rim. "As if I'm remotely interested in that sort of thing!"

"Your customer bought something for Laura?" I held my breath.

Nonchalantly, Sidney said, "A tennis bracelet, yes. But Laura was only a passing fancy, not an important conquest, if you know what I mean. He has many lady friends. I just sized an engagement ring for him. Not the first."

"He's engaged?"

"I gather he plans to pop the question soon. He's picking up the ring tomorrow. And his intended is no lightweight, as well you know."

"As well I know?" I repeated.

Sidney said mysteriously, "Let me show you the ring."

We left the table. Yale Bailey had plowed a swath through some of the best families in the city. We all assumed he was shopping around for just the right combination of looks, brains, money, influence and sex appeal before he chose a wife. Who was he chasing now? I wondered.

The cat accompanied us down the hallway, swishing his tail against my legs. I nudged him away with my foot. It wasn't a kick. Just a nudge. Really.

Sidney used a double key system to open one of the heavy metal drawers in his vault. He withdrew a tray and carried it ceremoniously to the coffee table in the shop. He put the tray beside the footed sauce-boat and turned on a Waterford crystal lamp. Then he opened the mint-green velvet cover on the tray. Three diamond rings lay on the velvet. Sidney picked up the largest of the rings. Lamplight flashed in the thousands of facets of the enormous emerald-cut diamond that was the centerpiece of the ring.

"I knew you'd be moved by this piece," Sidney said, seeing my tears.

"Sidney, it's beautiful." I wasn't exaggerating. I used my handkerchief to hold back an allergic gush from my itchy eyes and bent to get a closer look. The huge diamond was surrounded by sprays of smaller stones that managed to soften the shape but increase the dazzle of the primary jewel.

"The young man wanted something outstanding, so I found this. It was created in the twenties, can't you tell? The workmanship! But he wasn't looking forward to ending things with Laura, let me tell you. He said she was going to go ballistic."

Maybe their breakup had turned into a murder scene?

Sidney looked at me sagely. "You see? Your jeweler knows everything."

I was trying to come up with an acceptable way of asking who Yale's most recent fiancée was when Jean Pierre leaped up onto the table. His hind paws landed squarely on a velvet-wrapped bundle.

"Oh, Jean Pierre, be careful!" Sidney cried. He snatched up the bundle, but the wrapping slipped and out onto the table slid a glittering silver gun.

I gasped.

"Don't be nervous." Sidney picked up the weapon with terrifying clumsiness. "I don't keep it loaded. I must have a gun, you know, for security reasons. But the bullets are in a drawer."

Jean Pierre leaped onto his master's lap and nudged the gun aside. He braced his front paws on Sidney's chest and began to lick the dribbled marmalade from Sidney's chin. "Darling boy," Sidney cooed.

I ruined the moment by exploding with a gigantic, splattering sneeze.

# Chapter 7

When I got back to the farm late that afternoon, Emma was there trying to unload a horse trailer by herself. I thanked Reed and sent him on his way, then walked across the lawn to the paddock. My sister was perspiring as she held a thick rope with both hands. The other end of the rope was clipped to the halter of one very annoyed horse that refused to exit the trailer.

"Need some help?" I asked.

"Not from you," she replied, not tearing her gaze from her adversary. "You'll muss your hair. This one bites and kicks."

I looked into the trailer where the wild-eyed animal stood glaring at us and dripping sweat, just like Emma.

"He's pretty," I said.

"He's a son of a bitch," she said. "But he's going to learn to jump tall buildings in a single bound."

"Only if he learns to get out of a trailer first."

"Well, yes."

"What's his name?" I asked, thinking something dramatic and inspiring like Sheik or Apollo might fit.

Emma spoiled my fantasy. "Mr. Twinkles."

I leaned on the fence to watch, careful not to get my St. Laurent coat dirty. "Em, what do you know about Yale Bailey?"

She quit glaring at Mr. Twinkles and came over to the fence. With one hand, she swatted a cloud of dust from her riding breeches. Then she bent down and retrieved a beer can from the grass. She took a thirsty slug and lit a cigarette. "Why do you want to know? God, he didn't ask you out, did he?"

Tartly, I said, "Is that such an impossible idea?"

"He's hardly your type."

"Rumor has it he was seeing Laura Cooper before she died."

"Doesn't surprise me. Yale goes after anything in pink panties."

"Including you?"

She blew smoke. "My panties aren't pink. And I'm not an idiot."

"You think Laura was?"

"You tell me."

"She was unhappy with Flan, I know. But why take up with a social climber like Yale?" I sighed, unable to make sense of it. "Unless it was the sexual thing that drew them together. She was a victim from the word 'go.' "

Emma watched me think. "What's up?"

"I talked with a police detective earlier today."

"That kid?"

"Detective Bloom doesn't act like a kid. He wants enough evidence to make Laura's death a homicide case. And he has some incentive for me to help him."

"Incentive?"

"He found Grandmama's sapphire on Laura. He'll trade it for information I dig up."

Emma whistled. "What are you going to do?"

"I could turn him in for blackmail or coercion or something."

"But . . ." Emma prompted.

"I could," I argued. "I could squeal on him."

"But you'd rather cooperate and avoid opening a scandal, which makes perfect sense, knowing you."

"Why does that sound insulting?"

Emma shrugged and had another sip of her beer. "What does the boy detective think you can find out?"

"Who else Laura stole from."

"It'll be a long list."

"It will be shorter if I can narrow it down to just the people who attended the Cooper party Friday night. Would it surprise you to hear Oliver might have paid people to keep quiet about Laura's stealing?"

"Oliver's not exactly driven snow."

"Firsthand experience?"

She shook her head. "I don't do the Viagra set. But he cheated on Annabelle for years. I saw him with one of Mama's friends at the Devon Horse Show one year, in somebody's horse trailer."

I pushed aside the mental picture before it sharpened in my mind. "Do you know anything about Sidney Gutnick?"

"That pawn broker?"

"He's not a pawnbroker. He buys and sells jewelry and silver."

Emma shrugged. "Sounds like a pawnshop to me. I never met him. Why do you want to know?"

"I figured he was a good place to start. People have bought and sold valuables through him for decades, and he's a gossip. But I left his place with more questions than I went in with. What about Tempeste Juarez? Do you know her?"

Emma frowned. "She used to sashay around the polo fields when I played a few years back. She paid attention to the men, not to a kid like me. She had tons of jewelry, though. She a pal of Gutnick's?"

"To hear him tell it, they're mortal enemies. But I'm not sure that's the truth."

Emma finished her beer and put the empty can on top of a fence post. She didn't look drunk, but I had begun to worry about her need to have a six-pack within easy reach all the time. Her recent broken arm—and the leg she'd broken more than a year earlier in the car accident that had killed her husband, Jake—were still stiff, I knew. Her injuries caused her to lose the job she'd had with the top-notch professional Grand Prix trainer since she was sixteen. I wondered if she was using beer to deaden her pain. Not just her physical pain.

"Listen," Emma said. "I'm not crazy about you helping your detective friend. If somebody got furious enough to kill Laura for stealing jewelry, they might get peeved if you start making accusations."

"I won't accuse anyone."

Our quiet voices must have calmed Mr. Twinkles because suddenly he gave a snort and came bolting out of the trailer as if fired from a howitzer. Emma dropped her end of the rope, and he went galloping past us and off into the unmowed paddock, kicking up dirt and hunks of weed in his wake. We turned and watched him rocket away from us in the falling darkness. He pivoted at the end of the enclosure and came cantering back, head up and nose to the wind. He looked magnificent.

I said, "He's really something."

"He's awfully stupid," Emma replied. "But I like 'em that way."

"Think you can get him into the barn tonight?"

"Hell, no," she said with a grin.

"Want to stick around and order a pizza?"

Emma's grin deepened into something more lascivious. "Can't. As soon as I figure a way to get my rope off that bad boy, I'm going home to take a shower."

"With anyone I know?"

As usual, Emma didn't divulge anything but the most basic details. "A rodeo guy I met at the horse auction. What about you? Mick stopping by later?"

I avoided her eye. "Not that I know of."

She let a loaded silence go by before suggesting, "Why don't you pick up the phone, Sis?"

"No. I don't think that would be wise."

"I don't get it," she said. "I was here the night he made risotto for you, remember? All that stirring and wine and butter and—hell, I left because the two of you were clearly headed for a three-day orgy. Next thing I know, you're alone again. What's the matter, for crying out loud?"

"There is more to life than sex, Em."

"Yeah, but sex is a good place to start. Plus, you care about him. It's so obvious."

"Yes," I admitted.

"And he cares about you."

"I know."

"So what's the problem? You waiting for a nice Amway salesman to come along, or you want the real deal? You're both lonely people who actually have the capacity to be happy if you'd just pick up the damn phone."

"We scored low on the compatibility test, okay?"

"Baloney," she said. "You don't want to give up on your marriage yet."

"Sound familiar?" I asked, more nastily than I intended.

Emma's face tightened. "I'm getting on with my life."

"Picking up every man you meet on the street is not getting on with your life."

"It puts me in charge. It's my way of controlling things."

"Well, this is mine."

She said, "I hear his father's in the hospital."

I snapped to attention, and all the fight drained out of me. "What? When? How did you hear that?"

"I stopped for gas in town. One of the guys who works there mentioned it."

"What happened?"

"Don't worry. He wasn't gunned down in a gangland shoot-out. I think it was a heart attack."

"Is he—? Will he recover?"

Emma shrugged again. "I don't know. You could call Mick and find out."

I hurried inside and dialed Michael's various phone numbers. He didn't answer any of them, so I left a message on his cell voice mail. Then I went outside again. Emma had managed to corner her new horse long enough to get the rope back. We talked as she locked up the trailer. Then she waved and drove away.

Back inside, I decided I had to get my mind off Michael's father, so I dialed the phone number of Annabelle Cooper.

Annabelle picked up at once. Her voice, a smoker's deep rasp, sounded frightened. "Hello?"

"Annabelle, it's Nora Blackbird."

"Nora!" Relief flooded across the phone line. "I was afraid it was more bad news. How nice to hear from you. Are you checking up on Flan?"

"Yes," I said, glad she knew me so well. "I figured you would know how he's doing. I don't want to bother him."

"He's just awful," Annabelle said succinctly. "I went over to that ghastly house yesterday and again today, despite that dreadful Doe hinting I wasn't wanted. I needed to be with my son. He's a wreck, Nora. So upset."

I could imagine Annabelle at that moment. She paced while on the phone, her slim, rangy figure probably dressed in sharply cut trousers and one of the boat-necked cashmere sweaters she favored. In black, to set off the silky white cap of her fine white hair. No doubt she was smoking, too, perhaps even lifting a cigarette from one of the packs she shared with her longtime cook, Margery. The two of them were closer than most sisters, bonded forever by their addiction, since it was ludicrous for a woman who was entirely uninterested in food to employ a cook.

I said, "Is there anything I can do, Annabelle?"

"Oh, you're so kind. You always felt the same way about Flan as I do. That he's special and needs protecting. But his brothers are standing by him right now, thank heaven, and so is Oliver, in his way. In a few weeks, though, Flan will need all his friends. When things quiet down."

When things quieted down, Flan would be left alone with his own guilt and regret, I knew. Yes, he'd need people then. I'd never been so grateful for my family and friends as I was during the few months after Todd was killed. Now it was my turn to make a difference for someone I cared about.

"And how are you?" I asked, knowing how Annabelle would throw herself into Flan's turmoil.

"You're such a sweetheart. I'm bearing up." I could hear her sucking tobacco smoke as she trapped the telephone receiver against her shoulder and chin. "I wish I could shoulder some of Flan's pain. I'm going to bail him out of debt, for starters, no matter what Oliver says."

I always had a hard time keeping up with Annabelle's fast and often fuddled way of talking. "I'm sorry?"

"Oh, you know Oliver. He gives those boys all the toys they can possibly want, then pulls the rug out from under them. Flan's never been cut out to help with the business the way Oliver wants him to. So naturally things went bad. Only now Oliver refuses to help. No wonder Flan's been so upset lately. He's going broke! That's one thing I can fix, isn't it?"

Softly, I murmured, "I had no idea Flan was in trouble."

Annabelle was in full mother mode. "Well, he'd never complain, would he? I only found out about it recently myself."

Too curious to stop myself, I asked, "Was Laura upset about their financial situation?"

"I haven't asked Flan that," Annabelle replied. "But she seemed clueless to me. Spending money recklessly. They've been limping along on his pittance of a salary and what little monthly interest her trust fund allows but then she started those silly house renovations. On a practically new home! Flan tried to put his foot down, but—well, I don't want Flan thinking Laura killed herself because he couldn't make ends meet until she takes control of her money next year."

"Oh, God."

"Exactly," Annabelle said. "Do you suppose your friend Lexie could help? Flan's such a fool with money, and he needs a good adviser."

Lexie Paine was the best in the business, but I doubted she'd be interested in holding Flan's hand. She had bigger financial fish to fry. Noncommittal, I said, "You could mention her name to Flan."

"I could just scream," Annabelle swept on. "Oliver

can take full credit for Flan's money trouble, the son of a bitch."

Her divorce wasn't fresh, but Annabelle was clearly still angry with the way her marriage had ended. Now her son's marriage was over even more tragically. I said, "Oh, Annabelle, you must be so distressed."

"I am," she said, suddenly sounding weary. "My poor Flan."

"Poor Laura," I said.

"Oh, the hell with her," Annabelle snapped. "I hate what she's done to my son."

I was surprised by her sentiment. But I recognized that Annabelle, blind to Flan's faults, would take his side in any situation. Was I doing the same thing?

I heard the unmistakable click of call-waiting, and Annabelle did, too. She got rid of me quickly, but politely. "We get our strength from friends like you, though, Nora, dear. Thank you for calling."

"If you think of something I can do, please phone."

"I will, dear. Bye-bye."

I spent the rest of the evening doing my laundry and licking stamps for the Big Sister/Little Sister invitations. But while my hands were busy, my heart ached for Flan. His life was a mess, and I knew he was suffering. I vowed to watch my feelings where he was concerned, though. I didn't want Annabelle's reflexive defense system to become mine, too. Flan did have faults. Maybe more than I wanted to acknowledge.

My mind wandered back to Laura.

She had been angry that she wasn't respected the way her family had been in Charleston. She had been badly utilized at work where her architectural skills had been ignored and her salesmanship of expensive "extras" caused her clients to belittle her. Her marriage was in trouble. Now I'd learned their financial circumstances were bad, too. And last but not least, she'd been seeing Yale Bailey, village tomcat.

There was still the disturbing detail of her appearance, too. Why had she made herself look like me?

My social calendar for Monday was completely empty, so I put on my hiking boots, grabbed an old ski jacket and set off walking to Frenchtown, the community across the river where I bought my groceries. If I cut across fields and hopped a fence, the trip was only a couple of miles. But on a soggy day, I chose to walk the longer route along the side of the road and hope passing motorists didn't turn me into roadkill. I felt I was safe enough from reckless drivers, wearing my bright pink jacket. I made the trip twice weekly and usually enjoyed the exercise. Even on a drizzly day, I figured I'd be back in time for lunch.

Head down against the light rain and with my hands thrust into my jacket pockets, I thought about the Coopers again. I wondered if Laura's funeral would take place here or in Charleston.

I reached the intersection, glanced up and down the highway and started to cross to the bridge. Suddenly a low black car whipped around the curve and blew past me—too close for comfort. I stepped back, startled that I hadn't heard it coming. The driver blew his horn before accelerating away.

After I crossed the road and started across the bridge, the black car returned. I heard it come from behind me and saw it slow down. I braced myself for a confrontation when the driver lowered his window.

"Hey, Nora," he said. "You got a death wish?"

It was Flan Cooper. Smiling.

I stared at him. "What are you doing here?"

"Out for a drive. C'mon." He looked and sounded remarkably amiable. "Let me give you a lift."

Hardly the grieving husband. I hurried around the back of his Jaguar and got into the passenger seat. It was the largest Jag built, very luxurious with leather seats and a cozy, cockpit feeling. But I smelled booze immediately.

He leaned over and kissed my cheek. "Hey."

I saw an oversized plastic coffee cup nestled between his legs and my heart skipped. "What are you doing?" I asked. "It's still morning."

He sat back, smiling blearily at me. "That's the first thing on your mind?"

"Of course it isn't." I was contrite. "Flan, I'm so shocked about Laura. Are you all right?"

"I'm plastered."

Another vehicle came up behind us and tooted. He glanced into the rearview mirror and put his foot on the accelerator. We crossed the bridge into Frenchtown, New Jersey. Driving left-handed, Flan reached for the plastic cup with his right hand and drank from it without taking his eyes off the road. Was he too drunk to drive? At the moment he seemed to be taking extra care.

I said, "Flan, you should go home. Be with your family."

He sent me another half grin. "I got in the car to get away from them."

"Why?"

"I just needed to get away. And I ended up coming here. Subconsciously, I must have come looking for you." He sent me another loose smile. "You were always good for me, Nora. How come we broke up?"

The liquor had made him woozy. Or was he faking it? Pretending he was drunker than he truly was? I wondered how long he'd been driving. Since breakfast? I steeled myself to see past his act. "We broke up for lots of reasons, Flan, and you know it. Let's go back to my house. We can call someone—"

"You're living at the old farm now, right?"

"Yes, and it's only—"

"How does that work?" he asked. "With you not driving? I always thought you'd live in the city."

"It's a challenge." I glanced nervously ahead as Flan guided the car around a sharp turn and headed out of town, going south. "Fortunately, I can walk to Frenchtown, and my sisters don't mind taking me places. And the newspaper hired a driver for me for work. Why don't we go back to Blackbird Farm? I'll make you some coffee."

He shook his head. "I don't need coffee. I'll be okay. It's just—it's been a hell of a couple of days." In a different voice, he said, "I can't believe she's gone."

"I'm so sorry, Flan."

"They won't even—we can't have the funeral yet. They're keeping her somewhere."

For an autopsy, I assumed.

"They say maybe they'll release her this afternoon. Meanwhile, we have the FBI crawling up our asses twenty-four, seven." He slurped from his cup again, and the car wobbled on the rain-slick road. "You know what? A package came for her this morning. She ordered a dress from a catalog on Friday.

I saw the pain contract in Flan's face. He didn't try to hide it, and I felt a flood of nearly forgotten emotion for him. Flan rarely let the world see behind the laughing mask he usually wore, the mask his father had doubtless helped him create in the misguided WASP male belief that strong men kept their true feelings hidden. I'd seen behind the mask, though. I remembered an afternoon long ago when a bunch of noisy and yes, perhaps arrogant college students played softball in a park. Flan had been the one who saw we'd commandeered a field the local kids used when the disappointed youngsters discovered us on their turf. He drafted them onto his team and rejoiced when they hit bobbling ground balls that eluded outfielders. I'd fallen hard for him that afternoon. A sensitive man lurked behind the loudmouth, I decided. And today I could see that sensitive man needed my compassion.

"Ordering a dress. Does that sound like the act of a suicidal woman?"

"No, it doesn't," I said softly.

"And her quarterly trust fund payment came today, too. But she's not here to sign the check. It's pocket change, but it would sure help with . . ."

I touched him. "I heard you found her, Flan. I'm so sorry."

"Yeah," he said. "At the bottom of the goddamn pool."

"Wasn't the pool closed for the winter?"

He nodded. "I put the cover on it myself two weeks ago. When I went down there, I saw right away somebody had unfastened the cover. That's why I turned on the lights. And there she was, in the deep end with that thing tied around her feet. I dove in to get her out, but she was dead by then."

"Watch the road, Flan."

"Listen," he said, suddenly intense. He looked at me with bloodshot eyes. "Everybody says she killed herself, but that's just nuts."

"What happened after the party?"

He worked to gather his thoughts. "We had another fight."

"Did you—? Did it get physical between you and Laura?"

"No," he said at once. Then, "Well, maybe I grabbed her too hard. She could really push my buttons. I never hit her, though. I know what everybody thought. The black eye—she got that on a construction site, she said. But I wondered. I was really mad at her that night." His voice cracked. "You were there. You remember. I was mad. But not— I didn't want her dead!"

I put my hand on his arm, and he began to cry. The car meandered into the opposite lane into the path of an oncoming car, but Flan had enough wits to pull the wheel back. The other driver blew his horn long and loud. At last Flan pulled off the road. We hit a rock, then a huge puddle. The car slowed to a crawl and finally stopped in a sea of roadside mud.

Flan let the tears roll down his face. Then he dropped his head forward on the steering wheel and wept. Rain spattered on the windshield, and the wipers gave a silent swipe to clean it.

I pulled up the parking brake and put my arm across his big shoulders. I murmured nonsense to him, but mostly just let him cry. Eventually, I dug a handkerchief out of my jacket pocket. I tried to press it into his hand, but he pushed it away and turned towards me. He gathered me up into a hug and sobbed into my hair. I held him, too, cramped in the front seat of the car but willing to do anything to help my old friend feel better.

Except he started kissing me. First my hair, then my face. Then his boozy mouth found mine and soon I had to wedge both hands against his chest.

"Flan—"

I pushed. He was strong and resisted me. But he was also drunk and didn't have much determination. I shoved harder and he sat back at last.

The shove seemed to sober him up. Running one

hand down his face, he said, "I don't know what I'm doing."

"It's okay," I said, trying to catch my breath.

"She wanted to be like you, Nora."

"Flan, I don't understand that."

He rubbed his face with the palm of his hand. "It was crazy. I didn't see what was happening at first."

"When did it start?"

"I'm not sure. She got this idea in her head that I still had a thing for you. And I do, Nora, but not like she thought. You're a friend. I married her, for godsake, and didn't look back. But she talked about you a lot—especially after your husband died. Wanting me to compare the two of you. Which one was more attractive, which one was better in bed—"

"You don't need to tell me," I said. "But why did she feel this way?"

He wagged his head. "I don't know. Her family is some kind of minor royalty down South. They were born on some famous street, and it makes them important. When she came up North, all that didn't matter. People here don't care about anyone else's history. She used to fume about not getting the same treatment she did in Charleston."

"But she married into your family."

"That wasn't good enough for her. The Coopers aren't real Old Money, not like your family. Then Laura and I started having money trouble and—and, okay, maybe I mentioned how you were coping with being broke. Wearing the old clothes and watching your pennies. That's when she dyed her hair and started to dress like you. Except she kept buying more clothes that looked like yours. Our credit-card bills are worse than ever. We were really just hanging on until she took control of her trust fund next year."

I said, "What happened the night she died? After the party?"

Flan tried to focus. "Most of the guests left before eleven. The Red Barons had planned a dinner that night, so they all went down to the airstrip around midnight. I didn't go, but I thought Laura tagged along."

With Yale Bailey, I thought to myself.

Flan continued. "The whole compound quieted down after the planes took off. I went to bed. I drink too much. I know that. I woke up when I had to go to the bathroom. I went across the hall to see her—to apologize, I swear. She wasn't in her room, so I went looking for her." He removed the lid from the empty cup and looked morosely inside. Voice lower, he said, "It's only a matter of time, you know. They're going to come after me."

"Who?"

"The FBI. The cops." He laughed uncertainly. "It's always the husband. Don't you know that? Once my dad's nomination goes through, the cops are going to dig into Laura's death. It won't stay a suicide. And then they're going to arrest me."

"They'd have to prove you hurt her. They'll have to find a motive, and they'll need evidence." I could see arguing with him wasn't going to help. He was depressed and drunk, and in no mood to be reasoned with.

He shook his head slowly. "I need help, Nora. I thought maybe I could soften you up. Make you think about what we had back in college. A couple of kisses, you know, and maybe you'd help me. You figured out who killed Rory Pendergast. Maybe you can do the same for me."

Part of me still loved Flan. I didn't need kissing to remind me of the young man who had captured my heart many years ago. My first love. The one who made my breath catch when I caught sight of him, the one who could make me ache with love and newfound sexual longing. The one who helped me grow up.

I could picture him that night, contritely going across the hall to make peace with his wife. With me, he'd been more sensitive than he'd let on to the world, and I knew he must have loved Laura with all his big heart.

"You don't need to play games with me, Flan. I'll do everything I can to help. But you have to meet me halfway." I shook his forearm gently. "You have to help yourself."

"I can do that," he said. "I'll do whatever you tell me to do."

He trusted me. With that trust came responsibility. "Let's get you sobered up first," I said. "Do you have a phone?"

He pulled a cell phone off his belt and handed it to me. I flipped it open, but the battery was dead. Typical. It was my observation that cell phones never worked at crucial moments.

I said, "You'll have to drive us into town. It's just a couple more miles, Flan. Be careful. We'll find a phone and figure out what to do next."

Obediently, Flan drove his Jaguar along the Delaware to Lambertville. He didn't slog into any more puddles or crash into any cars, trees or postal boxes. The rain had stopped, but the road was still wet. My heart was in my throat the whole trip. I wanted only to get him out from behind the wheel and in front of a large cup of coffee as soon as possible.

But the car reached the town limit and ran out of gas.

We had just enough momentum to coast down

North Main. We were within fifteen yards of the gas station when the car finally drifted to a stop in the middle of the street.

Directly in front of Michael Abruzzo's garage.

"Hell," Flan said, pleased to find himself staring at the gas station. "What better place to run out of gas? My luck is changing already."

I wasn't so sure.

Flan blew the car horn.

At the sound, a tall figure came out of the dark garage, wiping his hands on an oily rag. He squinted into the car. It was Michael, looking like a pirate king or a very tall rock star. He had his hair tied back with a bandanna and some kind of wrench slung through a loop on his stained overalls. He saw me and ambled over to see what the trouble was.

I got out of the car and intercepted him. "I'm sorry about this."

Considering we had argued just two days ago, I felt ridiculous coming to him for help. But I had no choice.

He must have seen the urgency in my face because he said only, "What's up?"

"I'm with a friend," I said quickly, aware that Flan was fumbling with his seat belt and trying to get out of the car. "He's drunk and shouldn't be driving. The car ran out of gas, thank heaven, but I don't want him to drive again until he's sober."

"No problem. This is a Jag," Michael pointed out. "I'm sure we can find something wrong with it."

Flan got out of the car and reeled around the hood. "Hey, buddy," he said with a tone that bespoke a lifetime of being obeyed. "Give us a hand, huh? How about pushing this baby over to the pump?"

"Sure," said Michael, but he didn't move. Already, a cadre of his employees had wandered out of the garage to see what was going on. One spat on the asphalt. The rest of them carried tools and looked like mercenaries readying to pillage a car dealership. I was startled to see my nephew Rawlins among them. On a school day, no less.

Michael glanced over his shoulder and communicated some silent code, so the gang came over to push Flan's car out of the middle of the street. Avoiding my eye, Rawlins opened the driver-side door and reached in to steer.

Flan called, "Hey, kid, watch out for the upholstery."

Then he put his arm around me and stood back to watch his car. His arm felt like a three-hundred-pound weight on my shoulders.

Michael went on cleaning his hands. "Not a great day for a drive in the country. Looks like you got into some mud. Why don't you go get some lunch and we'll clean up the car?"

"Great idea," I said. "I'm starving. What do you say, Flan?"

Flan shrugged. "Okay. I gotta take a leak first."

Michael pointed around the side of the garage.

Flan let me go and headed for the rest room.

Michael said, "When he gets back, you going to introduce me to Prince Charming?"

"It's not what you think. His wife just died."

"The same woman we talked about on Saturday?"

"The very one."

Michael cocked an eyebrow at me. "Looks like he's getting over her pretty fast."

"He's upset and he's drunk and he's—oh, never mind. I don't have to explain."

"No, you don't," he agreed. "But you brought the asshole here."

I didn't get angry, exactly, but I felt a zing in my blood pressure. "He's not an asshole. What is my nephew doing here on a school day, may I ask?"

He smiled. "Vocational training."

"You, of all people, should advocate the importance of a good education to a young person like Rawlins."

"It's Columbus Day, Nora. No school. Give the kid a break. And me some credit."

My face got hot. "I'm sorry. I don't know why I'm being—well, never mind. Can I use the phone? I'll call his brother."

Out of his pocket, he handed me his cell phone. Then he sauntered over to the Jag and asked Rawlins to open the hood.

Of course, Michael's phone worked perfectly. I dialed information, then connected with Chaz Cooper's home telephone line. A woman answered, not his wife, but perhaps a housekeeper. I started to leave a message with her, but she interrupted and suggested I reach Chaz on his cell phone. I dialed quickly, but Flan came out of the rest room just then. Michael called him over to the car.

I spoke with Chaz Cooper at last, and he sounded relieved that his brother had turned up safe. He agreed to come for Flan as soon as he could humanly get there. I hung up in time to hear Flan shouting at Michael.

"The car was running perfectly until you got your hands on it, and now it won't start? Who gave you permission to open the hood?"

"I did, Flan." I hurried across the asphalt. "I'm sorry. I thought I heard a noise."

"We'll have a look at it." Michael appeared not the least affected by Flan's red face and belligerent tone. "Go get some lunch. It'll be good as new when you get back."

Flan muttered more abuse, but allowed me to drag

him down the street to the Lambertville Station Restaurant where he ordered the alligator chili and a Coke. He ate a few bites, then turned dejected. Oddly enough, his change of mood made me feel better. At last he was starting to act like a man who had lost someone he loved.

When we walked back to the gas station an hour later, I was relieved to see Chaz Cooper talking with Michael outside the garage, apparently discussing motorcycles.

Flan was too dulled by his drinking to ask many questions, so Chaz and I bundled him into the other car.

Chaz was the oldest of the Cooper boys, the one who had stepped up to run Cooper Aviation as their father drifted into the political arena. At a distance, he could pass for Flan—bulky through the chest and shoulders, fair-skinned and blond. But close up, Chaz had unmanicured nails and no dimple. He was the serious version of Flan. I knew he'd married the girl next door, Jennifer, a lawyer who mostly did pro bono work for families. They had three young children. Chaz often flew around the country on aviation business, meeting with shareholders, lawyers and customers but always making time to attend Little League games in the evenings.

He was the least likely family member to hold Flan's behavior against him.

"Thanks, Nora." Chaz took my hand and gave me a perfunctory kiss on the cheek. "I appreciate the call."

"I'm glad to help, Chaz. I'm very fond of Flan."

Even his smile was serious. "You always had a weakness for people in trouble. Instead of my brother, you ought to have a bunch of kids to look after now. Or are you on a career path these days?"

Conscious of Michael beside me, I said lightly, "I hear it's possible to do both." Then, "Chaz, I'm so sorry about Laura. Is there anything I can do to help?"

"You've helped plenty." He jerked his head to indicate Flan safely stowed in the car. "We're all sorry about what happened at the party, Nora. You and Flan, I mean, then Laura getting in on the act. He was paying her back, you know."

"Paying her back?"

Chaz glanced uneasily at Michael, not comfortable making a full disclosure without some privacy. "He interrupted her earlier in the evening. Caught her with someone. So he was retaliating, I guess. I'm sorry you got mixed up in it."

I couldn't ask for more details. Chaz clearly wanted to let the subject drop. "Come on," he said, jerking his head toward his car. "Can we run you home?"

"That's okay," I said, staying under the overhang of the garage. "I'll get a ride."

Chaz's gaze flicked from me to Michael and back again with only the slightest twitch of an eyebrow. He nodded. "Okay. See you around." He put his hand out to Michael. "I'm Chaz Cooper. Maybe I'll come back and look at that bike when it's running."

Michael took his handshake. "Mick Abruzzo. Come any time."

Chaz had turned away before Michael's notorious name sank in, and I could see his step falter as he absorbed the information. Chaz glanced back at me, but his manners were too good for anything more.

Flan was already asleep in the passenger seat when Chaz drove off. As we watched them depart, I said humbly, "Thank you, Michael."

"No problem. We'll take Cooper's Jag down to his place later this afternoon." He put his shoulder against the doorway and leaned there to look down at me. "The brother is nicer than the asshole."

"Yes, Chaz is very sweet."

"Sounds like you had a pretty good time at their party."

"Not really, no." I decided he didn't need to hear any more about the Coopers, so I went on the offensive. "Emma says your father is ill."

"Yeah, I heard that."

"You haven't seen him yet?"

"Nope."

Closed door.

Clearly, Michael wasn't going to talk about his relatives. I'd read every scrap of newspaper coverage of the Abruzzo family and even dug into the *Intelligencer* archives to learn more. "Big Frankie" Abruzzo was a well-documented East Coast criminal who associated with a man commonly referred to as a "kingpin." After the kingpin went to prison for a stretch likely to last into his next few incarnations, Big Frankie branched into gambling and eventually became the focus of several racketeering investigations. Most recently, those investigations had resulted in the arrest of Michael's brother.

Big Frankie's photos—those not snapped as he held a magazine over his face—made him look like a brawny lounge singer, not a mob boss.

I said, "I telephoned you last night. I assumed you were at the hospital with—well, it doesn't matter."

"I got your message," he said, giving no excuses. "You okay?"

I glared at his buddies, who watched us from inside the garage, grinning as they ostensibly gathered around the pieces of a dismantled motorcycle. Doc, the heavyset bruiser with a greasy ponytail, sported a T-shirt that read DRUNK CHICKS THINK I'M HOT.

With all those men around, Michael didn't look

lonely to me. But Emma had dropped a remark that had stuck with me. Was he lonely?

"I'm fine," I said. "I heard about your father, that's all."

"Okay." He dismissed that subject. "Reed says you talked with Detective Gloom yesterday."

"Is that part of Reed's job now? Reporting back to you?"

He held my gaze steadily. "I thought you didn't want to get mixed up in another murder investigation."

"If Reed's job description now includes babysitting me, perhaps it's time to—"

"He mentioned it in passing, that's all. His job description includes making sure you're safe."

"I'm perfectly safe in the company of a police officer."

"Depends on the officer," he shot back.

"You would know." At once, I felt like an idiot. "Oh, for godsake, now you've got me talking like I've time warped back to junior high."

"Maybe that's a good thing."

"What's that supposed to mean?"

"You could cut loose once in a while," he said. "Or is that what happened at your boyfriend's party?"

We glared at each other. Pistols at forty paces sounded like a great idea to me.

He collected himself first and said, "Do you need a ride home?"

"Yes," I said shortly. "Please."

"Okay, then. Rawlins! Take Nora home, will you?"

He put me into my sister's minivan and slammed the door without another word.

# Chapter 8

On Tuesday I came up with a plausible reason to telephone Tempeste Juarez.

Upon hearing my proposal, she immediately invited me for tea that afternoon at the Cassatt Room in the Rittenhouse Hotel where she was staying in Philadelphia.

I wore Grandmama's Diane von Furstenberg wrap dress and arrived at three, and I encountered a stampede of tourists fleeing the room. Behind them, the air was hazed with blue smoke that didn't smell like tobacco.

"Miss Blackbird!" Tempeste bellowed, waving a champagne bottle. "We're back here, darling! Do join us!"

Under normal circumstances, the Cassatt Room was a lovely, dignified oasis. The furniture was plush, the tablecloths immaculate. Tall windows overlooked a charming patio garden. The walls were painted with murals depicting the lush landscape of the Du Pont estate. Tall potted palms enveloped each table in a veil of quiet privacy.

Today, however, there was no privacy.

"Pull up a chair!" Tempeste roared.

I stepped over the heap of shopping bags and empty bottles that littered the floor around her table. A waiter cowered a few yards away.

Tempeste waved away smoke so she could get a better look at me. Her hair was covered by a sequinned turban she must have copied from a Charles Addams cartoon. Embroidered on her flowing Chinese robe was a red dragon with a long orange tongue.

"By God," she shouted from behind dark glasses. "You don't look anything like your father!"

Since my father was barely five-six and hadn't had a single hair to comb over his head since 1969, I appreciated the compliment. "Thank you, Miss Juarez."

"Call me Tempeste," she commanded. "You already know my guests, I believe."

Doe Cooper was barely visible behind the platoon of bottles on the table. She looked ashen as she breathed Tempeste's secondhand smoke. "Hello, Nora," she croaked, clearly in the throes of an allergic attack. Her eyes were pink, and her face blotchy.

Grandma Cooper's wheelchair had been drawn up on Tempeste's left, and the elderly woman clutched an empty champagne flute in her hand. "Hi there, little filly!"

Doe got hastily to her feet. "Mother Alice," she said with a wheeze, "I think it's time we went home. Oliver will be worried."

"Nonsense, honey. We're just getting warmed up. Aren't we, Tempeste?"

"Run along, Mother," Tempeste said. "I'm going to be interviewed for the newspaper about my jewelry collection. Alone."

"Oh, poo," said Grandma. "I hardly ever get to have any fun."

"Be a good girl," said Tempeste, "and I'll take you shopping for a fur coat tomorrow."

"Fox?"

"If that's what you want, Mother, that's what you'll get. Here's one for the road." Tempeste refilled her mother's glass of champagne.

"I love fox," Grandma confided to me. "It's got sex appeal."

Doe had grabbed their wraps and seized the handles on her mother-in-law's wheelchair. She gave me the desperately grateful look of a woman being freed from ruthless kidnappers. "Nice to see you, Nora. I hope you don't mind us running off this way. But we've been here since ten this morning—"

"Don't worry, Doe," I said. "I'll take it from here."

She gave me a flying air kiss and wheeled Grandma out to the lobby so fast I thought Alice Cooper might get whiplash. Grandma Cooper lifted her glass in a good-bye salute and began to sing "The Yellow Rose of Texas."

I realized I hadn't given them my condolences about Laura, but Tempeste terminated any thought of chasing after them by grabbing my wrist with the strength of a starving bald eagle.

"What about a drink? Garçon! Where is that blasted waiter? Ever since I asked him to take off his shirt, he's been—oh, there you are. Darling, what would you like to drink?"

"I'd love a cup of tea," I said to the trembling waiter. "No sugar, no lemon."

"Belay that nonsense! Bring us another bottle of champagne." Tempeste waved an empty bottle at him. "No, wait! Let's take it upstairs, shall we? It's damn boring down here! And bring lots of glasses! Maybe we'll find someone promising in the elevator."

"Yes, ma'am," whimpered the dismayed young man.

Tempeste got unsteadily to her feet and sailed out

of the Cassatt Room with her Chinese robe flowing out behind her skinny body.

I glanced down at the table and realized Tempeste had left her snakeskin day planner amid the empty glassware. I snatched it up and rushed after her. "Tempeste!"

She plunged into the elevator and punched a button four times.

"So," she said, tipping down her dark glasses to give me a once-over. "You're Charlie Blackbird's granddaughter."

"Yes, I am. Here's your book."

She ignored the day planner I held out to her. "He wasn't really my type, but I wouldn't have kicked him out of bed. Or your charming papa, either. You're very pretty, *cherie*."

"Thank you."

"I suppose you're one of the widows?"

"My husband passed away about two years ago."

"Well, take it from me. It's better if you get back in the saddle. You're only young and nubile for a short time. Use it or lose it—words to live by!"

There was no way to respond to that remark with any dignity, so I said, "I'm so pleased you agreed to be interviewed about your jewelry. I'm sure our readers are going to enjoy the piece."

"Anything for the reading public! Let's go look at my sparklies!"

Without further ado, Tempeste escorted me past a pale concierge to the Presidential Suite. She fumbled with the key, clearly unable to see well enough to open the door, so I took over. Once the door was unlocked, she pushed past me, launching into a story about the last hotel she'd visited where the waitstaff anticipated her every wish. "Including midnight massages!"

She threw her sunglasses on the desk and headed straight for the bedroom. There, Tempeste's luggage had exploded across the king-sized bed and spilled onto the floor. Flamboyant blouses and lingerie lay heaped on the chintz armchairs, too.

But the mantel of the fireplace had been brushed clean of everything except a gleaming silver box. A recessed ceiling light had been focused on it.

"Don't mind Benito," Tempeste said, waving her hand at the box when she caught me staring. "He's seen everything. He likes to watch me undress, you know."

"Oh," I said faintly. The box contained the ashes of her first husband.

"Would you like to try on some of my nighties? He might enjoy a change of pace."

I hoped she was joking. Tempeste picked up the television remote and snapped on the set. She clicked through the channels until she found a triple-X movie.

"There," she said, as the room filled with the sound of moans and a tinny guitar. "A little mood music!"

I gulped. "Where do you keep the jewelry?"

"Right to business. I like that! Here, sit down."

Tempeste flung herself full length onto the bed. Her robe parted to reveal a silver Versace bustier with red ribbon trim. From beneath a heap of pillows she pulled three red leather Vuitton travel cases, each the size of a Whitman sampler. The moaning on the television became more energetic. I couldn't look.

"I love my sparklies," Tempeste said, hugging one of the cases. Then she winked. "Almost as much as I love publicity! Climb in and settle down."

"You don't keep your jewelry in the hotel safe?"

"The hell with that," she said. "I can't enjoy my

things if they're hidden away. Besides, hotel security is better than ever these days, and trust me, I know all about hotels!" She thumbed the tumblers on the lock of the first case.

I picked a pair of rhinestone-studded jeans off the bed to make space for myself. Under the jeans lay a pith helmet, I swear. I folded the jeans and laid them atop a suitcase. There was no space for the pith helmet anywhere but on my own head. Which is where I put it.

"Ninety percent of my time is spent in hotels," Tempeste said. "Or cruise ships. I love to cruise. Plenty of booze and dancing, two of my three fave activities. There!"

How she managed to unlock the case with her bad eyesight, I'll never know. I leaned closer to have a look at the blindingly bright collection of rocks and precious metals that lay tangled in the case. "Wow."

Between her thumb and the long nail of her forefinger, she plucked a brooch fashioned in the shape of a lizard as it ate a dragonfly. "See this piece? I bought it from the Windsor estate. Cute, huh?"

"Lovely," I said, although my taste didn't run to creatures devouring each other. Still, it was hard not to goggle at a pin made of several dozen diamonds, each at least a karat apiece. "Do you buy most of your pieces from estates, or shops?"

"Wherever I can find 'em, honey."

"There's a good shop here in Philadelphia. I wonder if you know it? Sidney Gutnick's place."

She didn't bat an eye, still intent on the contents of her cases. "Gutnick? Is that old queen still in business? Still selling that junk of his? Yeah, sure, I bought some things from him back in the old days, when I couldn't afford anything better. Haven't seen him in years."

Tempeste fished around in the tangle for a hammered gold necklace with the profile of an Egyptian queen cut into the metal. "Ah, now we're getting somewhere. This little beaut came from a very naughty Saudi fellow. He wanted to make me his number-one wife. Oh, the pleasure dome! Here, try it on."

Okay, I really intended to stick to my professional duties, but how many times is a girl invited to put on a necklace that weighs as much as the Heisman Trophy?

Tempeste grinned. "Can't resist, can you? C'mon, *cherie*. Live a little."

She fastened it at the nape of my neck and I went over to the mirror. My reflection stared back at me, somewhat goggle-eyed. Which is why I was preening in front of the mirror while Tempeste lolled among the bed pillows when the waiter stepped through the door with champagne.

At that exact moment, Tempeste said to me, "It'll look better if you take off your dress."

The waiter bobbled his tray and two glasses went flying. I dove in time to rescue the champagne, but the glasses were beyond hope. Despite the thick carpet, the glasses broke. I thought the poor young man was going to cry.

"Oh, buck up!" Tempeste thumped his back as he forlornly stood over the mess. "What's your name, anyway?"

"Julio, missus."

She laughed and began to rub his shoulders. "My favorite! I once had a very virile lover by that name. C'mon, Julio. Sweep up the glass and relax, honey. The champagne is safe, so no harm done."

Tempeste opened the first bottle and the waiter tried to clean up the broken glass, while mesmerized by the action on the television. I got some drinking glasses from the bathroom, and Tempeste urged young Julio to take a load off. He obediently perched on the edge of the bed, knees together and eyes very wide as he alternately stared at the TV screen and at Tempeste's fabulous jewels.

I'm not sure how it happened, but soon the three of us were guzzling champagne and rooting through Tempeste's jewel boxes while listening to her tall tales. She lit up a joint and had no trouble convincing Julio to join her. Their smoke filled the air, and I had a harder and harder time trying to remember what questions I wanted to ask.

Tempeste fastened a diamond earring to Julio's ear and coaxed a smile out of him by tickling him under his chin. We saw bracelets and anklets and necklaces, and the travel cases kept opening. Along with fabulous diamonds, she showed us nipple rings and a pair of engraved ben-wa balls, which fascinated Julio.

"I've had rings in places Britney Spears never heard of," she confided, making him giggle.

All right, I'm normally in control of myself and careful about what I say and do. I spent a lot of years watching my parents misbehave, and I know about all the consequences firsthand. So I usually watch my step.

Usually.

But after a few glasses of champagne and all that secondhand smoke, Tempeste's argument—use it or lose it—began to sound like brilliant words of wisdom.

She lit up another fat joint and urged me to take off my shoes to try on an ankle bracelet that had come from an Indian maharaja. I reclined on the bed with my foot in the air to admire the way the little gold bangles adorned my ankle.

"You have very pretty feet," Tempeste remarked. "Don't you think so, Julio?"

Julio agreed, looking pink in the cheeks. The champagne was delicious. The room had gotten very warm, too, and he unbuttoned his shirt.

Tempeste made a toast. "To fine jewelry and the men who give it to us!"

I made a toast, "To garage mechanics!"

Julio lifted his glass. And burst into giggles.

"Hear, hear!" Tempeste began helping him off with his shirt.

"Now, with all this beautiful stiff," I said, trying to get down to business, "I mean, *stuff,* have you ever had anything stolen?"

"Oh, sure, honey." Tempeste sighed, collapsing back into the pillows and snuggling with Julio's semiconscious and half-nude form. "But what's the point of collecting sparklies if I have to keep them locked up?"

I fought hard to keep my brain on track. "But you're so fond of it all. Every piece has a wonderful story. Don't you get upset if something goes missing?"

"I've had only one thing disappear that I really miss," she said, running her fingers through Julio's hair. "And, sure, it pisses me off that she had it."

"She?"

Tempeste lifted her glass to the ceiling. "May she rot in hell."

"Tempeste, do you mind me asking some questions off the record?"

"Sure, *cherie.* Anything you want to know." She smiled at me with a glowing gaze. "But you look awfully warm. Wouldn't you like to get comfy? You look so miserably hot."

"The piece that was stolen from you. Did it disappear while you were traveling?"

She sighed. "Nope. In fact, I was never closer to the bosom of my family. The ring was a very pretty little number that came from a dear friend. . . ."

I didn't really care where the ring came from, but I poured the last of the champagne into my glass and listened while she recounted a tale involving Errol Flynn without his pants.

"And what did it look like?" I asked. "The ring, I mean."

"It had a diamond the size of my big toe. With a gold snake wrapped around the stone. Gorgeous. God, I'd give a lot to have that back! It had sentimental value, which that bitch knew perfectly well, I'm sure, and that's exactly the reason she stole it from me."

"Laura Cooper?"

"You betcha. But now, I carry protection! And I'm not afraid to use it!"

With that, she began rummaging among her belongings. She dislodged a shopping bag, and I caught a glimpse of the mint-green paper sliding to the floor before Tempeste sat up and hauled a small, pearl-handled derringer out of somewhere. At first, I thought it was another trinket from one of her many famous lovers. Then my soggy brain absorbed it was an actual gun.

Julio yelped and disappeared under the bedspread.

"Is that really real?" I demanded.

"Of course it is. I can wing a pigeon at fifty paces. Get it? Wing a pigeon?"

Normally I don't find puns terribly hilarious, but this one struck me as funny, and I burst out laughing.

Then Tempeste was leaning closer. "Want to try on one more necklace?"

"Why not?"

"It's so large, you'll definitely have to take off your dress. See? It's African. Kikuyu, I believe."

She handed over the panel of colorful beads, fashioned to tie around a woman's neck with leather thongs. I stared at the beads as they flashed in my fingers.

"Where did you get this?"

"Oh, nowhere special." She began to untie the wrap on my dress. "People all over the world keep their eyes out for things I might like. Here, let me help. Oh, what a lovely bra. Don't you think so, Julio? And now the necklace. Oh, stunning. You like?"

It could have been a great coincidence. Marian Jefferson had lost a rare Kikuyu necklace. And now Tempeste had one.

I tried to make my brain focus. "Tempeste, did you get this necklace here in Philadelphia?"

"Who knows? It could have been Cairo, I think. Or maybe London. There's a sordid little flea market there—"

I sat up and let my voice get too loud. "It's important, Tempeste. Where did this come from?"

Her eyes widened. "Why do you want to know?"

"Did it come from Sidney Gutnick?"

"Of course not!"

She was a bad liar. Or maybe she'd just had too much marijuana.

Sidney Gutnick got the necklace from Laura Cooper, I was willing to bet, who stole it from Marian Jefferson when she took it off to brush her teeth. At least, that's what the carousel in my mind came up with in that hazy moment. Sidney Gutnick had lied to me. No surprise, of course. He was accepting stolen goods from Laura Cooper. And now Tempeste was lying, too.

I was on the brink of demanding more information from Tempeste when I realized that we were no longer alone in the hotel suite.

Someone called out from the front door of the Presidential Suite, and we could hear him getting closer, calling Tempeste's name.

And there I was, standing in front of Tempeste Juarez's X-rated television wearing a pith helmet, an Indian ankle bracelet and an African necklace and little more than my slip, when Jack Priestly walked into the bedroom.

# Chapter 9

Jack took me downstairs and ordered two cups of coffee in the farthest recesses of the hotel restaurant where I hoped I became the invisible woman. Cocktail hour was just getting under way, so the dining room was quiet except for two waitresses murmuring near the kitchen door.

"I don't know what I was thinking." I gulped coffee with both elbows planted on the table to stop it from spinning. "I don't usually behave like an idiot."

"You looked very nice, actually." Jack sat with one relaxed leg crossed over the other. "Feeling better?"

I groaned softly. "Only if the floor swallows me up and sends me to China."

"You didn't know about Tempeste's predilection for voyeurism?"

"No." I put my face into my hands. "Can I bribe you to keep this a secret?"

"A bribe would be illegal. Compounding your crime." He laughed. "The smoke was so thick in that suite, I got a little high myself."

I wrapped my hands around my coffee cup again. "Thank you."

"For rescuing you from a fate worse than death?"

"That. And for trying to make me feel less like a fool."

"I don't think you're foolish," he replied. "I'm

wondering why you went to see Tempeste in the first place."

I drank more coffee and attempted to sober up. One more glass of champagne, and I might have danced naked on the nearest tabletop. Who suggested I should cut loose once in a while? I couldn't remember.

I said, "I'm doing an article for the *Intelligencer* about Tempeste's jewelry."

"Really? I thought perhaps you had a different agenda."

I tried to collect my expression, but I wasn't having a whole lot of success controlling anything more than basic motor skills at that moment. "What agenda?"

Jack remained in his relaxed posture, but his voice sounded slightly different. "Listen, Nora. You're a smart and attractive woman, and I'd like to get to know you better. But I work for a man who'd frown on me seeing somebody who planned to undermine my job."

"Undermine your—?"

He passed me the other cup and saucer. "I'm supposed to make sure Oliver Cooper becomes the next secretary of transportation. I can't have a lot of extraneous issues cropping up right now."

I needed time to get sober. "Has there been much political fallout for Oliver?"

He tapped his fingers on the table twice. "A lot of condolence messages have come up from Washington. So far, Laura's death hasn't become an issue for us."

"So far," I repeated. "You don't think suicide is the real story?"

"I don't know anything about that," he replied, sounding like a politician. "The best we can do is let the experts handle everything. I did notice one thing.

Laura's recent change in appearance. She wanted to look like you, Nora. Her husband said she wanted to *be* like you. Why is that?"

"I didn't know her well enough to even guess."

In his sweet Appalachian twang, Jack asked, "Do you have an alibi for the night of her death?"

I felt my spine stiffen. "Of course I do. My driver took me home. I was in bed before midnight."

"Well, that's good," he said, in a tone that indicated he might be willing to buy a bridge somewhere. "Were you alone?"

I could only glare at him.

He spread his palms innocently. "You could have gone out again. Except you don't drive. At least," he added, "you claim you don't drive."

A lightning bolt hit me between the eyes. Or maybe it was just the beginning of a monster hangover. Suddenly I knew why the FBI hadn't come knocking on my door yet.

Because Jack Priestly had already interviewed me.

I drank the last swallow of coffee and marshaled my thoughts.

"Can you confirm you were at home all night?"

I felt a red-hot bolt of anger inside again. "Have you confirmed everyone's alibi? Where was Oliver, for example?"

"With me—at least, until one in the morning. Then a Secret Service agent remained outside his bedroom for the rest of the night."

"And you?" I asked. "I suppose you were surrounded by people all night?"

He smiled. And ignored the question. "I'm sorry I've upset you."

"I'm not upset by you. A young woman is dead, and somebody is getting away with killing her—that upsets me."

Jack nodded. "Everyone needs closure. The funeral is being arranged. Maybe that will help. The body will be released soon, so the family has started making plans. It's going to be a private affair, I understand. By invitation. And frankly, Nora," he added, "I'm not sure you'll be on the invitation list."

I realized my mouth was open, and closed it quickly. Then, "Because of my argument with Laura? Or my relationship with Flan?"

"Because of your relationship with someone else."

"Someone else?"

Jack said, "You associate with a person with whom the Coopers would prefer not to be linked in any way. We must keep Oliver above reproach right now."

"What person?" I demanded.

"Big Frankie Abruzzo."

"I've never met the man!"

"But you've been seeing his son."

"I haven't—well, all right, I know Michael, but I never laid eyes on his father."

"His father is gravely ill, I hear."

"Yes, I—I heard that."

"And if he dies?"

"I don't understand what you're driving at."

"If Big Frankie Abruzzo dies, who do you suppose will take over his business?"

"I haven't the slightest—" I stopped myself. "It won't be Michael."

"No?"

"Of course not. They don't speak. Michael has no connection to his father's activities."

"You're sure about that?"

"Yes, I'm sure."

I wasn't, of course. Not completely certain. I knew Michael had interests in all kinds of peculiar businesses, and I assumed none of them were more ominous than the Marquis de Sod and a string of gas stations.

But it occurred to me that maybe I shouldn't be discussing Michael Abruzzo with a government lawyer or FBI agent or any other guise Jack cared to wrap himself in.

Perhaps Jack saw my thoughts because he shrugged and said benignly, "Well, I'm sure you know what you're talking about."

I cleared my throat and reached for my handbag. "I'm going home now."

Jack reached over and restrained my hand. "If you don't mind my saying so, Nora, you're wandering into some dangerous territory. I'd like to help you stay safe, if I can."

"I can take care of myself."

"Well, good. Shall I take you home?"

I gathered up my handbag composedly. "Thank you, but that won't be necessary."

"Then you'll be allowing the Cooper family to mourn their daughter-in-law?"

I stood up. "I wouldn't dream of intruding on the Coopers."

He walked me to the street. I went home with Reed, making only one stop along the way. I ducked into a quick market to buy some Excedrin and load up on local newspapers. As Reed drove, I prepared to read up on Big Frankie Abruzzo's medical condition.

But first I opened my handbag to stow the Excedrin.

Inside my handbag lay Tempeste Juarez's snakeskin day planner. I had forgotten to give it to her.

I couldn't resist. I opened the book.

And discovered it wasn't Tempeste's at all.

Instead, I found myself looking at Doe Cooper's detailed entertainment notes. It was Doe who had left the book on the tea room table.

I flipped through page after page and discovered that Doe had written down every guest she ever invited, every meal she ever planned, every caterer she hired, what she wore and even—I couldn't believe it—what color her lipstick had been. Her tiny, perfect handwriting was compulsively neat. She included Polaroids of flower arrangements so she'd be sure never to repeat herself. Lists included the best invitation engravers, calligraphers and postage services.

She had a separate section for special notes about specific guests.

Under my name, for example, she had written *Newspaper contact, friend of Lexie Paine, reads books, hates Jamie Scaithe, Flan's lover.*

Being somewhat of an entertaining aficionado myself, I knew many women kept track of their parties so as not to repeat mistakes or pair two people who despised each other at a dinner table. But I had never seen such accuracy in my life.

Under Laura Cooper's name, Doe had written only *Keep away.*

Naturally, a good hostess would have wanted to spare her guests Laura's thievery.

I had to return the book as soon as possible. I could see Doe having a meltdown if she thought she'd lost her Bible.

At home, my answering machine was blinking like crazy.

I returned Libby's call before telephoning Doe.

I could hear her children in the background making the usual dinnertime hubbub. She said to me, "You have to come with me tomorrow to my OB appointment."

In all the concern for Laura Cooper, I had forgotten about offering to help Libby through her labor and delivery. I felt as if she'd thrown a bucket of cold water over me. "What's wrong?"

"Nothing. I just want you to come."

"Am I officially your Lamaze coach?"

"No, I found somebody else for that," she said. "I'll pick you up at nine."

"Okay," I said, ready to ask for more details, but she had already hung up.

There was no message from Michael, and I decided not to risk my pride by leaving any more messages on his voice mail, either.

With a splitting headache, I went to bed and vowed to call Doe first thing in the morning.

I overslept and woke with a humdinger of a hangover. I drank a glass of tomato juice and took a limp carrot out to the barn to feed Mr. Twinkles. While he crunched it, I tried to will my headache into submission. Libby arrived in a spray of gravel and blew her horn, which nearly exploded my eyeballs. I crawled into her minivan, determined not to whimper, and she set off for her doctor's office. She wanted to know all about Big Frankie Abruzzo.

"Why do you imagine I know anything?" I asked, trying to rally. In my mouth, the taste of moldy mothballs had resisted several toothbrushings and made speaking difficult. "You've read exactly the same newspapers I have."

"Is he going to live or die?"

"I don't know!" I snapped, then winced as the invisible knife sliced through my head.

"Well, what does your friend say about his father?"

"I haven't spoken to Michael in days."

"Really?" She shot a surprised look at me. "Still trouble in paradise?"

"There is no paradise," I snapped. "Keep your eyes on the road, please."

"Jeez, who bit you on the ass?"

"Sorry. Really, I'm very sorry. I had a bad night and I'm taking it out on you."

"You're forgiven." She managed to keep quiet for eight seconds before bursting out, "But aren't you curious? About what's going to happen if his father dies? I heard on the radio there might be a gangland war. They might go to the mattresses."

I couldn't stop myself. "Do you know how ridiculous that sounds? There isn't going to be a gang war over a few video poker machines."

"If you say so." Libby sounded doubtful as she shot a wary glance at me "Did you know your friend has a different mother than the rest of his siblings?"

"Yes."

"His mother was his father's mistress."

"I know, Libby. I read the papers, too."

"What a family! Do you think it's a great idea for my future nieces and nephews to grow up in a criminal culture?"

"Can I even come close to guessing what you mean by that?"

"If you decide to have children with that Abruzzo person," Libby said, "you should think about the influences they'll be exposed to."

"Is that why you wanted me to come along today?" I demanded. "Is this excursion part of your campaign for me to have a baby?"

"Who said anything about a campaign?"

"I have no intention of having a baby in the near future."

"But you will," she predicted. "I can see you're getting the urge."

The only urge I had was the urge to scream.

"What was he in jail for, anyway? Do you know?"

I sighed. There was no use keeping the truth from her. "Stealing motorcycles. He went to a juvenile facility first, but he got into trouble fighting there, and was sent to an adult prison for a couple of years."

"Oh, dear. Did he have any weird sexual things happen behind bars?"

"Libby, sometimes I wonder if you were raised by wolves while I wasn't looking."

"It's a logical curiosity. Don't you watch any daytime talk shows?" She braked for a traffic signal. "Red light!" she cried. "Do your kegels!"

"What?"

"Your kegel exercises. Every time you see a red light, you're supposed to strengthen your pelvic muscles by doing your kegels. C'mon!"

I looked at my sister, who glared very hard at the red light overhead. I said, "Maybe I should have you hospitalized. You've lost your mind."

"Do your exercises," she commanded. "That Abruzzo person will thank you."

OB-GYN offices came in two varieties, I decided once we arrived for Libby's appointment. One was the type with fuzzy romantic pictures of sunsets on the walls and a toy box full of mismatched Fisher-Price toys in one corner. The other kind had anatomically correct posters of the uterus tacked up beside the nutritional pyramid.

Trust Libby to find something out of the norm.

The receptionist wore a caftan and rushed to give Libby a hug, which was quite a feat since both of them were hugely pregnant. While they gushed over each other, I peered around the waiting room. The lights were dim, scented candles flickered on the table that functioned as the receptionist's desk and the recorded sound of night crickets chirped from hidden speakers. I could smell an earthy scent in the air, like fresh rain. I felt as if I'd walked into a womb.

The room was filled with huge La-Z-Boy chairs with pastel slipcovers. One expectant mother snored peacefully in the chair nearest me. In a different corner, another young woman had her feet up as she nursed a very small infant.

Libby introduced me to Tara, the receptionist, who made us each a cup of herbal tea and talked to Libby about her bladder. I wandered over to check the selection of magazines.

Before I had to choose between *New Baby* and *Cosmo,* a nurse opened the opposite door to call for the next patient. I was glad to see she had a stethoscope around her neck and wore standard medical scrubs with sensible shoes.

"Rebecca?" she said to me.

"No, I'm just visiting."

She didn't respond with effusive perkiness, but had a friendly, knowing smile. "Checking us out for the future?"

"I'm here with my sister, Libby Kintswell."

She looked past me in Libby's direction and nodded. "Well, we're not as nutty as we look. Come back when you need us. Is Rebecca here?"

The nursing mother adjusted her clothing and struggled up out of the chair with her baby in her arms. A large purse and bulky diaper bag dragged on the crook of her elbow and banged her knees.

"Here." The businesslike nurse went to her rescue. "You won't need all that stuff. Maybe Libby's sister can hold the baby while you see the doctor."

They both looked at me, and Libby and the receptionist did, too.

"Okay," I said after only a heartbeat.

All of a sudden the four of them wanted me to learn everything there was to know about holding babies, and I began to suspect Libby's plot had more operatives than the CIA. They settled me into one of the chairs and adjusted the baby's head on my arm with a lot of cooing and fussing. Of course I'd held Libby's children when they were babies. But for some reason, everybody thought I needed a crash course in gentleness.

"His name is Aaron," the new mother said softly before she departed for her exam. "He's four weeks old today."

Then they left me with the baby.

The dim lights and scented air were hokey, and the sound-effects tape seemed ridiculous to me. But that tiny boy blinked and mewed in my arms, and I suddenly shut out all the foolishness. He kicked his little legs until a satisfying burp escaped, and he looked so pleased with himself that I found myself smiling down into his face like a complete sap.

I touched Aaron's perfect fingers as he closed his eyes.

In my arms, he turned his head, instinctively seeking his mother's breast as he dozed. His delicate mouth made wistful sucking motions.

My mind wandered to Laura Cooper. Would she have been happier in general if she'd had children? Would she have been so concerned about her position in society if another human being depended upon her? Would she have been less self-absorbed if she had enriched her life with a family of her own?

If she'd had a child, would Laura have felt the need to reinvent herself as someone else?

The baby drifted to sleep as I looked down at him. The tiny blue veins in his eyelids were more fragile than the threads of a dandelion puff. And who wouldn't be affected by that intoxicating baby smell? I trailed my fingertips along the downy tips of his dark hair. It curled against his fragile head in tiny ripples.

Unmarried, with no children of my own, wasn't exactly the place I had imagined for myself at thirty-one. All right, a part of me wanted exactly what Libby had—lots of kids to hug at night and coach through their homework and cheer from the sidelines of a baseball field. But things hadn't worked out for my marriage, and I'd known for at least two years before Todd died that children weren't going to happen for us. When the drug life finally got him killed, I thought my own future had been blown away, too. Even as little as a few months ago I was still buried deep inside myself, destroyed by what he'd done to himself and to us. But now, looking at the child in my arms, I wondered if maybe I had come up to breathe the air at last.

Libby stole past me for her appointment, and I barely looked up.

# Chapter 10

When I got home late that day, I finished sealing the Big Sister/Little Sister envelopes while listening to the messages on my answering machine.

My boss, Stan Rosenstatz said, "Hi, Nora. Nice job on the zoo story. I'll call you later in the week if we have more assignments for you."

If? Strange. Usually Stan had a long list of events Kitty refused to attend.

Lexie Paine's voice came next, shouting, "Sweetie, I've got two seats to *La Boheme* next week. Save me the agony of taking my mother, will you? We'll have a bitchin' dinner somewhere and throw spitballs into the orchestra pit. What do you say?"

Libby came on next, muttering, "I think I dialed the wrong number."

I should have called them all back.

But Doe Cooper's day planner lay on the kitchen table and called to me.

I knew I should pick up the phone and call Doe to tell her I'd found her book.

A niggling voice in the back of my head suggested, however, that I keep it a little longer.

I skipped returning phone calls and instead took Doe's book upstairs to read. In the bathtub, I flipped through a few pages, not sure what I was looking for. Endless details of Doe's life were carefully cataloged on the pages. I kept thinking some useful clue might jump out at me.

Then Detective Bloom telephoned.

"Got anything for me?" he asked.

"Have you noticed we never have any small talk?" I said, putting the day planner on the floor while pinning the portable phone between my ear and bare, wet shoulder. "I don't know anything about you."

"What's wrong? You okay?"

I listened for some emotion in his voice, but wasn't sure I heard any. He sounded concerned, but in a professional, practiced, coplike sort of way. I could hear a whirring sound behind him.

"I'm feeling contemplative," I said. "Probably because I spent the day with my sister, and she's enough to make anyone take stock in life. We even had our faces done at Bloomingdale's, but it didn't seem to fix anything. I'm babbling."

"A little," he agreed.

"Never mind. No, I don't really have anything for you."

"Nothing?" he pressed.

"Well," I said, and stopped. I ran more hot water into the tub.

He waited until the water stopped running. "Well?"

At last, I admitted, "There's a relationship between Tempeste and a jewelry expert I know, but I can't make sense of it yet."

"Sidney Gutnick?"

"Yes." I poured more bath oil into my palm. "Did you know I'd seen him?"

"I know lots of stuff."

"Well, he wasn't at the Cooper party, so I suppose

we can write him off our list of suspects." When he didn't respond, I prompted, "Right?"

"He might have been seen at the Cooper house earlier that day," Bloom said. "Not at the party, but in the afternoon."

I put the bottle of bath oil on the floor. "He might have been?"

"Okay, he was there," Bloom admitted. "He brought some jewelry for Doe Cooper to wear that evening. Apparently she borrowed something from his shop."

"That's not uncommon." Especially among people who socialized a lot but didn't have a supply of good family heirlooms. "Did anyone see Sidney leave?"

"No, oddly enough. I thought maybe you could ask around about that."

"Have you learned anything about Sidney?"

"Vice tells me they've been looking at him for fencing some of the jewelry that was stolen over the years, supposedly by Laura Cooper. Some of the less-valuable stuff ended up on the street. Not in this city, though. Internationally."

"What other cities?"

"South American, mostly. And the Far East."

"Tempeste Juarez," I said. "She travels to places like that."

"What did you learn about the Juarez woman when you saw her?"

I said, "Are you following me?"

He didn't respond, so eventually, I said, "I didn't learn anything pertinent from Tempeste."

"Try me."

"She likes watching other people in sexual situations."

"You mean X-rated videos?"

I cleared my throat. "That kind of thing, yes."

"Think Laura Cooper was mixed up in something like that?"

I had learned several things about Laura. She'd had an affair with Yale Bailey. She and Flan were having some money trouble. She wanted to be as respected in Philadelphia as her family had been in Charleston, South Carolina. And she stole jewelry. I couldn't figure out why she stole, but Laura had probably given it to Sidney Gutnick to sell. But X-rated videos? No way. "I sincerely doubt it."

"Me too."

"She was caught in a compromising position at the Cooper party, though. Had you heard that?"

"Who was she with?"

"A man who runs a casino in Atlantic City. Yale Bailey."

"Is he one of the Red Barons, by any chance?"

"Yes. His plane was at the Cooper house during the party. I was in it myself."

"You were? What did you notice about the plane?"

I frowned. "That it was very tacky inside. Not at all what a corporate jet usually looks like. Very Austin Powers."

"Besides bad interior decorating, anything?"

"I don't think so."

Sounding as though he had a checklist in his head, Bloom said, "Okay, then. I need to know about the Red Barons. They flew to a restaurant after the party, around midnight, I hear. Who went?"

"Are you guessing that someone took Laura and murdered her elsewhere? And brought her back by plane?"

"It's possible."

But unlikely, I knew. The Red Barons were a social bunch who radioed each other during flights and lit cigars upon landing. Camaraderie was important. And lots of airport people were around, too. It would be hard to smuggle a dead body past all the friends and hangers-on.

"Chaz Cooper, Yale Bailey, Jamie Scaithe." I listed a few more Red Barons I knew, then added, "Their wives or dates, too, I suppose. But Flan didn't go that night. He'd been drinking."

"Maybe Laura went without him."

"She was at the estate, drowning, remember?"

"The Red Barons left around midnight. She died later."

Guessing where he'd gotten his theory, I said, "You saw the autopsy report, didn't you?"

Without answering my question, he said, "She may have had time to fly somewhere before she turned up in the pool."

"Was drowning the cause of death?"

"Yes. But she'd been pretty banged up, too."

"The bruise on her wrist," I remembered. "And on her face. I saw those at the party."

"The ME said those were old injuries. What about her neck?"

"I didn't see any bruises on her neck." I closed my eyes and tried to remember what Laura had worn. "No, I think her neck was fine."

"She was found with rope burns on her neck," Bloom said. "Bad ones, not self-inflicted. From the same rope used to tie the concrete statue around her legs. It was a thick twine used to bundle up some cornstalks that had been delivered to the estate earlier."

I nodded. "Doe had decorated the garden for Halloween with cornstalks. What else can you tell me about the autopsy?"

"Nothing."

"Detective Bloom, I could be a lot more useful if I had something to go on."

We listened to each other decide for a minute, and I wondered where he was. I continued to hear the whirring noise behind him, so he wasn't at his desk. Was he calling me from a car? From his home, wherever that might be? From his own bathtub, maybe? I began to wonder what a police detective looked like in a tub full of warm bubbles.

Eventually, he said, "The water in Laura's lungs didn't have any chlorine in it."

"No chlorine," I repeated. "That means she drowned someplace besides the pool. No wonder you're asking about the Red Barons."

"You get a gold star," said Bloom. "We're checking water samples now. Why don't you see what you can find out from some of your friends?"

"Who do you think I should I ask first?"

"Pick a Red Baron," he suggested. "Any Red Baron."

"All right. I'll see what I can do."

Another moment passed before he said, "I never got the impression you wanted small talk."

"What?"

"You said we never have small talk."

Aha. This was a change of pace. I said, "Well, we don't. You're always busy fighting crime, I suppose."

"And you go to parties. Why aren't you at a party right now, in fact?"

"I get a night off now and then."

"Oh," he said. "I get a night off now and then, myself."

I waited a while, but he reverted to being younger than I was, so I gave in to curiosity and asked, "Where are you right now?"

"Now? I'm on the treadmill."

"The treadmill."

"I'm at the gym."

I tried to decide if a call from a treadmill was anything to get excited about. Or insulted about. I didn't know why I was flirting with Bloom.

I was experimenting, perhaps.

Experimenting to see how it felt to be with a man who wasn't Todd and wasn't Michael. A man who was on the right side of the law, for once.

"You okay?" Bloom asked

"No," I said lightly. "But what else is new?"

We said good night and I got out of the tub.

While I wrapped myself in a towel, the phone rang again.

I picked up immediately. "Small talk requires a topic—something from which we can digress."

Michael said, "You mean like the weather, or can we talk about what's gone wrong between us?"

"It's you." I dropped my towel and hastily bent to grab it. "I thought you'd given up on me."

He said, "I've been busy. And you've been playing detective again."

I wrapped the towel around myself. "You talked to Emma."

"She says you don't think the asshole killed his wife."

"He's not an—" My relaxed mood evaporated fast. "Look, he has problems, but that's not who he is."

"I know who he is." Michael sounded more surly with every passing sentence. "And believe me, the idea that you slept with him has pissed me off for days."

"That was years ago."

"Maybe for you. Not for him."

"How's your father?" I asked, as long as we were pushing each other's buttons.

For a second I thought he'd hung up on me.

But then he said, "How's your investigation?"

I discovered I was hugging the towel so tightly around me that my arms had begun to cramp. I tracked wet footprints into my bedroom and sat on the bed. My heartbeat steadied. Reaching for the bottle of lotion I kept on the nightstand, I said, "I think I need to speak to a man by the name of Yale Bailey. He runs a casino in Atlantic City."

"Why him?"

"Because he's one of the Red Barons." I pinned the phone against my chin and squirted lotion into my palm. "And he had a connection to Laura Cooper."

"What kind of connection?"

"An intimate one, as a matter of fact."

"The dead lady was sleeping with Bailey?"

"Yes."

"So much for marriage vows."

"Yes."

Michael was silent while I massaged lotion onto my legs, so I said, "I'm not in love with him, you know. He's an old friend who asked for my help."

Heavily, he said, "Well, you're loyal. I'll give you that. Thing is, you don't know when to cut your losses. Or," he added, "maybe you do now."

My heart twisted. "I'm not ready to cut you out of my life, Michael."

He kept that awful silence for another long moment. Then, "When were you planning to talk to Bailey?"

"As soon as I can."

"At the casino?"

"I suppose so."

"What's your plan?"

"Do I need a plan?"

He laughed. But he didn't sound amused. Then he

stopped laughing, and I wondered if he was allowing the felonious side of his mind to ponder a plan. Sometimes it made me nervous that he had such a different perspective on crime than I had, but at other times it was very useful.

Then he said, "Listen, Nora, I need some help understanding this whole Tackett thing—the old house I bought. I know I don't get it. What I call a simple business deal, for you is some kind of Holy Grail—a way of objectifying your family or—"

"Who have you been talking to?"

"What?"

"Objectifying," I said. "Good heavens, are you in therapy?"

"No!" Then he admitted, "I have this friend, a psychologist friend, who thinks you and I ought to talk rationally about this before things go completely bad. I don't," he said, gaining momentum, "I don't want to lose you, Nora. I mean that. We've got some real chemistry going, and God knows I want to take you to bed more than breathe, but I feel like we've got a shot at riding into the sunset together, too. This is a first for me, and I don't want to screw it up. So can you just help me out here? Tell me what to do?"

I felt my head give a dizzy little spin. "I can't tell you what to do."

"Just give me a sentence with a verb in it. I'll do whatever it takes."

I couldn't help smiling. "You'll figure something out."

"How about a clue, at least? Just a hint?"

"Let's talk rationally," I said. "That sounds like a good start."

"You mean it?"

"Of course."

"Okay, let's go to Atlantic City."

"What?"

He said, "I'll pick you up in twenty minutes."

He did hang up on me that time.

In nineteen minutes, I was miraculously dressed, combed and smelling fabulous, if I do say so myself. He arrived wearing a leather sport coat over dark trousers and a crisp white shirt, open two buttons. I nearly asked if he'd father a child for me then and there.

I had rushed into a French-made lace camisole that weighed almost as much as a Kleenex and put on a fitted, low-cut Calvin Klein jacket along with very snug slacks that made no secret of my behind, so I skipped the underwear.

He came into the house, looked me up and down and said a very rude phrase in a prayerful tone. Then he backed me against the refrigerator and kissed me until my insides did something that usually happens on a trapeze.

While he'd explored my mouth and unbuttoned my jacket to touch me, I ran my fingertips across places I had only thought about in bed. Things had simmered too long and needed only to come to a quick boil for us both to feel much better. And things were definitely near boiling. I could hardly breathe for the fierce slamming of my heart against his.

"Wait," I managed to gasp with my head thrown back in a position only possible on the covers of romance novels. "I thought you were taking me to Atlantic City."

His voice was husky. "Can we get a room there?"

"We're not going to bed for the first time in an Altantic City hotel room."

He kissed my throat again with melting heat. "It could be a very nice room."

"We're not going to do that."

He stopped trying to undress me and looked into my eyes. "We're going to make an occasion out of it, huh?"

"Oh, yes. Somewhere romantic."

"Okay."

"Somewhere memorable."

"Okay."

"And very sexy."

"No problem there."

He kissed me more gently for a while longer, then released me slowly. "I'll think over some options and get back to you."

In the car and sounding surprised, he said, "You know, that really cheered me up."

"I'm sorry you've been upset."

He shook his head. "It's not just you. The phone's been driving me crazy. Everybody wants to know about Big Frankie, how he's doing and what's going to happen. But I don't want to talk about it tonight, okay?"

"All right."

Instead, we talked all the way to Atlantic City about everything we'd done during the two months we'd been apart over the summer. I told him that society editor Kitty Keough threw fits if I went to the office, so I was still e-mailing my stories to the editor. Lily Pendergast had taken over running the *Intelligencer,* much to the dismay of the staff. Michael told me that Rory Pendergast's will had forgiven all of Michael's debt to him, which turned out to be a considerable windfall. Michael had decided to use some of his newly found spending money for a fishing expedition in Scotland. He planned to travel with three friends—his lawyer, a fishing magazine–writer buddy and a male relative who baked bread. They all sounded like better company than his usual crew.

The car was one of Michael's old behemoths with a very large front seat and lots of silver chrome. He seemed very pleased to be driving it, and it rode as smoothly as a magic carpet.

When we crossed the Pennsylvania state line, he said, "You know that car Cooper left with us?"

"Flan's Jaguar? Yes."

"One of my guys took it back, and guess who met him in the driveway. A repo company."

"Flan's car was repossessed?"

"I guess he's so upset about his wife that he forgot to pay his bills. I wonder if the FBI knows."

Another nail in Flan's coffin, I thought. I said, "I'm sure they do."

"Have you been visited yet?"

"By the FBI? In a way, yes."

He glanced at me. "What does that mean?"

"We haven't been formally introduced," I replied, "but someone questioned me."

He stopped at a traffic signal, and I remembered Libby and her kegels. I began to laugh. In the glow of the dashboard lights, Michael looked at me and smiled as if he understood exactly what I was thinking.

We reached the bright lights of Atlantic City around nine and cruised past Bally's and the Trump Taj Mahal. When I got out of the car, I could smell the ocean. The hotels also pumped out the scents of exotic food, expensive perfumes and a fragrance I can only describe as cold hard cash. We left the car with a valet outside the entrance of the casino managed by Yale Bailey and followed the red carpet inside.

Michael seemed to know where to go. A horde of people rushed past us in the direction of the ballroom where a former sitcom star would perform later, according to the posters. We strolled among the slot machines, listening to the bedlam of bells, coins and Frank Sinatra singing about luck and ladies. Cigarette smoke was thick, and the average customer appeared to be a sixtyish woman wearing clothes that glittered. The hotel lobby—all crystal and water fountains and shiny marble—merged out of the slot machine area. There, the music was more subdued, the atmosphere expensive. A long check-in counter stretched before us, manned by a line of smiling assistant managers dressed like Thai banquet slaves.

Michael went over and spoke to a concierge—who wore a business suit, not a slave costume—and I thought I saw money slide between them. The concierge made a phone call while Michael chatted with a starry-eyed young woman behind the desk.

In a few minutes, we were given an okay from the other end of the telephone and the concierge escorted us to a key-operated elevator. Michael stopped outside the open car and kissed me quickly. "Be careful, all right?"

"Aren't you coming?"

"I'm feeling lucky," he said. "I'll go roll some dice. You'll handle Yale better without me, anyway."

The door closed between us. I smiled through the glass at Michael. He stayed where he was and watched me *whoosh* upwards. Until we couldn't see each other anymore, we smiled like two kids with a big secret.

At the top of the casino, the concierge and I stepped off the elevator into nearly total darkness. Only a small, lighted sign gave any indication we were still inside the building.

It read YALE BAILEY, EXECUTIVE MANAGER.

We walked away from the elevator along a glass block wall and reached an expansive office that took up the entire penthouse floor. No lamps or overhead light fixtures were turned on, but all the surfaces of metallic desks, sleek leather chairs and tall windows seemed to have electric moonlight gleaming on them. Tall windows overlooked the black ocean on one side and Bally's rooftop on the other. Brilliant lights gleamed from the other casino. The only artwork on the walls of Yale's office consisted of lurid posters for old vampire movies. Plenty of dripping blood.

A flick of movement on my right made me flinch. What I thought had been the glass block wall was actually a huge fish tank built to serpentine around the top floor. I had never seen an aquarium so large outside of a zoo. As I stepped back, a shark nosed out of the darkness and looked at me with its flat, black eye. It swam lazily past me, but I had the feeling I'd been earmarked for a light snack.

By more than the shark. Above my head, I glimpsed the glitter of a video camera's eye.

Yale Bailey came towards me out of the silvery darkness where he'd been in conference with a man and a very tall young woman. "Nora," he said. "Nora Blackbird. What a surprise."

"Hello, Yale. Thank you for seeing me."

We exchanged a quick, not-quite-friends kiss on the cheek, but also shook hands. Hard. I remembered how painfully he'd squeezed me at the Cooper party, too.

Yale countered his handshake with a bland smile. "It's a pleasure," he said.

He had grown up in New York, if I remembered correctly, and managed to infiltrate my social circle in Philadelphia by way of a Princeton classmate at first, then by virtue of his own persuasive personality. He attended a lot of charity events—at casino expense, I was sure—and over the last couple of years had made his way through many women of my acquaintance. He had fiery red hair and lots of orange freckles, but he managed to turn those features into assets. He generally wore earth tones, and I noticed his clothing made a striking statement among the cold metal and glass surfaces of his office.

"You look great," he said, releasing my hand from that wincingly powerful grip. "I'm glad you came up."

"I can see you're busy." I indicated his associates and the desk where his computer glowed and various notebooks lay open for his study. A bank of television screens showed live video feed from around the casino. "I don't mean to interrupt you."

"I could use a break," he said. "Can I get you a drink? A glass of wine? Something stronger?"

"You're having coffee," I guessed by the cup on his desk. "That suits me, too."

"Coming right up. Tiff?"

The tall young woman obeyed him by going to a butler's tray near the shark tank. To the concierge who had delivered me and the man who'd been talking with Yale when I arrived, he said, "Why don't you fellows give me ten minutes with my friend?"

They gathered up their notebooks and departed for the elevator with such speed that I figured they were sent away often.

I could see Yale was curious about my visit, but he made polite conversation first. "How's your sister Emma? I haven't seen her since last spring."

"She's fine. She broke her arm earlier this year, but it's mending."

He looked sympathetic. "That's tough. She was just getting over the broken leg, right? Must make riding difficult."

"She's bought a horse of her own to train. I think she'll do fine."

"She's fine, all right." Talking more to himself than to me, he said, "I should give her a call."

The tall woman returned with a china cup and saucer for me. She had an exotic face with almond-shaped eyes and arching brows balanced by a wide, luscious mouth painted dusky purple. She wore a short-skirted business suit—no blouse, just cleavage—large gold hoop earrings and a pair of very expensive Italian spike-heeled shoes with no stockings. Very Wall Street meets Vegas. Her face was cold when she handed me the coffee.

At once, I saw the bruise on her wrist.

"Thank you," I said.

The young woman made a snorting noise I wasn't supposed to hear. She left the room very quickly, leaving me uncomfortable and Yale smiling.

"Don't mind Tiffany. Jealous type." He grinned. "Want to meet my pet?"

"Uh, sure."

"We can talk while I feed him."

I carried my coffee cup with me while Yale led the way to a small fish tank in the corner. It was teeming with large goldfish, their colors flitting beautifully in the odd light. Yale said, "Is this a social call, Nora?"

"Not exactly. I know this is strange," I said, watching him lift the glass lid from the fish tank. "I'm doing a favor for a friend, and I thought you could help."

If he was dismayed to hear I hadn't come looking for love, he hid it well, but I had made it clear from the moment I arrived that my visit was only business, and he had gotten the message. "Whatever you need," he said. With his left hand, he picked up a long-handled net.

"I used to be close to Flan Cooper, you know. We were together in college."

He glanced up from the fish. "I didn't know that."

"We're still good friends, you see. He's very upset about Laura."

"I'm sure." It was difficult to be sure in that strange silver light, but I thought his freckles looked brighter orange than before as he bent over the goldfish again. "I'm very sympathetic, Nora, but what does this have to do with me?"

"Flan's worried that the police will eventually decide he killed Laura."

He flicked the net into the tank and captured a wriggling fish, but nearly dropped it when my words sank in. "Killed her? I thought she drowned herself."

"That was everyone's first impression, but I think that ruling is going to change."

"Someone killed her," Yale said. Looking believably stunned, he stood for a long moment, holding the net in midair while the goldfish gasped. "That's hard to believe."

I wondered if his response was a performance or genuine shock. "Thing is, Yale, the first step is to piece together what happened during the party and afterwards. Has someone from the FBI talked to you already?"

He carried the goldfish across the room, indicating that I should follow. "Yeah, sure, a couple of days ago. But they never mentioned anything about murder."

"I wonder if you remember what happened after the party broke up. You're a Red Baron, right?"

"Yep."

"And you went out with the Red Barons after the party. You took your plane and went to dinner."

He nodded as he unlatched the lock on a much larger fish tank and climbed two steps to stand over the open water. "Yeah, we went to a place near Pittsburgh. It was a beautiful night for flying."

"Do you remember who went on the trip?"

He named the same group I had identified to Bloom, then added, "Flan Cooper didn't go. He was three sheets to the wind."

"What about Laura? Did she travel with one of you?'

"No," Yale said at once. "She got waylaid before we took off."

"Waylaid?"

"Yeah, she was having a talk with Mrs. Cooper."

"Doe?"

Yale waggled the net, and droplets fell into the large tank, disturbing the surface of the water. He watched the gasping goldfish without really seeing it. "They were going at it pretty good, so we left without Laura."

"Laura and Doe were arguing?"

Yale shrugged. "Something about ruining the party. Doe was steamed."

I raised my brows and let a question hang.

Yale grinned. "Okay, so I'd been with Laura earlier in the evening. We were just fooling around, nothing serious, but Flan came along and caught us. He blew up, did some shouting, and Doe—well, Doe was worried the other guests were grossed out. She took it out on Laura later on the patio, said we'd ruined the night."

"You heard their argument and decided not to take Laura on your plane?"

He looked up at me, still suspending the poor flopping goldfish over the water in the tank below. "Right."

"Did you happen to see her at the airstrip with anyone else?"

"To be honest, Nora, the only thing I really noticed

about Laura that night was the fight she had with you."

I tried not to look at the desperate little fish on Yale's net. "I see."

"Everybody heard her yelling. And we saw you chase her up the stairs. Even the FBI asked me about it."

I said, "Yale . . ."

"What is it, Nora?"

"The fish. It's dying."

"Oh, right!" He laughed. "You distracted me. Here you go, little buddy."

He dropped the goldfish into the tank and it plopped deep into the water. At first it was stunned. Then I saw it revive with a happy wriggle and begin to swim.

But out of the darkness came the shark. It whipped into sight, slashed its tail and snapped the goldfish into its jaws. Instantly, the goldfish disappeared. Devoured.

Yale smiled. "Spectacular, don't you think? I love watching this guy eat."

I put down the cup and saucer before I dropped it on the floor. I felt my head go light and the dark cloud of unconsciousness start to whirl around me. I fought down the faint. Yale had wanted to horrify me, and he'd done it. But I was also suddenly angry, and that made me bold. I said, "I heard you had been dating Laura Cooper before the party. Having an affair with her."

Yale climbed down from the open tank and shook his head. "Nora, do you know any woman I haven't been seen with one way or another? Besides you, that is. And believe me, I was just allowing you a decent period of time after your husband died."

I supposed that was meant to flatter, but I looked at him with loathing.

He twirled his empty net. "Sure, I saw her for a while. We had a few laughs. But it was a fling. We both understood it was a short-term thing."

"Could Laura have interpreted your relationship as a serious affair?"

He waggled his head. "That girl was a nutcase, but even she wouldn't have assumed we were anything more to each other than some afternoon fun. I guess she couldn't get what she wanted at home."

He smiled again, showing lots of teeth.

I felt my insides curdle.

Over his shoulder, I caught another glimpse of the shark tank. The beast inside cruised past again, tail sashaying slowly.

Suddenly I wondered if the opening in the tank was large enough for Laura Cooper to fit through. Had she been drowned here and returned by plane to the Cooper estate, then left in the pool? If Yale could feed helpless goldfish to his shark, was he capable of drowning Laura?

"Besides," Yale said, "I'm in a one-on-one relationship now."

"Oh."

"It's the real thing," he assured me. "I'm a lucky man. I'm going to marry her."

"How nice."

"And you know the lady, too."

Okay, I have a terrible prejudice against men who call the women in their lives "The Lady." Either they want to be sure you know she's above all moral reproach or it's the name of their childhood dog that they want to perpetuate or something. I couldn't even plaster a small smile on my face. "Really?"

"Sure. Lexie Paine."

I stood very still and hoped my expression didn't look as horrified as I felt.

But I had no time to find out more.

We were interrupted by the tall young woman.

"Yale," she said, from the shadows, "we need your attention."

"Excuse me, Nora."

While I gathered my thoughts, they murmured together and were joined by another man in a maroon jacket with a casino logo printed on the breast pocket. They conferred seriously. Yale nodded and turned back to me.

"Nora, I'm sorry, but there's someone I need to take care of. I have a thousand employees, but all the real dirty work falls to me."

"Of course. I've kept you too long."

"Not at all. There's just somebody I need to escort off the property. We can't be too careful. Our business is highly regulated, and we have to police our guests or risk losing our license. Shall I ride down with you?"

The four of us got into the elevator and were joined on a lower floor by two more large men in snug-fitting maroon jackets. Before we arrived at the lobby level, I knew who they were kicking off the premises.

"Hey, Yale," said Michael, smiling broadly as he stood in the lobby in the company of all those maroon-jacketed security guards. "You want rid of me?"

"Hey, Mick." Yale looked far from worried as he returned Michael's handshake. "Sorry about this. But you understand, right? I can't have anybody thinking Big Frankie's operation is moving in here, you know?"

Michael didn't mind being thrown out of the casino. But I wished he'd stayed long enough to bring down whatever legal entity policed the gambling industry. I wanted nothing more than to see Yale Bailey out of a job, flopping on the sand as helplessly as a beached goldfish.

# Chapter 11

I called Lexie and ordered her to have dinner with me the following night.

She agreed, on the condition that Michael join us at her current favorite, a new Japanese restaurant near Rittenhouse Square, my old neighborhood.

I arrived late. The two of them were already at the table, talking about the stock market and drinking rice wine.

Lexie was saying, "Darling, I understand the need for liquidity, but really. Get out from behind the vegetable cart and into the stock market. And no mutual funds! You're much more the hands-on type."

They both got up to kiss me hello. Michael looked amused.

"Sweetie, you look absolutely fabu," Lexie cried. She was wearing at least four thousand dollars's worth of very simple Armani with a Wilma Flintstone–style necklace made of green stones that looked like kryptonite. Her gleaming black hair was pulled straight back from her flawless face in a cheerleader's ponytail. People from the sushi bar were craning to get a glimpse of her, probably because she looked as if she were worth tens of millions, which she was. "Fabu," she declared.

I smiled. "Are you comparing portfolios?"

"No, no, dearest. I'm just trying to woo your beau into giving me a peek at his assets. He could probably take us both to Paris with his pocket change, so I think it's high time he did something interesting with his dough."

"Paris," said Michael. "Now that's an idea."

"I'm sorry," I told him. "I used to go there with my husband."

"I'll keep thinking."

He excused himself. To go look for some pretzels, he said, but it was to leave me alone with my friend for a few minutes.

We sat down and Lexie grabbed my arm. "Sweetie, that man has made every woman in the room go positively gooey. Why don't you hibernate with him for the winter? See how the bad girls live, for once?"

"Because I'm trying to prevent Flan Cooper from going to jail. My second reason is keeping myself out, too."

"Darling," said Lexie, looking alarmed, "tell all."

I gave her the short version, asking halfway through, "Have you ever had any jewelry stolen while you were around Laura?"

"I lost a bracelet at a benefit once. My great-grandmother's pearl thingy with the double clasp. The whole Cooper clan was seated at my table, but I never thought for a second that one of them could have—" Lexie frowned. "Well, it's possible, I suppose. Good heavens."

I continued the story and finally got to my trip to Yale Bailey's lair. I slowed down and filled her in completely on what Yale had told me himself. But she couldn't let me finish.

"That devious little social-climbing shit!" she said, loud enough to turn heads.

"Well, that's a relief," I said. "I was afraid you'd gone insane."

"That—that—bastard!" she sputtered with anger.

"What does he think I am? I had drinks with him once and sat with him at—what presumption!"

"I didn't think you'd fall for him."

"Of course not! How many times has that rat been engaged in this town?"

"Lindsay Fiske last year."

"And Westie Cunningham before that! He's given trinkets to every heiress in town by now, all in a laughably obvious effort to marry himself a meal ticket!"

"It was no trinket he was getting ready for you."

"What?"

I told her about my visit to Sidney Gutnick's shop and the stupendous ring he'd been readying for Yale Bailey.

"Oh," she said, blinking. "Well, I do love a nice piece of jewelry."

"Which any fool could figure out, Lex, so it was part of his plan, I'm sure."

"But why me?" she demanded. "Isn't there some stupid young millionairess climbing out of a finishing-school window in search of a husband?"

"Why choose a young millionairess when you're richer than Madonna?"

"Because I'm just not his type, dear. He maneuvers a girl into bed first, and everybody knows I'm more interested in cash than copulation. There's a lot to be said for abstinence, you know."

"You are preaching to the choir."

"Oh, heavens, yes, sorry, darling."

"Lex, did Yale ever—?"

She read my mind. "He gave me the creeps, yes."

"He was physically rough," I guessed.

Lexie raised her elegant brows in acknowledgement. "I had a feeling he leaned that way. My radar, you know. My God, did he go after you?"

"No. Why should he? I'm poor and gun-shy."

"Gun-shy, indeed. With every reason, sweetie." Lexie lifted her glass to me and we clinked rims. Then she knocked back the last of her rice wine without a blink. "No wonder you stayed away from Yale. All you need is another man with bad habits. You were such a Sherpa for Todd, Nora. Tell me. Are you in over your head with this new beau, too? Are you in love with another dangerous man?"

One of the best things about having good girlfriends is cutting to the chase. I'd known Lexie half my life, and she'd been through it all with me. She moved in with me after Todd died and understood things I didn't share with my own sisters. I knew about the cousin who broke her collarbone when she was eleven and raped her when she was thirteen. We'd been known to discuss life and death over cartons of Cherry Garcia ice cream on dormitory fire escapes and the deck of her mother's yacht.

"He's not dangerous." I said. "Not the way Todd was, at least. In love with him?" I couldn't stop my smile. "It's a slippery slope, Lex."

"Does he make you cry?"

"Heavens, no."

"Well, then, he has my vote." Lexie pushed aside her glass to focus on me. "Sweetie, nobody's happier than I am to see you getting your sparkle back. I don't care if it is your beau or your job. After those horrible years with Todd, it's wonderful to see you laugh again. But have you gone to the other extreme? You protected Todd like a lioness. A misguided lioness, maybe, but you did it. Is that what your knight-in-tarnished-armor is doing for you now? Protecting you?"

"Maybe so," I admitted. "And it's a nice change, frankly."

"But is it an equal partnership? And I'm not talking about *The Kama Sutra*."

"It's not a partnership," I conceded. "Not yet."

She sighed. "Well, life can be a roller coaster or a train wreck. Just keep your seat belt fastened, okay?"

The waiter came with more rice wine, but it hasn't been very good so we waved him away politely.

"Lex, will you promise not to scream if I ask you something really corny?"

My friend smiled with affection. "Cross my heart, sweetie."

"What's your thinking on the whole baby issue?"

"Oh, God, are we talking about Libby now?"

"No, not Libby."

She stared at me. "Good grief. Your beau really has you in the spin cycle."

"It's not him that's got me thinking. Maybe I'm needy for some unconditional love right now. Or I'm looking to create a stable family for myself. That, along with the usual hormonal insanity. But I don't think that's all. I look at my life and wonder where everything went, Lex."

"Up Todd's nose."

I laughed again, unsteadily this time.

"Sweetie, if all you needed was unconditional love, you'd have six cocker spaniels. No, you Blackbirds have big families. It's part of who you are." She sat forward. "You told me after Todd's funeral that you needed to get yourself back on the right path. And for you, that path always included having a passel of kids."

"Emma says I can't get married again."

Lexie grinned. "You believe in that widow curse?"

"I can't ignore it," I said. "Can I? Then there's the whole issue of being broke."

Lexie waved off my poverty. "You can count on

me for extravagant baby gifts, darling. And who needs a husband in these days of growth stocks, not to mention turkey basters? Meantime, why don't you give me a few dollars and I'll try to make a nest egg for you?"

"First I have to fix the roof."

"Put a bucket under the leak," Lexie advised. "Now, here comes your beau. See how everybody watches? He's so yummy. Michael, darling, Nora tells me you know that snake Yale Bailey."

Michael slid into the chair opposite mine. He had found a bottle of wine at the bar and brought us clean glasses, too. "He's not a snake. Well, not a poisonous one."

"No? He seems to be slithering into our crowd. Oh, God, I sound like a snob, don't I? Well, he's been known to hit women, so that makes him a snake in my book."

Michael stopped opening the wine with the corkscrew attachment on his pocket knife. He looked at me. "And I left you alone with him?"

"Don't worry about Nora, dear. She can take care of herself." Lexie patted his hand. "How do you know our Mr. Bailey? From Princeton?"

Michael laughed and pulled the cork. "The closest I ever got to Princeton was scalping tickets outside a football stadium. We bumped into each other when he—well, when he got started in the gambling industry."

"Oh? How interesting." Lexie leaned forward on her elbow. "Can you tell me more? Or must you plead the fifth?"

Michael smiled at her and poured the wine into our glasses. "Don't start quoting mafia movies next, okay? It'll give me indigestion."

"Sorry, sweetie."

He put down the bottle and said, "Bailey's an accountant at heart. If he smacks women, that just confirms it. No guts."

I tasted Michael's wine selection. A crisp white, very dry. "Yale had something more than accounting going with Laura Cooper. When he broke it off, apparently to put the moves on Lexie, Laura turned up dead."

Michael eyed Lexie. "He put the moves on you?"

"I didn't notice," said Lexie. "What a nice little wine."

To Michael, I said, "You don't think he's a poisonous snake? You don't think he could have killed Laura?"

He shrugged. "If he hurts women, he's more into preliminaries. Killing her would have spoiled his fun."

Faintly, Lexie said, "Oh, goodness."

Unless he had a reason for wanting her dead, I thought.

But it was Flan who had the stronger motive. Killing his own wife to inherit her trust fund might ease his current financial problems. I immediately wondered whether Laura's entire inheritance would go to Flan or revert to her own family now that she was dead. It was customary for the current payout of a trust fund to go to the surviving spouse, but the rest of her share of the Hayfoot fortune might, also.

Was it possible Flan could profit from his wife's death? The idea made my head swim.

Michael reached across the table and put his hand on my arm. I became aware that he and Lexie were looking at me with concern. Shaken, I said, "Someone else must have had reason to kill her."

Michael sent a communicative look to Lexie.

"You think it was Flan?" She shook her head.

"He's a bumptious lug, but hardly the passionate type. Surely it takes passion to murder someone."

"Passion," Michael said, amused. He released my arm. "Okay."

"You disagree?"

"Most murderers I know aren't passionate," he said, making Lexie turn pale and me feel a twist of horror. How many murderers did he know, for heaven's sake? Unaware that what he'd said was anything unusual, he continued. "They're nuts. Or strung out. Or stupid."

*Or desperate,* I thought.

"It has to be someone else," I murmured.

"Why did she doll herself up like you?" Michael asked. "That's the part I don't get."

"I do." Lexie sipped her wine. "Laura wanted to be part of the inside crowd. In Philadelphia, that means Old Money, old family. You can't get bluer blood than Nora's. She wanted to be you, darling."

"But she stole stuff," Michael said. "That's pretty low-down."

"To have something from the people she wanted to be," I guessed. "Maybe she thought she could put on our things and become one of us."

Lexie agreed. "What it takes to be accepted isn't money anymore because everybody has gobs of it. And spending it is so easy. So Laura needed something else. A symbol. Crazy, maybe, but you have to understand what it's like to be in a closed, elite society."

Michael sat back and laughed outright.

Lexie had the good manners to blush. "Oh, dear. I've done it again, haven't I?"

"What about Doe?" I asked, my turbo-charged thoughts traveling through suspects.

"You mean Dull Cooper, the trophy wife? What a

bore she is. Can she get worked up about anything more exciting than centerpieces?"

I thought about all the details in Doe's day planner—still in my possession, I remembered with a twist of guilt—and wondered if Laura had truly jeopardized Doe's chances of becoming the premier hostess she wanted to be.

"What about Oliver Cooper?" Michael asked. "Isn't he the guy who stands to lose the most if Laura's stealing becomes public knowledge?"

"He may have already bribed people to keep quiet," I agreed.

Lexie nodded. "He thinks he doesn't have to play by the rules because he's got a fat checkbook."

"But he was covered by his security detail all night," I said. *Unless,* I thought, *Jack Priestly had lied about Oliver's alibi.*

Which got me to thinking about Jack, too. Was he so wrapped up in proving the president made the right choice for the cabinet post that he might have taken Laura for a real threat?

"My money's on Sidney Gutnick," Lexie said. "I bet Laura was going to expose the shady side of his business. He deserves to be horsewhipped for taking advantage of so many old ladies. Like your grandmother, Nora. She kept him in business for years."

I nodded. "Sidney values his reputation very highly. But could he have strangled Laura, held her underwater until she drowned, then thrown her body in a swimming pool?"

"He and Tempeste Juarez could have done it together."

Lexie and I looked at each other and blanched at the mental picture of two people ganging up to kill a young woman. Murder wasn't a parlor game, I reminded myself. It was brutal.

Michael opened the menu. "Anybody else hungry?"

Lexie recovered first because she could be ruthless when called for. "Yes. Let's order some food to go with this lovely wine and get Nora's mind off murder for a while."

Lexie distracted us after that by firing questions at me about the Big Sister/Little Sister outing I was organizing for Halloween. The trip details were nothing special, but she pretended to be fascinated. Michael's gaze rested on me often, and I could see he was worried. I tried to relax.

After dinner, we walked outside together.

"What's going on?" Lexie asked when we encountered a crowd on the sidewalk. Flashbulbs exploded in our eyes, and we could hear the rushing click of cameras. "Some movie star must be in town."

She looked around for someone famous.

"Oh, shit," said Michael.

With a shock, I realized the photographers were taking his picture. He gave me a little shove, but it was too late. Lexie and I had been photographed with the son of the notorious Big Frankie Abruzzo.

The first person to show me the newspaper photograph of myself and Lexie Paine alongside the future boss of the New Jersey underworld was my sister Libby.

"See? I knew it would come to this!" She flapped the paper in my face as she drove. "The picture even managed to catch him squinting. He looks terrible!"

"Don't say that," I told her. "I'll have to get your kneecaps whacked."

"Don't joke about this. I thought you broke things off with him. He's dragging you down, Nora. And isn't Lexie mortified?"

"I think she's pleased as punch. She'll probably get new clients out of this publicity."

Libby had picked me up on her way to her Lamaze session with the plan of dropping me at my weekly Israeli commando self-defense class. We'd have lunch afterwards. Her boys had come along and were poking each other in the backseat while they argued over who had the cooler costume, Spiderman or Batman. When we reached the Episcopal church, I threw the newspaper on the seat and bailed out of the minivan ahead of her. The twins, Harcourt and Hilton, hoisted their camera gear out of the van, still squabbling.

"Stop it, you two." Libby got out of the van with surprising speed, grabbed two large white pillows and waddled after me. "Hey, I learned something for you at my doctor's office yesterday."

"You went back to the doctor's office? Already? Is something wrong?"

"I had some Braxton-Hicks, that's all. Nothing out of the ordinary." She caught her breath and shoved her unruly hair out of her face with one hand. The other arm clamped the pillows. "But I learned a tidbit about Laura Cooper."

I pulled Libby away from the crowd walking around us—the self-defense class and the pregnant women with their pillow-carrying coaches. We went over to the steps of the church sanctuary. "What did you learn?"

She dropped one of her pillows on the top step. "Well, I can't be one hundred percent sure, of course, because doctors and nurses have all those confidentiality things going on, which seems pretty silly when the woman is dead, but—"

"What did you learn, Libby?"

She plopped down on the pillow and blew a sigh. "She was pregnant."

I took the other pillow from her. "Are you sure?"

Libby worked at getting comfortable. "Yes. Tara wouldn't say anything to me, of course, but while I was waiting, I heard her talking to the nurse in the next exam room. You know—while they changed the paper on the table. So when Tara made me some tea, I asked her. She danced around and claimed I must have misunderstood, but I kept pestering her. She finally admitted it. See? You're not the only detective in the family."

At last I noticed Libby was looking less than her perky pregnant self. Her face looked puffy and she was gray around the eyes. The beer keg that was her stomach seemed lower, if that were possible. "There's no need for you to start detecting, Lib. I think you have your hands full at the moment."

"Not to mention my bladder," she added, stretching out her legs uncomfortably.

"You okay?"

"Sure. Getting ready to pop, that's all." She massaged her belly as if it ached.

I tried to wedge the other pillow under her. "The doctor says you're all right?"

"Yes, of course. Gaining too much weight, but what else is new?"

I decided to make one last attempt to get her to see the light. "I'm worried about you, Libby. You need to take care of yourself. Maybe I should stay with you until the baby is born. Give you a hand around the house and with the kids."

"That's silly. Rawlins is being surprisingly useful these days. But . . . well, maybe you could come after the baby's born."

"It's a deal. Seriously, have you thought more about delivering at the hospital instead of the Jacuzzi?"

She sighed again. "I had to give up on the Jacuzzi idea. I'm so big, there's no room for any water. I'm going a different route now."

"A different route?"

"Yes." She brightened. "Did you know that some women actually have orgasms at the moment of delivery?"

"You're kidding, right?"

"No! I've been reading. A truly centered, peaceful childbirth can culminate in a very powerful sexual experience. I've been working with my sensual yoga tapes. I think it's quite possible. Would you be interested in going with me to one of those X-rated bookstores along the highway to look for—"

"No, Libby, I wouldn't."

She looked disappointed. "I didn't think so. Well, I'll manage without gadgets, I guess. Of course, the big drawback is my coaching."

"You haven't found a coach?"

"I have. Two, as a matter of fact." She became absorbed by the condition of her cuticles at that moment.

"Am I supposed to guess who they are?"

She slanted a quick look up at me. "You're going to disapprove."

"Since when has that mattered to you?" I softened. "Try me."

"Okay," she said. "RickandGabe."

"What?"

"The florists. They have a shop on—"

"I know who they are. They're very sweet men, but why—"

"Oh, I know they're not exactly Harrison Ford and Russell Crowe, but they're very interested in the whole process. They're thinking of finding a surrogate to have their child, you see. They're very open-minded about the whole sensual angle, too, and I think they're going to work out fine. I'm not terribly attracted to either one of them, of course, but maybe that's a good thing in the long run."

"I'm sure it is."

"But yesterday," she said, "I discovered hypno-birthing."

"Do I want to know what that is?"

"Hypnosis! I met this very interesting man at the grocery store who told me—"

"Libby," I said, "picking up weirdos at the grocery isn't what I meant by taking care of yourself."

"Oh, nonsense. Everybody is nice to pregnant women."

*Not everybody,* I thought, reminded of Laura Cooper's pregnancy. The question was, who fathered her child?

And who had known about her condition before she died?

# Chapter 12

I had a phone message waiting for me when I got home that afternoon.

"Nora," Stan Rosenstatz said, trying to sound jolly, which was instantly suspicious. Stan's voice usually sounded as if he were headed for the gallows. "How about stopping in the office as soon as you can?"

That didn't sound good. I phoned Reed, who came to pick me up in the Town Car. We arrived at the *Intelligencer* offices shortly after 6:00 P.M. I took the elevator up and met many of my colleagues as they departed after putting the finishing touches on the Sunday edition.

Stan was busy with another writer, but he spotted me when I entered the large room. He looked like a gawky stork—long, skinny legs holding up a lanky body that had subsisted for too many years on newsroom coffee and stale bagels. He had tufts of gray hair on a smooth, shining skull, and his hands toyed nervously with a yellow pencil. He finished his business with the other writer, then came over to me, tucking his pencil behind his ear. His brown sweater-vest had begun to unravel, I noticed.

And he couldn't meet my eye.

"Come into my office, Nora."

He even closed the door behind us.

"What's going on, Stan?"

"Sit down. Be comfortable." He hurried around his desk and sat on his squeaky swivel chair. Still, he couldn't look at me. He began shuffling papers. "I want you to know this has nothing to do with how I feel about you. You've been doing a great job for us, and I've been more than pleased with your work."

I felt the bottom drop out of my stomach.

"The general manager feels we need to make a change. I wish I could do something, but this has come from the top. We're going to put you on temporary leave, Nora. I'm sorry."

"Why?"

"It's complicated, but the paper's reputation is at stake."

"How?" I demanded.

"The publisher is unhappy that you—"

"Wait a minute. It's because my picture was in the paper, right? I'm being fired because somebody thinks I'm connected to the Abruzzo family?"

He let out an explosive breath. "The Abruzzo connection makes it worse, but it's really the whole Cooper thing. The Laura Cooper thing. The general manager felt we shouldn't be printing your byline if you're a murder suspect."

"I'm not a suspect!" I cried. "Stan, I had nothing to do with Laura's death."

"All right, maybe suspect is too strong a word. The guys in the newsroom have been chasing this for a couple of days. Some police sources are starting to think you're involved in Laura Cooper's death somehow. We're running more on the Cooper story tomorrow, and your name keeps—"

"Police sources?" Surely not Bloom, I thought. But who? The only other official I had spoken with was Jack Priestly, and I wasn't even sure what branch of law enforcement he represented. No, I thought. Not Jack, surely? Why would he want me to look guilty?

To get me off the case, of course.

Stan continued. "I talked the general manager into giving you half pay, but that's the best I can do until this mess is cleared up."

Half pay? I could barely survive on the full-time pittance I received every two weeks!

"Let me get this straight," I said. "You mean everyone here at the *Intelligencer* really thinks I'm a suspect in Laura's death? Have you consulted the legal department on this? You really think you can get away with firing me for an alleged involvement?"

Stan looked over my shoulder for an instant, then snapped his attention back to me. "Look, Nora, I'm really sorry, but my personal feelings aren't—"

"Kitty's part of this, isn't she?"

Stan looked ludicrously surprised. "Kitty?"

"Kitty's hoping I'm a viable suspect," I went on. "She's hoping I'll disappear, and she'll have the keys to the kingdom again, isn't she?"

Stan looked past me again, and this time I turned around. Standing outside Stan's office was Kitty herself, dolled up in a red evening dress that made her garish yellow hair even more startling. She had pushed an ostrich feather down through the hairdo, and a double twist of fat pearls clung to her throat. Obviously, she was on her way to a social function.

I don't remember getting up, but suddenly I was out in the newsroom. I snapped, "You are even lower than I first thought, Kitty. This is absolutely beyond reason."

She couldn't conceal her triumph. "So sorry to hear about your little trouble with the police, Sweet Knees."

"I have no trouble with the police, and you know it. You're trying to manufacture a story just to get me kicked out of here. And what you're doing to the Coopers! You're making their terrible situation even worse."

Kitty shrugged and turned away. Over her shoulder, she said, "I can't make it any worse than that idiot Doe already has."

"What have you got against poor Doe? Just that she can't throw a party to your specifications?"

Kitty spun around and her face hardened. "I tried to teach her how to play the game. Unfortunately, she's a slow learner."

"Just because she didn't pay you enough homage. What happened?" I demanded, reckless with anger. "She forgot to send you flowers after you mentioned her in a column? She didn't pay the right kickback?"

Kitty swelled up like a blowfish. "How dare you suggest—"

"It's your game, Kitty, with your rules. God help the person who tries her best and fails. Doe made a few inconsequential mistakes or made you feel unimportant, so you punish the whole family."

I thought she was going to argue further. But she controlled herself and said with smug pleasure, "That's the way the cookie crumbles, Sweet Knees."

Stan came up behind me. "I'm really, really sorry, Nora. My hands are tied. This will blow over, I'm sure—"

I stopped listening to him and went down to the street. It was a gusty day and I was hit by a blast of wind that nearly knocked me off my heels. I reached the parked car and climbed unsteadily into the front seat. I surprised Reed so much that he dropped the book he was reading. He snatched it up again before I could see the title.

"I'm sorry," I said, slamming the car door. "I don't want to sit in the backseat right now."

He hugged his book and looked astonished to find me sitting next to him instead of in the back. "What's the matter?"

"I just got fired. Well, not quite," I corrected. "But as close as you can get without standing in the unemployment line."

"Wow," he said, warily watching me for signs of hysteria.

"I'm not going to cry." Although I wasn't too sure about that. "I'm just stunned. I need a minute to pull my thoughts together." My hands were trembling, and I used them both to tightly grip my handbag.

Reed asked, "You want me to take you home?"

I shook my head. "No. I need to do something. I can't let this happen right now. Losing my job, I mean. I just . . ."

He waited, frozen, dreading the onslaught of blubbery sobs.

I hung on to my composure. "I need to figure out who murdered Laura Cooper."

"What's she got to do with your job?"

"Reed," I said, "let's go park on Jeweler's Row. I need time to think, and that's as good a place as any."

Reed put his book in the door pocket beside him and complied. In a few minutes we were sitting at a parking meter just four doors down from Sidney Gutnick's shop. Most of the store owners appeared to have closed their businesses for the day. One man came out of his store, locked the door, pulled down the iron gate and padlocked it, then grabbed the hat on his head and barreled down the sidewalk as if propelled by a hurricane. A ragged piece of newspaper tumbled after him on the darkening sidewalk.

"This okay?" Reed asked.

"Fine," I said.

My life was a mess.

I was just getting the hang of having a job for the first time, and now this. Was employment supposed to be this complicated? This difficult? Why couldn't I just do my work and collect a paycheck like everyone else?

Reed stayed very still, as if dreading an explosion of tears.

But I started to feel angry instead. I glared out the windshield. "See that shop up there on the second floor, Reed? With the lights on?"

"Yes."

"Let's just watch it for a little while," I suggested. "Maybe we'll see the owner."

"The man we brought here the other day?"

"The man who seems to have had a lot to do with Laura Cooper."

All roads led to Sidney Gutnick. That much seemed obvious. He had lied to me about his relationship with Tempeste. He probably received stolen goods from Laura. He sold bracelets to Yale Bailey. There was more to be learned from Sidney. I just needed to ask the right questions.

Reed suddenly said, "Is that a drag queen?"

Tempeste Juarez climbed out of a cab and charged down the sidewalk, swathed in scarves and carrying an umbrella that had blown inside out. In her other hand, she clutched one of Sidney's mint-green shopping bags. Big sunglasses concealed her face, even though it was after dark. She looked like Mata Hari on male hormones.

I sat up straight. "That's Tempeste Juarez! She told me she hadn't bought jewelry from Sidney in years."

"They look pretty chummy now," Reed observed.

Sidney, who'd declared his intense dislike for Tempeste, must have been waiting for her just inside the door. Short and round, his figure was unmistakable beside her rangy frame. He opened the door to allow Tempeste to slide inside, then glanced furtively up and down the street.

Reed and I instinctively scrunched down on the front seat of the car.

Satisfied he hadn't been observed, Sidney closed the door. They disappeared together, presumably upstairs.

"Now what?" Reed's voice was hushed.

I stared the Sidney's shop and wondered what a real detective would do. "I don't know."

"This is like a stakeout." For once, Reed sounded like a young man barely out of his teens.

I grinned at him. "It is, isn't it?"

"Should I turn off the car?"

"I think so. Otherwise, we'll look pretty obvious."

He shut off the ignition. A moment later, enthusiasm fading, he said, "I shoulda gone to the bathroom before this started."

"Oh," I said. "Do you have to?"

"Not yet."

Five minutes passed, and we didn't observe anything more exciting than a young woman walking a large pit bull. An occasional spit of rain landed on the windshield. Inside the car, I started to get cold. And I began to think about my bladder, too.

Finally I said, "Are you going to teach me to drive soon?"

"The boss says you faint all the time."

"I do not. Well, once in a while, maybe."

"He says you have to go six months without fainting; then I can teach you to drive."

"Why does he have a vote in this?"

"He's my boss," Reed said, as if that were enough.

I shifted uncomfortably in my seat. "Maybe I should phone Sidney. While Tempeste is there. Think that would accomplish anything?"

"It would scare 'em."

"Do you have a cell phone?"

He looked at me as if everyone on the planet had a cell phone but time travelers from the sixteenth century. Then he pulled out a tiny phone and handed it to me.

But just then a taxi pulled up in front of Sidney's store, tooted its horn and waited at the curb.

"Hang on," I said.

A minute later, Tempeste came out of Sidney's door and dashed for the cab. Reed and I scrunched down in the front seat again, but I felt safe since we were parked several cars away. Still, Tempeste looked in our direction just before sliding into the cab. Sidney closed the door and disappeared again. The cab whisked Tempeste away.

Reed sat up. "Should we follow?"

"No. I'm going up to Sidney's now myself."

"Wait!"

I had already put my hand on the door handle when a second car drew up in front of the store. It was a black Mercedes with a vanity plate that read OLLIE. He parked at a meter down the street, got out of the car and walked up the sidewalk to Sidney's door.

"Oliver Cooper," I said, staring at the familiar figure. "I don't believe it."

Oliver banged on Sidney's door, making no secret of his presence on the street. The girl with the pit bull came back, and the dog sniffed Oliver's legs as they went by. Oliver banged on the door again. Reed and I didn't budge.

At last Sidney appeared, looking flustered this time

as he opened his door to Oliver Cooper. They went inside.

"This is strange," I said aloud. "Why would Oliver come to see Sidney?"

To come to an agreement over Laura's dealings with Sidney? Or was he tailing Tempeste for some reason?

I said, "I'm going up there."

Reed croaked, "You can't do that!"

"Yes, I can. I'll be back soon."

"Wait!" Reed cried. "Mick will kill me!"

I popped open the car door and slipped out into the gusty night air. I set off for Sidney's shop entrance on cat feet.

I put my hand on the rain-slick door handle and hesitated, listening. Then I pulled the door open.

In the next second, somebody grabbed me from behind.

The man's hand came around my head and clamped over my mouth. His other arm snaked around my waist and pulled me backwards against his body in a grip that drove all the breath from my lungs. It wasn't Reed.

Instinctively, I bit his hand. I kicked back with one foot and connected with his shin. He yanked me off balance, but I braced my body against his and stomped my heel down into his shoe. It was instinctive, quick and as forceful as I could manage.

He swore but didn't let go. Then I jammed my elbow into his ribs.

"Dammit, Nora," Jack Priestly said in my ear, his Kentucky twang strangled with pain. "Stop that!"

I froze and tried to speak, but my mouth was immobilized by his hand.

He drew my body backwards into the shadow of a nearby doorway.

Then I realized someone else was in the street, walking fast towards us, head down against the wind, hands thrust into the pockets of a dark raincoat, shoulders hunched. From his short stature, I recognized the fast-moving figure instantly. Yale Bailey.

Jack and I flattened ourselves against the bars of an iron security gate. From that vantage point, we could both see Reed, who had gotten out of the car and was coming in our direction with a tire iron in one hand. Only seconds had passed since Jack had grabbed me, and Reed was on his way to my rescue. I put up both hands in a signal to stop, and thank heaven Reed obeyed, faltering to an uncertain halt just at the hood of the car. Jack loosened me and raised his hands over his head in silent surrender. I pointed towards Yale and signaled Reed to get back into the car.

He melted backwards, unwillingly.

In my ear, Jack said, "Hold still."

I obeyed, and we both watched Yale Bailey approach Sidney's shop door. The wind had made the night noisy, so he didn't hear us or see Reed ease along the side of the car. When Yale got close, I could see he was smoking a cigarette. He threw the smoldering butt into a puddle before reaching for Sidney's door.

He went inside, and the door closed behind him.

I took a step away from Jack and spun around to face him. "What are you doing here?"

He looked surprisingly messy. His hair was windblown, his coat wet with rain. He was out of breath, too. "I could ask you the same thing."

"Are you following Oliver? Of course you are. This whole street must be crawling with the Secret Service." I glanced up and down the block to see if I was right. "I guess they're more concerned about Oliver than a woman being attacked right under their noses."

"I didn't attack you," said Jack, cradling his right hand. "Where were you going, by the way?"

"To see Sidney Gutnick, of course."

"Why?"

"Why?" I sputtered, hoping I sounded genuine. "Last time I checked, this was a free country. What is Oliver doing here?"

"Buying jewelry, I presume. Maybe something for his wife." Jack peered at the palm of his hand. "You really bit me."

"You're lucky I didn't do worse," I retorted. "What makes you think you can go around grabbing people like that?"

"To keep you out of harm's way," Jack snapped.

"Harm's way? Why did you let Yale go up just now, if you're protecting Oliver?"

"I didn't know Bailey was going to be here." Jack shook his hand out. "Look, were you really going up to see Gutnick?"

"Why else would I be here?"

"Then go," Jack said, sounding urgent. "Go now, Nora. Yell if you get into trouble."

"You want me to—? Now what? You're going to pin something else on me?"

"You'd be helping," he said. "Go on. I trust you."

"It's not mutual. Good Lord," I said, suddenly understanding. "Oliver doesn't know you're here. You're in the dark as much as I am."

Jack said, "I don't know what you're up to, Nora, but I'm counting on you not to murder the next secretary of transportation. So run up there and—"

He didn't have time to give me further instructions. Beside us, Sidney's door burst open and Oliver Cooper charged out into the night air, looking frazzled and angry. Jack and I plastered ourselves out of sight again, but it wouldn't have mattered. Oliver was too upset to notice us. He spun around and grabbed something from his pocket. An instant later, he threw it onto the sidewalk and almost ran up the street towards his car.

Sidney Gutnick waddled outside. With a garbled cry, he flung himself onto the sidewalk and began to pick up what Oliver had thrown. Money. I could see the soggy bills as Sidney hugged them to his chest. He scrambled to his feet and rushed inside again.

I turned around to stare at Jack.

He was silent and frowning, clearly as puzzled as I was. "Look, Nora, I think it's best if you forget what you saw here tonight."

"You're covering Oliver's tracks."

Suddenly sure of his decision, Jack said with more conviction, "It will be in everyone's best interests if you drive away right now."

"What are you covering up? If it's Laura Cooper's murder, I can't believe you think you can get away with that."

A sharp noise spun us both around. Then glass breaking, another pop, an echo, and a whine that bounced around the buildings on either side of the short block.

"What in the world was—?"

"Oh, shit." Jack pushed me hard against the iron gate. "Stay here."

He took off at a sprint, heading for my car.

From several points around us, the street suddenly came to life with people. Like mice just released from a maze, they scurried out of dark corners. I caught my balance on the gate and looked past Jack's running figure at the car. Squarely in the center of the windshield was a hole.

A small, single hole in the windshield.

"Reed," I said.

I went after Jack at a dead run. "Oh, Reed, please, no."

I grabbed the passenger-side door handle and hauled it open.

Reed was sitting upright, very still. Tiny shards of glass were in his lap.

Then he moved, stiffly reaching with his right hand for his shoulder.

Jack was already in the car, pushing Reed to the middle of the front seat. He was saying, "It's okay, son. You're okay."

Reed said in a very young voice, "I'm hurt."

And he began to breathe in shallow, painful gasps.

"Get in," Jack said to me.

He slid behind the wheel and started the car. I climbed in beside Reed and somehow managed to end up on my knees with my arms around him. There was blood on his shirt already. Jack passed me a handkerchief. I took it and pressed it against the blood, holding it in place with the flat of my hand. Jack pulled out of the parking space. He rolled down the window and spoke to someone in the street as the car gained momentum. I wasn't listening. The man he spoke to got into the backseat while the car was moving. He told Jack to make a left at the corner. Reed's head lolled against my neck when the car made the turn.

"Hurry," I said to Jack.

Reed whispered, "I can't breathe."

It took forever, and I don't remember what I said, but I know I talked to him and held the wet handkerchief against his thin chest to hold in the life. When the car whirled under the lights of a hospital canopy, he passed out and I began to cry.

# Chapter 13

I didn't faint until after the doctors took Reed away and Jack said he had people to talk to. Then I went down like a sack of potatoes at the feet of a startled intern.

When I fought my way out of the dark again, I was flat on my back on a hospital exam table and could hear Michael's voice on the other side of a white curtain. He was telling someone to get out of his way or he'd tear their head off.

I sat up too fast, and as he came around the curtain he caught me before I fell off the table.

"I'm so sorry," I babbled. "So sorry. This is all my fault. Is he—is he—?"

"He's alive," Michael said.

I wrapped my arms around him. "Reed was going to teach me to drive. He said as s-soon as I stopped fainting, he'd teach me. And now—"

"He'll teach you," Michael said. "He'll be okay."

Poor Reed, paying a terrible price for my stupid behavior. He was a shy, steady, determined boy who deserved every good thing that came his way. I had his blood on more than my clothes.

Holding me, Michael said, "Do you know who did the shooting?"

His voice was low and full of purpose.

I sat back and hiccoughed. "No."

He touched my chin with his fingertips, a gentle caress that didn't match his tone. "Did you see anybody?"

I shook my head. Then I looked at his face and my pulse skipped. In his narrowed gaze was a cold light that frightened me. It snapped my brain back into functioning mode. "Michael, you can't do anything about this yourself."

"Who else is there?"

"No," I said. "This night is horrible enough already."

"Just give me some possibilities."

Jack arrived, looking cheerful as he brushed the white curtain aside. "Okay, it's all taken care of."

Michael turned on him, six-feet-four inches of towering rage. Suddenly he had a grip on Jack's shirt and jammed him against the wall so hard that something crashed to the floor. Jack's face turned red and a nurse cried out behind me.

I got up hastily and jammed myself between them. "Stop it, Michael!"

There we were, the three of us fused together while every other atom in the emergency room went motionless.

"Mick Abruzzo, I presume?" Jack said cordially.

Michael said something he shouldn't have, and Jack replied, "You're only making more trouble I'll have to clean up."

"You don't know how much trouble," Michael replied.

"Let's not have a fight," I said. "Please. Please, Michael."

Mocking, Jack said, "Please, Michael."

For an instant I thought Jack was going to be torn

into very small pieces and squished into the floor. But then Michael was overcome by a Zenlike stillness.

He released Jack so carefully that I knew he'd learned this lesson a very hard way.

Two large men from Michael's posse came around the curtain and stood like a pair of sumo wrestlers ready for battle. They trained their eyes on Jack and dared him to budge.

Curtly, Michael said to me, "I have to take care of something. You have to leave the hospital. Aldo will make sure you're safe tonight."

I glanced at one of the henchmen standing close by, then back at Michael. "Where are you going?"

"I have to see Reed's mother."

Of course he did. "Let me come, too."

He shook his head. "I made some promises to her. I need to talk to her alone."

When Michael left the hospital, I turned to Jack. "You've hushed this up, haven't you? A young man has been shot, and you've made sure everyone will keep quiet."

"It will be better for everyone this way," Jack soothed, touching my arm. "My more immediate concern is getting you out of harm's way, Nora."

I pulled away from his hand. "I'm perfectly safe."

"You were the target tonight." Jack looked me dead in the eye. "You know that, don't you?"

"Yes."

"So let me take you somewhere where we can watch you."

"You wanted me to go up to Sidney's shop tonight," I said. "You wanted me to make something happen. Well, this happened instead, Jack. My confidence in your judgement isn't very high right now."

# Chapter 14

My husband and I quarreled the evening of his death. I distinctly remember the moment I gave up, and he—relieved, and maybe even happy—went out the door to score his last cocaine. Hours later, when he was in the hospital, dying, I saw the whole argument flash in my mind and I wished that I had never stopped fighting him.

I wondered if Reed's mother felt the same way tonight. Blown apart by her inability to protect the one she loved.

When Aldo stopped the car, I had no idea where I was.

He said, "Boss told me to bring you here."

The river ran close by. I could see the silver water slipping swiftly past in the moonlight, going in the wrong direction. I realized we were on the New Jersey side of the Delaware. Wind hissed in the leafless trees overhead. A ramshackle house stood back from the water among the trees. I could make out the tall apex of darkened windows that overlooked the river the way a chalet might view a mountaintop.

"Where are we?"

Aldo jerked his head. "C'mon inside. You can call somebody, if you like."

His black hair was gelled into elaborate duck wings and a thick necklace nestled in his hairy chest.

A heavyset man, he hobbled with the gait of a peg-legged pirate.

"Are you okay?" I asked.

He limped ahead of me. "Yeah, sure. Just my knee didn't heal so good."

"Oh. Some kind of surgery?"

"No," he said. "Gambling problem."

He found a key that had been hidden under the wooden deck. With a series of grunts, he laboriously climbed the steps. I heard a lock click, and he shouldered the door open, leading the way inside and flipping on a light.

It was Michael's house. I knew it as soon as I edged inside. The first floor was all one room like a summer cottage. A huge fireplace commanded the rear wall with a kitchen to the right. I could see copper-bottomed pots hanging from a rack over a stainless-steel stove. Fishing gear and a daunting collection of boots were left by the door. Mismatched bachelor furniture was arranged in front of a large television. A heap of automotive magazines spilled onto the floor from a thrift shop coffee table that looked like it was also used as a footstool.

Not speaking, Aldo systematically searched the house and returned to the television, which he switched on with a remote. While the sound blared at us, he took a cigarette lighter from his pocket and went over to the fireplace. The room was cold, and he lit the firewood that had already been laid, complete with tinder. A flame danced up immediately.

Aldo flopped down on the sofa with a thankful groan and looked up, surprised to see me still standing just inside the door. "You want to phone somebody? Maybe get some clothes brought over? A toothbrush?"

"I can't stay here."

He shrugged and looked at the television. With the remote, he began to click slowly through the channels.

I said, "Really, I can't stay here."

His attention was already glued to the screen. "Phone's in the kitchen."

A Turkish prison guard might have more flexibility.

I went into the kitchen and found a portable telephone hidden under a pot holder shaped like a fish. First I dialed the hospital, using the card I'd been given by the patient liaison. I was told Reed's surgery was going well and was expected to be over in an hour. The update didn't make me feel any better.

Next I dialed Emma. When she answered, sounding lush and languid, I explained everything that had happened and my current predicament.

She woke up fast. "Wait, reload. You okay?"

"I've been better."

"Somebody really shot at you?"

"Reed got hurt instead. Em, I'm so afraid for him."

"Jesus," she said again. "And you're staying at Mick's?"

"Not for long."

"You want me to bring you some sexy underwear in the meantime?"

"Emma!"

"Look, the kid is going to be fine. You might get yourself killed if you go home. Mick's got the right idea. You'll be out of trouble at his place."

"I feel as if I'm in bigger trouble here," I muttered.

"Scared to spend a night with the love machine?" Emma laughed. "It's like riding a bike, Sis. I'll be over in a little while. How do I get there?"

I handed the phone to Aldo, who gave succinct directions to my sister.

After they hung up, I sat on the sofa and watched

the clock between glimpses of a television program called a "smackdown" that featured men who all seemed to look like Aldo, except with very small, patriotic costumes. I tried not to think about Aldo in a red-white-and-blue codpiece.

After about ten minutes, Aldo said, "You want to make us some food? Some pasta or something?"

"No," I told him.

He sighed. "Feminist, huh?"

Emma arrived half an hour later with a duffel bag of clothes that turned out to be hers, not mine.

"I can't fit into these things," I protested, pulling out the pants as we stood on the deck, out of Aldo's earshot.

"They'll fit," Emma promised, smirking. "Leather is very forgiving."

"I don't wear leather!"

"It's time you tried."

I yanked out something made of black satin. "And what's this? It laces up the back!"

"No, that's the front. You don't wear a bra, see?"

"I'm not going to dress like a hooker, Emma."

"So don't wear anything." She handed over a plastic shopping bag, too. "I stopped and bought you a new toothbrush and some shampoo and stuff. I figure Mick's not the herbal type. And a few condoms might come in useful until you can get on the pill. I needed a new box anyway."

Rummaging in the bag, my hand had already found several foil-wrapped condoms. I took one look at the neon packets and hastily shoved them back into the bottom of the duffel. "I can't believe you're my sister."

"So this is Mick's hideout, huh? Any suspicious characters around?"

"You have no idea."

"I gotta go," she said with a grin. "I've got a date."

I looked past her at a red monster pickup truck idling in the driveway. Its tires looked like they'd been inflated by a fairy-tale giant. I couldn't make out the figure sitting in the driver's seat, except for a very large cowboy hat. Tartly, I said, "What if that huge truck is his way of compensating for an anatomical limitation?"

"It isn't," Emma reported. "Oh, one more thing. I heard the coroner released Laura Cooper's body. The funeral's in South Carolina tomorrow evening."

"The Coopers are going?"

Emma nodded. "One of Chaz's kids takes riding lessons from a friend of mine and was complaining that the whole family has to fly down to Charleston tomorrow. G'night, Sis." She waggled her eyebrows. "Hope you get lucky."

I went into the downstairs bathroom to change. Taking off my clothes, I discovered Reed's blood had even soaked through my bra. I rinsed it out in the sink, tears streaming off my nose and into the soapy water. Then I opened the duffel and pulled out some of Emma's choices. I decided I would almost rather wear bloodstained clothing than put on Emma's idea of alluring attire. The pants fit, but only if I didn't inhale. The black satin top made me look like an intergalactic milkmaid. I had cleavage I'd never seen before.

Fortunately, Michael had left a flannel shirt on the back of the door, so I put that on instead and was relieved to discover it came down to my midthighs, thereby covering everything embarrassing.

By the time I changed, washed my face and put the rest of my clothes into the sink to soak, Michael had arrived. I heard him dismiss Aldo in an exchange of low voices. I came out of the bathroom just as Aldo went out the door and Michael shut the sound off on the television. He was holding his telephone.

He looked exhausted in the firelight.

"Have you talked to the hospital?" I asked from across the room, hardly able to control my voice.

He pulled himself together before he turned towards me. "Yes, just now. Reed's out of surgery, in recovery. It went well. They didn't have to remove any of his lung. Just patched him up."

I put my hands over my face and felt the relief well up fiercely inside me.

"Hey." Michael came over and pulled my hands down. "He's young. He'll be fine."

I couldn't speak, just shook my head.

Michael pulled me to him and held me tight. "I took his mother to the hospital. Even she's not as upset as you are."

"It wasn't her fault," I managed to say against his shoulder. "She didn't put him in harm's way."

"It was one of those things," Michael said. "Hell, I gave him the job. And his mother insisted he drive you around. She reads your column. She thought you'd be good for him. You're beating yourself up too much."

"How is she?"

"His mom? Stronger than anyone I know. It's okay, Nora. He's going to be okay."

Against his chest, I said, "Reed could have been killed. If I hadn't asked him to take me to Jeweler's Row . . ."

"What were you doing there?"

I told him I'd gone to Sidney's because the newspaper put me on leave.

"I should have let the police take care of this," I said fiercely.

He slid a strand of my hair behind my ear, and his touch lingered there. "One big difference between you and me is that you assume the justice system works."

I looked up at his face. "But—"

"We'll handle this," he promised.

"Oh, no." I pushed him away as if I could also physically reject what he was saying. "No, Michael. Something truly horrible is going to happen if you do anything. Please, I have terrible luck with men. I couldn't live if you—"

"Stop." He pulled me down onto the couch and put an arm around me. "Take it easy."

"I don't want you involved," I said. "Not you. Not anyone else. Let the police do their job."

He smiled a little. "I'm not a puppy on a leash, Nora."

I felt my eyes start to sting and closed them. Too many uncontrollable people. Too much chaos to bring into order. I blurted out, "I know. That's what scares me."

He slid his hand up the back of my neck. "Let's be glad everybody's alive. Can we do that? Reed's fine. Let's just go to bed and—what are you wearing exactly? Are those leather? Is this my shirt? Hell, you look great!"

"You've seen me in some of the most exquisite designs ever created on earth, and this is what turns you on?"

He smiled. "It's you that turns me on."

The adrenaline that had gotten me through the last few hours was suddenly making me tremble. Or maybe it was because I was alive with Michael and feeling too weak to resist what we both wanted.

I gave him a shaky smile. "You're too tired."

"Never."

"I'm too tired."

"I can make you feel a whole lot better." His touch turned seductive. Softer, he said, "I've been a good boy for you, Nora."

"Have you?"

Something in his expression changed. "Well, pretty good."

"What does that mean?"

"Well," he said again and stopped.

I saw the truth and tried to pull myself together. As lightly as I could manage, I asked, "You didn't spend the summer pining for me?"

"I was seeing somebody," he admitted.

"Somebody who? Is she the psychologist?"

He paused to organize his thoughts. "She's an old friend. We've been together off and on for years, but neither of us ever took it more seriously than an occasional release of—of sexual tension when we needed it."

"So you slept with her?"

"A hundred times." Quickly, he added, "Over the years, I mean. Not this summer, though. It's been convenient. When the two of us are between serious relationships, we just—" He shrugged. "She's someone I can talk to."

"What's your girlfriend's name?"

"She's not my girlfriend."

"Your lover, then."

"Oh, shit. Nora, please."

I laughed unsteadily. I touched his face. I almost told him it didn't matter, but it did. I almost said I wanted to make love right there in front of the television wrestlers and make him forget about all the other women he'd ever been with.

But I didn't.

Because my nephew Rawlins came knocking at the door.

"What the hell?" Michael said.

"Hey," Rawlins said, when the door was opened for him. He strolled into the house, baggy jeans nearly falling off his hips and several rolled-up papers under his arm. He looked surprised to see me there. "Hi, Aunt Nora."

"Hello, Rawlins."

He shoved the rolls of paper at Michael. "I brought these over. You said you wanted to see them. Looks nice and cozy in here. You guys having some dinner?"

I heard the wistful note in his voice. "Are you hungry?" I asked.

Rawlins grinned. "Starved. Mom's at home breathing heavy with two totally bogus guys who wear matching tassel loafers and bring us salads all the time."

Michael looked confused. "What guys?"

"Libby's Lamaze coaches," I supplied.

"They chant." Rawlins rolled his eyes.

"What are those? Blueprints?" I couldn't help noticing the way Michael eased the rolled-up plans out of Rawlins's possession. The guilty expression that flitted across Michael's face was as unmistakable as Rawlins's unspoken angling for a free meal.

Rawlins said, "Yeah, some kind of plan for a house. We got 'em out of the car."

"Out of what car?"

"That big Jag you were in the other day."

"Rawlins," said Michael, "why don't you go see what's in the fridge? I might have some cold pizza or something."

"Wait a minute," I said. "Flan's Jag?"

Michael put his hand on the boy's shoulder and spun him towards the kitchen. "Go."

"Hold it."

My voice stopped them. Rawlins looked instinctively guilty.

"It was an honest mistake," Michael said at last. "We needed to get into the trunk, but there was all this junk in there. We forgot to put these back in, that's all. I was going to ask you to return them. Really."

"What are they exactly?"

"I don't know. Blueprints, I guess."

I took one of the rolls from him. We spread the plans out on the kitchen counter. Rawlins raided the refrigerator while Michael and I looked at the unrolled blueprints.

"Big place," Michael said. "A hotel, maybe?"

I stared at the blueprints. "It's Oliver's house."

"Oliver Cooper's?"

I pointed to the bottom of the first page where the architect had printed *Cooper Residence* beneath the name and logo of the construction company that had built the home. "It's where the party was Friday night. Where Laura drowned."

Then I flipped to another page, and we both bent closer.

Michael whistled. "Wine cellar? Screening room?"

"These are Laura's copies of the blueprints. She must have designed all the extras for Oliver's house and left these prints in the trunk of her car."

"And these other ones must be left over from her other jobs?"

I glanced at the corners of some of the remaining pages. "Looks that way. We have to return them, Michael."

"To who? She's dead."

"To someone." I still had Doe's day planner, too.

"Maybe not yet," Michael said. "You never know what might come in handy."

"And," I added, hoping I sounded sincere, "I don't want to bother them at this difficult time."

Michael nodded. "Sure."

"I found the pizza," Rawlins called in triumph. "Hey, cool television!"

Michael and I watched him sprawl out on the sofa.

In unison, we sighed.

Rawlins ended up spending the night, parked contentedly in front of the television except for forays into Michael's refrigerator. By midnight, he'd even started in on cornflakes.

Michael took me upstairs to his bedroom and made sure I had a clean towel before he kissed me good night and went back downstairs. I could not get into his bed. I stood over it and wondered how recently he'd slept there with his longtime lover.

I didn't begrudge him a sex life. Frankly, I'd have been surprised if a man of Michael's age and constitution didn't have a lot of former partners. Still, it was disconcerting to look at that bed and imagine him there with somebody else.

I pulled the quilt off, curled up in an overstuffed chair under the window and wondered if I could possibly sleep.

I woke up in the same position seven hours later, so stiff I could hardly stand. I hobbled into the bathroom, which had a huge tub and a shower with jets. The hot water helped immeasurably. Afterwards, I put on Emma's pants and Michael's big shirt again.

Downstairs, Rawlins was asleep on the floor in front of the fireplace, tangled in a sleeping bag and snoring like a young lion that had eaten an entire hippopotamus by itself. Michael was making breakfast.

"How's Reed?" I asked, first thing.

"Awake and complaining about the liquid diet. They're talking about releasing him in a couple of days. I guess that's a good sign, but I want to see for myself." He leaned across the counter and kissed my mouth. "I'm going to run into town later."

"I want to go, too."

"Sure."

I went around the kitchen counter. Michael had pulled on his jeans, white socks and an obviously beloved, threadbare shirt, still unbuttoned so that the broad contour of his bare chest was visible. He took a saucepan of hot oatmeal off the stove and began portioning it into blue bowls with a wooden spoon and a practiced, wrist-flicking technique.

He said, "Your nephew ate everything but my oatmeal. Even the bananas."

"You must have eaten the same way when you were his age." I leaned my hip against the counter.

"At his age, I was in jail," Michael said, and my heart contracted. He added, "Food was not my primary concern."

He had not shaved yet, and yesterday's five o'clock shadow had become a rough second-day beard with tiny flecks of gray. Watching him cook made my insides ache. I thought that if he hadn't derailed his life as a teenager, he could be making breakfast for his own children by now.

"What *was* your primary concern?" I asked.

He returned the saucepan to the stove, pulled two spoons from a drawer and laid them beside the bowls. Then he snagged a plastic bear full of honey from a cupboard. He accidentally got some honey on his thumb and sucked it off without thinking. He didn't answer.

Maybe it was the plastic honey bear that did it.

Or maybe I couldn't stand being pushed away just when we'd started to get close.

So I backed Michael onto a sturdy kitchen stool and climbed into his lap. I wrapped my legs around his hips and locked my ankles behind him, bracing my knees against the kitchen counter for added balance. Then I put my arms around him until my braless breasts were snuggled against his chest.

"Hey," he said. "This is interesting."

I kissed him. His mouth tasted of warm honey, and he smelled like oatmeal and something less wholesome. I slid the soft shirt off his shoulders and let it slip to the floor. Then I smoothed the strong contour of his back and felt the heat of his skin beneath my palms. He said my name against my lips and slid his hands up under my shirt until he cupped my breasts. His kisses traveled down my throat and across my collarbone. His thumbs traced irresistible circles, and I felt all my blood vessels dilate.

The magic caught me by surprise. I was ready, I knew. Ready for the pleasures of waking up with someone, of making slow love in the golden morning light and laughing over breakfast while still languorous from the exertion. I wanted wet kisses and hot sex. A rekindled life. I was ready to take a chance on someone else, trust that he'd hold up his end of the contract, turn me on, make me happy and sometimes angry, but always alive.

Against his mouth, I said, "You spent the summer with the wrong girl."

I could feel his smile. "Whose fault is that?"

We kissed a little longer, his hands warming parts

of me that already felt molten. We didn't dare move for fear of falling off the stool, but managed to explore and tease until our breathing was ragged. I laced my fingers into his curly hair and tightened my thighs around him. With Rawlins so close by, we were very quiet except for the slam of our hearts.

Finally the kiss melted away. We bumped foreheads and looked into each other's eyes. His were luminous blue. Then I whispered, "Will you tell me sometime? About your family and your life?"

"Nora—"

"Because it isn't going to ruin things between us. I just want to know who I'm falling in love with."

He didn't breathe for a long moment.

I said, "Let's make a deal. I'll let you slay a dragon for me once in a while if you'll let me inside your armor. I want to know about your father and your jail time and everything else. Think you can talk to me? Let me be your friend as well as your lover?"

"It's for your own good that—"

"No," I said. "I want the whole package."

"Nora," he said patiently, "somebody's shooting at you. Doesn't that make you see how bad things can get?"

"Somebody shot at me because I'm getting close to the right answers."

"Getting close," he repeated. "You're not still—"

"I'm on the right track."

He eyed me. "You're going to continue playing detective?"

"You said yourself we can't count on the police. The FBI and the local cops are obviously fighting over territory, putting people at risk and missing the obvious."

"Which is?"

I tangled my fingers in his hair again. "Last night I saw Tempeste and Oliver and Yale all going into

Sidney's place for whatever reasons. That can't be a coincidence. They're all connected to Laura and to the stolen jewelry."

"But one of them saw you and realized you are figuring things out."

"Hence the gunfire."

"That doesn't scare you?"

"Of course it does. But I know in my heart that Flan is innocent. I just haven't gone after this with any kind of logic. We need a plan."

"I like the sound of 'we.' "

"I thought you might be able to help with a strategy."

His hand found a soft curve. "Can I take you upstairs first?"

With Rawlins in the house, we both knew the bedroom was out of bounds for us. "I think strategy comes first. But not on an empty stomach."

He grinned and kissed me once more before helping me off his lap. Once on my feet, I poured coffee into mismatched mugs. Michael passed me a steaming bowl and a spoon.

I climbed onto the other stool and pushed the plastic bear towards him. "I thought about Laura Cooper in the shower."

"Damn. Not me?" He took the bear and proceeded to squirt a thick layer of honey on top of his oatmeal.

"Well, after you. I think she sold the jewelry she stole to Sidney Gutnick."

"Gutnick is the pawnshop guy? The one who might have shot Reed?"

"He's at the top of the hit parade, yes."

Michael stirred the honey into his oatmeal. "Should I go see him?"

"He'd turn tail and run at the mere sight of you, and that wouldn't get us anywhere."

"So, what are you thinking?"

"Laura and Flan were in financial trouble. Oliver's known for being a cheapskate with his sons unless they devote their lives to the company, and Laura only worked part-time for a contractor. Maybe Laura gave the jewelry to Sidney to sell to raise some cash."

He licked his spoon. "How do you find out for sure?"

"While I was in the shower this morning—it's a lovely shower, by the way."

"This used to be a weekend house for some rich New Yorker."

"Lucky for you. Well, if Sidney doesn't have the jewelry, it has to be somewhere else. Being in the shower made me think about Laura. She was an expert at tubs and closets—all the extras people put into their luxury houses. And now that we have the blueprints for Oliver's house—where Laura was living—maybe I should look around a little. To see if there's any jewelry hidden somewhere."

"Haven't the police done that already?"

"Maybe they didn't know what to look for, or maybe they were looking in the wrong place. After studying these plans, I might have better luck."

Michael ate a spoonful of oatmeal and gazed at me. "You want to break in."

"Pay a visit," I corrected. "Flan asked for my help, after all. That's pretty much an open invitation, right?"

He gave me a wry smile. "Well, that's an interpretation a good lawyer could work with. When were you thinking of taking him up on his kind offer?"

"Laura's funeral is in South Carolina tonight. The whole family's going."

"Think they'll leave somebody behind to look after the old homestead?"

"Maybe, maybe not. We'd have to figure out a way to distract that person. And there's a security system to worry about, too."

Michael pulled the blueprints over and opened them again. He pinned down the corners with the salt and pepper shakers, his coffee cup and one elbow. Then he ate his breakfast while studying the drawings.

Oatmeal does wonders for cholesterol. And I discovered it was good comfort food for watching Michael plan a felony.

He finished his breakfast and rolled up the blueprints. "It'll take one person on the inside, one person outside. Wouldn't hurt to have a third."

"And the security system?"

He leaned over and kissed my forehead. "Piece of cake."

# Chapter 15

After breakfast, we went to see Reed. I met his mother, Rozalia Shakespeare, a daunting woman with a strong Christian faith and a booming voice prone to rising in praise of the Lord even in a hospital room.

She said to me, "I didn't want my son shot on a street corner, but it happened anyway, just in a better neighborhood. Don't you feel bad, Miss Blackbird. God moves in mysterious ways. We can't know what He has planned for us, but we must believe He knows what He's doing."

"You're very kind."

"I hear you need a dog," she said. "I think I can help you with that."

"Oh, I don't really—"

"No, no. A woman alone needs a dog."

Reed was embarrassed to be caught in the undignified position of his hospital bed, but his eyes widened when he saw me in Emma's leather pants.

"See?" I said to him. "I finally changed my clothes, just for you."

His throat was sore from the ventilator, but he managed to croak, "I like your other clothes just fine."

Which made me want to cry again, so I patted his arm and went out into the hall.

While Michael lingered in the room with Reed and his mother, I pulled myself together and went looking for a phone. I called Emma and told her machine not to plan anything for the evening.

Then Michael took me to The Home Depot, where he purchased a long list of innocent-looking items that seemed to have new, nefarious purposes.

I had never been inside The Home Depot before. I liked watching Michael banter with the sales guys, debating the virtues of nylon rope and steel clips. He rocked back on his heels to study an array of hardware that all looked the same to me, and the limber motion of his hips was mesmerizing. When he reached for a length of wire, his economy of motion made me think of a really good tennis swing. Or other physically skillful activities.

Okay, I should have slept with him long ago.

"That's it," he said, checking his list. "Do you have a ladder?"

My brain had taken a fantasy tour, and I couldn't comprehend what he meant. "We're going to need a ladder?"

He looked more closely at me. "You okay? Are you having second thoughts?"

"No."

We had lunch at a diner where everyone knew him and stared openly at me. I had a BLT and the best piece of lemon meringue pie I've ever tasted. Then he dropped me at Emma's place and said he had other things to take care of.

Emma and I debated the best wardrobe for breaking and entering. We settled on the black leather pants for both of us—she had pairs in various styles depending on her mood—and black turtleneck sweaters, no jewelry. She also had some cheap scarves, which we used to tie back our hair. Emma wondered if we should darken our faces just in case, but I voted against it.

At seven, Michael turned up again. He took one look at the two of us and burst out laughing. "What is this? Lucy and Ethel go to Harley-Davidson?"

"Admit it," Emma said. "We look good."

"I don't think I can handle two biker chicks at the same time."

"Want a drink for courage?" Emma was sipping from a tall glass.

"I think I'd better keep a clear head. Did you manage to borrow your friend's vehicle?"

Emma lived in a spare apartment over an antique shop in New Hope. She led us down the back stairs to the rear parking lot as the huge red pickup truck roared into view. Out stepped her rodeo boyfriend, a skinny, bandy-legged young man with a sweet smile and a glint of boyish mischief in his eye. He had a thatch of blond hair and wore tight jeans, pointy-toed boots and a perfectly ironed white shirt with the professional bull rider's logo stitched above the yoke. He took off his Stetson to me and shook Michael's hand, but he couldn't take his eyes off Emma, who didn't kiss him hello or mention his name. She jerked her thumb for him to follow her upstairs to her apartment, and he hurried after her like a little boy who'd been promised Popsicles on a hot day.

Michael looked after them and said, "That boy is in big trouble."

Emma returned, carrying a glass newly filled with ice and clear liquid. "Ready?"

"That was quick," I observed.

"He'll wait," she said. "I've given him a few things to think about until I get back." She dangled his keys in the air. "Meanwhile, we can go for a ride."

Michael was looking at the red pickup. "I guess you couldn't find a fire truck?"

"Is it too ostentatious?"

"Not for a Fourth of July parade."

"It's the best I could do on short notice."

"Maybe I should go look for something a little less showy," Michael said. "Something that doesn't glow in the dark."

I vetoed that. "I don't want us to be caught riding around in a stolen vehicle."

"Who said anything about stealing?"

"This will have to do," I decided. "Let's get it loaded up."

He checked his watch. "And hurry."

We loaded the supplies from Michael's car into the truck, debating whether or not to go to the farm for a ladder. We decided against it. Afterwards, I took a sip of Emma's drink to quench my thirst and realized it was vodka.

"Maybe you ought to drive," I said to Michael.

But Emma took the glass and climbed into the cab. "I know the way. Let's go."

It was dark by the time we got to the Cooper estate. We went by the driveway once, all three of us peering down the lane to see if we could catch a glimpse of the house through the trees. Unfortunately, all the autumn leaves hadn't fallen yet, so we couldn't see more than a tiny light winking at us in the distance.

"Park here?" Emma asked, slowing down.

"Maybe in the woods," I suggested.

"If I tear the muffler off this sucker, Nora, it's your bill." Emma aimed the pickup at a heavily foliaged bank.

I checked my watch again. "We wanted to get transportation from an owner with an alibi. Is he going to get suspicious if we don't come back right away?"

"It's okay. He can't get out of bed."

"I have a feeling," said Michael, bracing himself against the dashboard, "that we don't want to know why."

"Handcuffs," said Emma, focused on driving. "Hang on!"

The truck bumped over something big, bouncing us against the restraints of our seat belts. Emma changed gears and rammed the truck up the slope. We narrowly cut between two trees and thumped over a fallen log. The headlights stabbed into a huge pine, and Emma yanked the wheel to avoid slamming straight into it.

My little sister gunned the engine, threw the truck into yet another gear before charging through the woods at a breathtaking rate of speed. Pine branches swiped past the windows, the tires bounced over rocks, and something loud crunched beneath us. Emma kept her foot hard on the accelerator, and both hands fought the wheel as we roared deeper into the woods.

Finally she jammed on the brakes, and the truck rocked to a halt inches from a creek bed. The three of us looked over the hood at the rushing water a few feet below.

"Hold up," Michael said. "Let me check the territory."

He unfastened his seat belt, opened the passenger door and slid out.

"This is fun," Emma said.

I said, "Handcuffs, for crying out loud." But I was thinking about the vodka.

Michael returned. "Leave the truck here. The rest of the way we'll go on foot."

We got out and joined Michael under the trees in the cool night air. Clouds were scudding overhead, occasionally obscuring the moon, but I could see well enough to walk without risk of breaking a leg. I worried about Emma, though, who didn't need another injury. She looked perfectly sober, but I couldn't guess how much she'd had to drink.

Michael strapped a tool belt around his hips. "Ready?"

"This way," I said, hoping I could remember the lay of the land as I had observed it on the night of Oliver Cooper's party.

We hiked about half a mile through the tangled forest—following the flicker of lights ahead. Emma muttered about poison ivy. Michael leaped lightly over a small stream. I jumped after him and landed on dry ground, but Emma stumbled into the water. She climbed out cursing, but unharmed. We reached the perimeter of the landscaped property in less than fifteen minutes. When we hunkered down behind a fragrant pine tree, I reached for the bird-watching binoculars I wore around my neck. They had belonged to Grandmama Blackbird, who used them at the opera. I scanned the house.

"Stay down," Michael warned quietly. "Don't move more than necessary. The security system is still functioning."

"How are we going to fix that?" Emma whispered. "They've probably got lasers and a SWAT team that comes by helicopter."

"Don't worry."

"If you say so." She sounded doubtful.

We stayed quiet. The night was cool, very still, very October. Beside me, Michael and Emma squinted at the house for signs of human habitation.

I swept the property with the binoculars. I could

make out the shapes of topiary bushes and Doe's overdone flower beds. At last, I trained the lenses on the airstrip at the far end of the property. "I see a bunch of parked cars. All the planes are gone."

Emma asked, "They've all gone to the funeral in South Carolina?"

"That's what we're hoping." Michael eased up beside me. "Lights in the house?"

"Lots turned on, but that doesn't mean anything."

Emma asked, "Do they have dogs?"

"I didn't see any dogs when I was here before. And Doe's allergic to just about everything."

"Okay," said Michael. "Let's find out if there's anybody in the house. First we try the telephone. Did you get the number?"

We had discussed this earlier. I pulled a piece of paper from my pocket.

He dialed. From inside the house, we could hear a faint telephone ring.

"No answer," Michael reported after several moments.

"Try the staff phone," I said. "It's the second number."

He consulted the paper and dialed again. We didn't hear a corresponding sound from the house, but Michael sent me a look that meant it was ringing somewhere.

"I think we're okay." He terminated the call. "Now, about the security system."

The three of us crouched silently behind the tree, all eyes trained on the house before us. Michael had a gadget in his hand. The moonlight faded at that moment, and I couldn't see what he was holding. Emma and I leaned closer. Emma's knee landed on a fallen branch, and it snapped, sounding like a gunshot.

We froze. Silence.

Then a sharp noise sounded behind us.

We hit the ground at once. I tasted dirt and felt Michael's hand tense on my arm. On my other side, Emma didn't move.

More silence.

"What was that?" Emma whispered at last.

"I don't know." Michael risked a peek. "It's too dark to see anything."

"This is starting to feel scary."

"You?" Michael asked her. "Scared of something?"

"Let's crawl around to the other side of this tree," I whispered.

Emma went first, slithering on her stomach. Michael went next, silent as a ghost.

But I heard the noise behind me again and stayed where I was.

The snap sounded again. And again. Footsteps.

Coming from behind me. Going slowly, as if stalking prey. I tried not to breathe. Had we managed to trigger an alarm already?

Suddenly a light blazed in my face. I yelped as if I'd been hit.

A voice above me demanded, "What the hell are you doing here?"

# Chapter 16

Behind the light, I could make out an enormous figure.

A familiar figure.

"Libby!" I exclaimed. "Someday I'm going to murder you!"

"What are you guys doing?" she demanded, shining the light on Emma and Michael. "I followed you the whole way from New Hope! What's going on? How come you didn't tell me you were going on a picnic?"

Emma cursed. Michael rolled over onto his back and started to laugh.

I scrambled to my feet and grabbed the flashlight from Libby. "Dammit, you shouldn't be running around in the dark like this! You could have fallen!"

"I already did." Libby sat down heavily, breathing hard. "I had to park on the road, and I couldn't keep up with you. I thought you were coming only a short way, but—does anybody have a diet Coke? I'm really thirsty."

"Gee, that's one thing we forgot." I flicked off the light. "What was I thinking?"

"What's going on?" Libby asked. She put her hand on her gigantic belly, but the gesture looked as hopeless as a single finger holding back a deluge from the Hoover Dam. "Where are we, anyway? Whose house is that? Is this one of your parties? You're in a costume! It's very flattering, Nora. Are you two the Spice Girls? Why are you waiting out here in the dark? Maybe they have some diet Coke at the party."

"Libby, you shouldn't be here."

"Why not?"

"Because you're a pregnant woman, and this is the middle of the woods. How are we supposed to get you back to your car?"

"I can walk perfectly well." She was still having difficulty catching her breath. "Trouble is, I think I dropped my keys somewhere. I slipped, you see, and they—"

Michael said, "We're on a tight schedule here."

"I know," I said.

"What?" Libby asked. "Am I bothering you? I'm not invited, is that it?"

"No, Libby—"

"Well, I certainly don't mean to spoil anyone's fun." She began to get huffy. "I'm only here because I happened to pass you in traffic on my way back from PTA, and I thought I'd join you for a few minutes. I'm going to have a baby soon, you know, and after that, nobody in their right mind will come see me. I'll be in total seclusion for months."

"Libby, we're not here for a party."

"What, then?"

Emma said, "We're breaking into Oliver Cooper's house."

Michael sighed. "This is a mistake."

"You're what?" Libby looked prettily thunderstruck. "Why?"

Michael said, "The more people who know, the worse this will get."

"Well, she's already here," I said. "I can't make her disappear in a puff of smoke."

He eyed her belly. "I guess not."

Emma said, "Isn't there a magician who makes elephants disappear?"

Libby's brows snapped down. "Are you making a remark about my size?"

"David Copperfield or somebody like that."

"Oh, he's so handsome," Libby said. "Don't you think so, Nora?"

Michael lay back down on the ground and looked up at the sky.

"Libby," I said, "I really wish you hadn't come. But since you did, I'm going to ask you very nicely to please stay right here while we do something we shouldn't do."

"Why can't I come? I'm dying to see the inside of the Cooper house. I hear Doe did some hilariously bad decorating."

Michael said, "Time's up. I gotta do this now, or we're screwed."

"Go ahead," I said.

"What's he doing?"

"Deactivating the security system," Emma said.

Michael lifted a gadget in his hand. We leaned closer to see what it was. A small digital screen glowed eerily green. Then it began to beep quietly.

"What are you doing?" Emma whispered finally.

"Making a phone call," said Michael.

"It's a cell phone!" I said. "Good grief, we thought you had some master criminal technical device—"

"Shhh," said Michael. Then, into the phone, "Skeet? Yeah, it's me. Shut it off."

And he closed the phone.

"That's it?" I asked. "Your plan for deactivating the security system?"

"What's wrong with it? It works."

"What did you do?" Emma asked.

Michael shrugged. "Guy owed me a favor. He works at the security company, so I asked him to turn it off for an hour. This is our only chance, ladies. So let's get going."

"Okay. Libby, stay here."

"I don't want to be left alone."

"You just trekked through the woods by yourself!" I cried. "What's wrong with staying here for a few minutes?"

"I don't feel very well," she said, petulant.

"What's wrong?"

"Oh, for godsake," Emma said. "This will take all night! Just let her come along and she can sit on the patio while we go inside."

Michael and I looked at each other.

He shrugged. "You're the boss."

"All right. Let's go."

Staying behind a long line of Halloween cornstalks, we crept closer to the house and eventually hid behind a garden statue that was lit from below—the figure of a voluptuous woman wearing a fruit basket on her head and sporting breasts that the most ambitious Las Vegas plastic surgeon would have refused to implant. If not for the weight of her ample hips, the whole top-heavy statue would have fallen facedown in the mums.

Michael led the way out onto the lawn. He moved as swiftly and as silently as a desert commando, sticking to the dark edges of the landscaping. I followed, with Emma close behind. I assumed Libby brought up the rear, but I didn't wait for her. We skirted an elaborate planting of yew bushes and found ourselves in the middle of a large garden of spent perennial flowers. I heard Emma yelp, then she tripped in the flower bed and landed in a koi pond.

Instantly, she was standing in eighteen inches of

water and saying words that would send a pro-football coach to confession. I pulled her out, dragging a few water lilies, too. Her shoes squished as we plunged ahead.

Michael dodged around the swimming pool and reached the edge of the patio first. He dropped on one knee in a shadow, looking up at the house. Moments later, Emma and I reached his side and knelt. I glanced behind us to look for Libby.

She was a long way back, laboring across the lawn like a drunken sailor. She reached the perennial garden and waddled safely around the koi pond.

"So far, so good," Michael reported.

We scanned the house for signs of habitation.

Libby arrived at last. She panted like a locomotive and clutched the small of her back. "Why didn't you wait for me?"

"Sorry," I said. "We're going to leave you here, Lib. Stay with Michael."

"Me?" he said. "Why me?"

"Because you aren't going inside."

"But—"

"If Emma and I get caught, we'll get into trouble, but we won't go to jail."

Emma added, "We'll take it from here, big boy. You can baby-sit."

"Hold on," Michael objected.

"I don't feel very well," Libby reported.

"You're just tired," I said. "Sit down and catch your breath."

"No, really. I don't feel well at all."

I looked at my sister. Despite the cool evening air, she was perspiring. Her face had a pasty shine, and a pinched frown knotted her brows.

"Libby," I said, "don't you dare."

She sank down on the ground. "I can't help it."

"What's wrong?" Michael asked.

"I thought I'd be fine," Libby went on, "but I'm starting to get little tweaks."

"Little tweaks," I repeated. "Are you saying what I think you're saying?"

"Oh, God," said Emma.

"What's she saying?" Michael's voice rose.

The three of us stared at my sister Libby as she lay down on the lawn, put both hands on her belly and let out a definite groan.

"No," Michael said. "Definitely no, no, no."

"We can't call an ambulance," Emma said. "We'll get caught."

"No, no, no, no, no."

"We have to get her to the truck."

"She'll never make it."

"And we only have an hour to get in and out of the house."

"We'll have to do this another time," I said.

"There is no other time," Michael said. "My guy at the security company will be history after tonight. This is it."

"Then I'll have to think of something else."

"Ooh," said Libby.

"We've gotten this far," Emma said. "We could split up."

"Oooooooh."

"Cut that out," Michael said, looking positively unnerved.

"I need a focal point!" Libby cried.

"Jesus," said Emma, "I'm breaking and entering with the Three Stooges."

Libby drew a cleansing breath and blew it out again.

"Well?" I asked as the three of us stared at her. "What's the verdict?"

"I think it's just a random contraction," she reported. "Nothing to worry about. I'll just lie here for a minute. Maybe Mr. Abruzzo would kindly check his watch."

"What for?" he asked.

"To time the contractions," I told him.

Michael looked skyward and began to beg for heavenly intervention.

# Chapter 17

Between Libby's contractions, we made hasty preparations. First we rang the doorbell and ran away like junior-high trick-or-treaters to make sure the house was empty. Then we systematically tried all the doors to see if one might have been left unlocked. No luck.

Michael broke out his various tools and sent me to look for an outdoor electrical outlet. "Plug this in." He handed me the end of a long orange extension cord.

I found a plug and unraveled the cord to Michael. He pulled out a soldering iron the size of an electric toothbrush and inserted it into the cord. While we waited for the iron to heat up, we looked at Libby. Another contraction began, and she started to breathe in short bursts.

Michael checked his watch. "Four minutes."

"Libby," I said, "how long were you in labor with Lucy?"

"Oh, not long at all, really," she panted. "It was the easiest delivery of all. Only an hour or so."

"Hurry up," Emma advised us. "The nearest hospital is twenty minutes away."

Michael tested the tip of the iron and looked at me. "You know what to do?"

I nodded. "I think so."

"And you memorized the layout of the house?"

"I was inside before, too. I can do this."

"All right," he said reluctantly. "I'd wish you luck, but I think I'm going to need it more."

Libby tried to get upright on her own, but couldn't manage. Emma grabbed her under one arm, and Michael took the other. Together, they hauled her to a standing position. But Libby immediately doubled over as if she'd been punched.

Emma said, "You'll need a forklift to carry her."

Michael said, "Good idea. Got one?"

"You'll have to go, too, Emma," I said. "Maybe the two of you can manage. Besides, you're too wet to go with me. You'll track pond water through the house."

They both knew I was right, but there ensued a short argument against leaving me on my own. Libby terminated the discussion when she let out a strangled yell.

"That does it," said Emma. "We're outta here."

Michael unbuckled his tool belt and dropped it at my feet. Then he handed me a stick of gum from his pocket and kissed the top of my head. "I can't believe I'm leaving you."

"Take care of Libby."

"We'll do our best. Be careful."

I watched them lug Libby across the dark lawn in the direction from which we'd come. I could hear my sisters squabbling as they went.

I tried to gather my wits. I was on my own, and time was running short. My hands shook as I unwrapped the gum and popped it into my dry mouth.

Dragging the extension cord behind me, I took the soldering iron to the French doors by the patio. From inside, lamplight illuminated the colors in the stained-glass design. The picture depicted birds and airplanes flying against a blue sky background.

Offering up apologies to the artist, I set to work.

I tested the metal stripping that separated the pieces of colored glass with my fingernail. Yes, it was lead. I chose the largest glass panel near the door handle. Carefully, I applied the hot tip of the soldering iron to the lead and watched a tiny curl of smoke float up. My pulse steadied as the lead began to soften. With an emery board, I peeled it away from the glass in small strips. In a few minutes the glass panel wobbled, so I took the gum out of my mouth and gently stuck it to the upper edge of the glass. A few more seconds with the iron, and the final bits of lead could be pried off.

The glass teetered for a second as the gum shifted, but I dropped the iron and used both hands to delicately lift the glass away from the rest of the window. I set it on the patio and let out an uneven sigh.

Cautiously, I tried to fit my hand in through the space left by the missing piece of glass. It wouldn't go. From my other pocket, I pulled Emma's contribution to the night's bag of tricks. A tube of lubricating gel manufactured by a company called Knights of Love. I squirted a lightly scented blob onto my hand, smeared it around and tried again to squeeze my hand through the hole in the window.

Success. I angled my wrist and felt around for the door lock. My lubricated fingers slipped on the mechanism, and for an instant I thought I was stuck there with my hand inside the house. Then my thumb caught the small lever just right, and the lock clicked. I struggled with the door handle for an instant, then popped the door open smoothly.

I managed to get my hand threaded out through

the hole again; then I paused to listen. No alarm. No sounds.

There wasn't time to repair the window properly. But I pulled a strip of lead we'd purchased that afternoon and prayed I could patch it up enough so my break-in wouldn't be too immediately obvious. I picked up the piece of glass I'd removed and stuck it back in place. I balanced it with my right hand and used my left to solder the new lead strip in place. I burned my fingers twice.

It was a hasty job, I decided when I finished and stood back blowing on my smarting fingertips, but it might not be noticed for a while.

I gathered up the mess I'd made and stashed it in the mulch around the patio bushes. I stowed Michael's tool belt under the same bushes and wound up the electrical cord, too. I didn't look at my watch. I knew too much time had passed.

At last, I slipped into the house.

Absolute quiet. I slipped through the corridor, avoided the powder room where Flan had tried to kiss me, and went past the dining-room doorway and into the enormous great room. The house felt cold. Even my quiet footsteps echoed up into the Gothic rafters overhead.

I knew what I had to find: at least one piece of jewelry that could tie Laura's stealing with the person who killed her. If I could trap one suspect in a lie, the whole story would come together, I was sure.

I ran up the stairs and found Laura's room with no trouble.

But the door was locked.

And no Michael to show me how to open it.

Frustrated, I took a walk down the hallway. I remembered from the blueprints that Laura's room had been one of a suite, joined by a shared bathroom. I took a chance and found the other bedroom door just down the hall. Unlocked. I slipped inside, past an elaborately pillowed bed. The nightstand boasted a water carafe with a crystal drinking glass upside down on top of it.

I went around the bed to a pair of doors. The first turned out to be a large closet. The second opened into a small breakfast kitchen—just a mini fridge, sink, coffeepot and microwave for the guest who didn't want to join the family at breakfast downstairs. Through the kitchen lay a short hallway and then the bathroom.

The bathroom door was ajar. A skylight provided just enough moonlight to see a marble Jacuzzi and a long counter with double sinks. A pair of heavy-framed mirrors reflected the moonlight. I crossed the tile floor and tried the opposite door.

Miracle of miracles. It opened.

I eased inside Laura's bedroom.

For a long moment, I stood in the doorway and thought about a young woman. She'd come from a respected family in an old Southern city, but she hadn't been able to break the glass ceiling of Philadelphia's social hierarchy. She'd gone about it all wrong. She'd wanted the acceptance of the Old Money crowd, but she hadn't been willing to spend the years doing good works, delivering Meals-on-Wheels or cultivating young musicians or electing good government. It wasn't enough to marry into a loaded family, and Laura hadn't a clue how to make herself part of a bigger picture.

Perhaps Laura Cooper was the first person whose cause of death was social climbing.

I went to the windows and pulled down the shades one by one. Then I snapped on a small lamp. On the dresser stood the large, cheap vase of dying roses. From Yale Bailey, I knew. They smelled like compost.

The police had been in the room; that was obvious. Laura's neat stacks of boxes and belongings had been ransacked by someone who didn't care how her things were left.

Where to start?

I flipped rapidly through her drawers, sure the police would have found obvious clues and removed them. I uncovered clothing—lots of it with expensive labels. Unframed photographs had been jammed under her collection of sleeveless sweaters. I paged through them and saw Laura and Flan in formal dress. The last, faded photo showed a man wearing tennis dress and holding a large trophy. A country-club sign stood behind him. I flipped the photo over. *Daddy* was written in neat script.

I put the photos back in the drawer.

More ideas began to zip around in my head. Like fruit on a slot machine, they kept reappearing and disappearing, not making any sensible pattern.

On the desk were stacks of glossy catalogs picturing enormous bathtubs, wine racks and even gun vaults. The false trappings of wealth nowadays.

On the nightstand, under a copy of a book that extolled eight ways to influence powerful people, and one that coached women on dressing for corporate acceptance. I found *Southern Names for Southern Babies*. I flipped through some of the pages and discovered she had highlighted names already.

So she had known she was pregnant.

Who was the father? The man she'd married but didn't trust? Or the animal she'd sought out for a brutal affair? Looking at the book in my hands, I knew Laura intended to keep the baby. She had been planning a name and a life for her child.

What a desperate woman she had been, I thought. Desperate to fit in, to dress herself so she could become somebody she thought mattered to others. But here had been her answer. A child would have made everything else insignificant.

Flan was still on this earth, I reminded myself. It was Flan who needed my help now.

I sat on the edge of her bed. There was no jewelry in the room, I noted. Not Laura's or anyone else's. The fact that she didn't keep even so much as a wristwatch in the bedroom struck me as odd.

Time was running out, I knew. I checked my own watch. The security system would be functioning again in twenty minutes. Galvanized, I left Laura's bedroom and retraced my steps.

Across the hall was another bedroom. A cursory search told me it was the room where Flan was staying. His distinctive aftershave stood on the bathroom counter; his clothes hung in the closet. No signs of Laura here.

Somewhere down the hall was an entrance to the safe room. The latest in luxury items, a safe room was a place where the paranoid modern homeowner could hide if a home invasion occurred. While psychotic burglars ransacked the rest of the house, the plan-ahead master of his domain could relax in comfort. I went down the hall past bedroom after bedroom and more sumptuous bathrooms. I opened a walk-in linen closet filled with lavender-scented sheets all tied in pairs with satin ribbons. Plush towels were arranged by color. Cotton and wool blankets sat in shrink-wrap. At the back of the closet hung a selection of linen tablecloths on oversized wooden trouser hangers, evenly spaced. Control-freak Doe had clipped a note to each tablecloth, listing the date when it was used and for which event.

*Schrager dinner party,* said the rose-colored one.

I pushed the tablecloths gingerly aside and found the safe-room door. The handle was recessed, and I pushed it. The door swung open like a vault, and a light automatically went on.

I stepped over the threshold, but kept one hand on the heavy door to prevent it from closing. The safe room was little more than a glorified bathroom equipped with television monitors, a toilet and sink, a case of bottled water and an unopened box of energy bars. No jewelry.

But sitting on top of the case of water stood a teacup with a dried brownish residue in the bottom of the cup. I sniffed cautiously. A faint fragrance of mint.

I closed the door and retraced my steps down the hallway.

I went back into the guest suite and made a beeline for the breakfast kitchen. I flipped on the overhead light and looked around.

No mint tea in the cupboard.

In the mini fridge, soft drinks and a jar of low-sugar strawberry preserves. In the freezer, frozen English muffins, a package of designer coffee and ice trays.

I closed the fridge.

Then opened it again. I took one of the ice trays out of the freezer.

My heart began to pound. I went to the sink and began to run hot water over the ice-cube tray. The cubes began to melt, and at once I knew I'd found what I'd come for. Rings in one tray, bracelets crammed in another. The third tray had two necklaces in it, frozen in the ice.

I recognized the ring Tempeste had described to me—a huge diamond encircled by a golden snake.

And Lexie Paine's pearl bracelet with the double clasp.

I didn't recognize the other pieces, but from the weight and quality of the stones, I knew they were all expensive, valuable jewels that had been taken from some of the prominent people in my social circle. Old Money heirlooms. Only the very best. The cheap stuff, Laura hadn't bothered to keep.

In my mind, the slot-machine clues started to make sense. I began to understand what had happened.

To a soft, humming sound, I piled the jewels back into the ice trays.

Too late, I realized the hum that reverberated around me was not the quiet motor of the refrigerator.

It was an airplane, coming in for a landing.

I shoved the ice trays back into the freezer and slammed it shut. I hit the light switch on my way out and ran for the staircase. I reached the first floor in time to see the flashing lights on the wings and belly of the incoming plane. It cruised smoothly past one window and I heard it touch down just a hundred yards from the house.

I couldn't leave the way I'd come. The arriving family would use that door to enter their home. And no doubt the first people through the door would be Jack Priestly and the Secret Service detail.

I ran for the back of the house, the kitchen wing.

I skidded to a stop on the tile floor of the kitchen. The security system had come on. I could see a red light beaming from the keypad by the kitchen door.

Trapped.

# Chapter 18

I waited two agonizing minutes. Adrenaline zinged in my veins, clearing my head, making me hyper-alert. I waited until I heard the patio doors open farther down the hallway, and the red light on the security keypad flickered. Then I shoved out through the kitchen door and took off into the darkness as if chased by a rabid dog.

I ran headlong into the kitchen garden and took a flying leap over a privet hedge before tearing out into the only part of the lawn the outdoor lighting didn't illuminate. I slid on the damp grass and cut left in search of shrubbery to hide behind.

At last I reached a landscaped island of trees and juniper bushes. I slowed and looked over my shoulder, barely breathing hard.

The lights of the house came on one by one as the Secret Service went through the building. I was on the opposite side of the house from the patio and landing strip, but I imagined Oliver or members of his family waiting there for an okay to enter. I could see figures through the windows, men checking all the rooms. In the kitchen, one man lingered, but I couldn't see what he was doing. I decided not to wait to find out.

I edged around the lawn, keeping myself hidden behind the trees.

I found myself in the perennial garden at last. I eased past the flowers, heading for the womanly shaped fountain.

Then I realized I had mistaken a human figure in the grass for the statue.

Doe Cooper turned to me and blinked. "What are you doing here?"

She had been taking a walk through her garden while she waited for the all-clear from the house. Dressed in a black suit and pearls and carrying a simple Kate Spade bag, Doe squinted in the darkness at me. "Nora?"

I stepped into the light so she could see my face. "Hello, Doe."

"What's happened?"

I took a deep breath. "I think you'll have to tell me."

She didn't pretend to misunderstand.

I said, "You were the one, Doe."

She mustered some belated indignation. "I don't know what you're talking about."

"You drowned Laura in your koi pond, didn't you? And then you put her body in the swimming pool, hoping nobody would find her until spring."

She transferred her handbag from one hand to the crook of her elbow and put one foot slightly forward as if posing for a photograph.

"I didn't understand why until I saw your linen closet. And the strawberry jam in the guest refrigerator. And this garden. There's nothing more important to you than impressing your guests."

"So? You, of all people, must understand the importance of good entertaining."

I shook my head. "You were afraid of her, weren't you?"

"Afraid of Laura? Don't be silly."

"You wanted to become a respected hostess in the city. But Laura's reputation for stealing things—that was starting to keep people away, wasn't it?"

Her face hardened.

"Even if you went to Washington, Laura would have followed you, wouldn't she? There's no way you could ever start over . . . unless you got rid of her."

Doe raised her chin. "What are you going to do?"

I shook my head. "The question is, what are you going to do?"

For the first time, she looked startled. "You're not going to turn me in?"

"I don't think I'll need to. Think about it, Doe. Think about Oliver."

"But . . ."

"The publicity is going to be brutal for him. He'll probably lose the job in Washington," I said slowly. "If you turn yourself in, though—if you take the blame yourself, you might spare him the worst."

"But . . ." she said again.

"You'll get a good lawyer," I suggested. "You'll be able to share Oliver's life eventually. But you've got to take the heat now."

She considered me thoughtfully. Across the dying flowers, we regarded each other for a long time.

"I can't do that," she said at last. "I'm going to Washington. I'm going to have a lovely home and give beautiful parties."

"I don't see that happening, Doe."

"You're the only one who knows, right?" She began to tremble with the effort of controlling herself. "If I can just make you be quiet, this could all go away."

"Doe—"

"What about money? We have enough money to take care of you, Nora. We'll pay you."

"Hasn't Oliver already paid people to be quiet? Sidney Gutnick, for example?" I stepped back from her. "You can't do it, Doe. There are too many people who know things. Eventually, somebody else is going to figure it all out."

"But not you," Doe said, coming towards me. "It's not going to be you. I drowned her, yes. I grabbed her and wrapped the twine around her neck to drag her to the pond, and I held her head under until she was dead. Then I hid her in the pool. I didn't have time to replace the pool cover. The Red Barons started to come back and I had to hurry. Tonight, I can be faster."

I'd thought because she was beautifully dressed and wearing high heels in the garden, she wouldn't try to overpower me. But I had misjudged her determination, and in a second Doe pushed me into a flower bed. I stumbled in the loose mulch, and she made a grab for my arm.

She was strong. All those days of digging in the garden and keeping fit for her husband had given her muscle I didn't expect. She twisted my arm and sent me down on my knees in the mulch.

"She was pregnant, Doe," I gasped. "Did you know that? She was going to have a baby."

"Shut up," she said. "I know that. She told me, the stupid slut. She said it would make her husband happy and save their marriage."

Telling Doe had been Laura's worst mistake. For Doe, a Cooper grandchild was just one more reason why she'd be stuck with Laura forever.

Doe hit me over the head with her Kate Spade bag.

I saw stars, but the blow wasn't enough to stun

me. She clubbed me again with the bag, then threw it away and latched on to my throat with both hands.

I gasped and tried to speak. But she gripped me so hard that it took all my strength to draw in oxygen. I felt her stubby nails dig into my skin. Her face was close to mine, her eyes narrowed to slits and her mouth drawn back in a feral grimace. She forced me backwards. Suddenly I slid down into the pond.

Knee deep in water, I seized her wrist and tried to pry her off me. No use. I flailed out at her clothing then, black stars dancing before my eyes. Blindly, I grabbed for her pearl necklace. It snapped, and the pearls went splashing into the water around me.

I couldn't see. I knew I was blacking out.

I yanked the scarf from my own hair and gathered all my strength to say one word to her.

"Polyester!"

Doe's grip lessened for a split second. My vision cleared enough to see her expression—fear and revulsion. I shoved the cheap scarf into her face, aiming for her eyes.

Doe cried out and staggered backwards. I clambered out of the pond and went after her, brandishing my only weapon.

"Get it away from me!" she cried. "Get that horrible thing away!"

She caught her heel as she fell, twisting as she landed on one knee. I whipped the scarf around her neck.

Doe began to scream with hysteria. Her breath was already wheezing, her eyes wide with panic. Any moment hives were going to break out on her face. I didn't need to keep her long. In seconds, Jack Priestly appeared in the moonlight, followed by the Secret Service.

"What the hell is going on?" Jack demanded. I could see him make all the right connections and reach the worst conclusion. Murder and politics didn't mix. His face loosened, and he said, "Damn."

# Chapter 19

Two hours later, Flan was standing in the spotlighted driveway next to Detective Bloom's police car. He'd been weeping, and he looked stunned. But he didn't look drunk.

I hugged him. "I'm so sorry it turned out this way, Flan."

He hugged me harder. "I know. Me, too. But it wasn't going to be any good, no matter what, Nora. Thank you. I know you did this for me."

"You're my friend," I told him, standing back and holding his hand.

He wagged his head. "I've been a pretty lousy friend. Not to mention a lousy husband. In fact, I'm basically a—"

"Don't," I said, mustering a smile. "You've always had potential, Flan. You've got a second chance now."

"Do I? I feel like my life is over."

I thought of Todd, of course. No matter what, my husband was always going to be present for me. I said, "You're alive. You need some time. Be with your family for a while. We'll get together in a few weeks. We'll have lunch or something, and you can tell me about CanDo Airlines. I'd like to help with that, if I have anything to offer."

"I should be the one offering to help you, Nora. If you ever need anything, you'll come to me, right?"

He could make a call to the *Intelligencer* and get my job back for me, but I figured now that Laura Cooper's murderer was caught, I'd be working again in a few days. I smiled. "Thank you, Flan."

He kissed my cheek and held the car door open for me.

I hitched a ride to the hospital with Detective Bloom.

"I hope you're happy," I said as we sped through the dawn. "Looks like the FBI wants to get out of Dodge as fast as possible. Thanks to me, you'll get credit for solving another high-profile murder."

For once, I saw Detective Bloom smile. "Thanks to you," he agreed. "Is Cooper going to be okay? If I'm any judge, I'd have him on suicide watch for a while."

"He'll be okay. We'll take care of him—his brothers and his friends. What do you think will happen to Oliver and Doe?"

"She'll go to jail. But if he really didn't know she killed Laura, maybe he'll just get a slap on the wrist for bribing people to keep quiet about their lost jewelry."

"And Sidney?"

"By seven o'clock, he'll be Philly Vice's main man."

"He was fencing stolen goods?"

"And selling it through Tempeste Juarez. She was stopped at the airport trying to blow the country, and she's squawking to the Feds about Gutnick. I guess she's hoping to save herself by turning against him."

So Laura had indeed kept the most prestigious

people's jewelry for herself. I said, "Tempeste and Sidney must have made a switch at the Cooper party. Sidney waited in the safe room for Tempeste to come upstairs and get the stuff. I saw her on the stairs with a bag from his shop."

"Does she carry an old derringer? Ballistics said the bullet that hit your driver came from an old two-bullet pistol."

"She had a little gun at the hotel. I don't know what kind it was, but I would recognize a picture," I said. "She must have seen me outside Sidney's shop and thought I figured out her arrangement with Sidney. She came back to scare me away. That's when she shot Reed. And what about Yale? What was he doing at Sidney's?"

"I don't know yet. What's your guess?"

I considered the question. "Something to do with the ring he'd planned to give to my friend Lexie. Or a bracelet he was supposed to give Laura. He just ended up there at the wrong moment. Oliver must have panicked when Yale walked in."

"What was Cooper doing at Gutnick's place?"

"Paying off Sidney, I suppose. Trying to prevent any more information about Laura from spoiling his chances in Washington. But you'll have a hard time getting anyone to tell you that. Speaking of secrets, you didn't tell me that Laura Cooper was pregnant. That information must have been in the autopsy report."

I had startled him. "How did you know that?"

"I know. Did Flan?"

"Not yet. We'll tell him when the DNA results come in."

I wondered how Flan would respond to that information. I was pretty sure Flan was the father of Laura's child, particularly because Doe had been so convinced Laura would be the millstone around her neck forever.

"How do you think he'll react?" Bloom asked.

I couldn't guess. But at that moment, I realized the father hadn't mattered to Laura. She had given up on Flan, and no woman in the universe could have considered Yale Bailey a suitable parent for anything but a monster. Laura had been choosing a name and planning for a new baby no matter who had fathered her child.

Slowly, I said, "The father wasn't part of Laura's equation."

She had wanted the baby.

"You all right?" Bloom asked.

"Yes."

Bloom pulled into the circular drive in front of the hospital. He stopped at the curb, put the car in park and turned to me. "You're a good deputy, Nora."

"Thank you."

He pulled a handkerchief from his pocket and unwrapped it to reveal my grandmother's sapphire ring. "You can have this back now."

"Thank you." I slipped the ring on my finger.

"You didn't really do it to get the ring back, though, did you?"

"No," I said. "Have you ever been in love, Detective?"

"Me?"

"Yes, you. Did you have a girlfriend in high school? Someone who made your heart go pitter-patter?"

"Josie Epstein."

I nodded. "Flan was my Josie Epstein. He might look like a buffoon to you, but I know what he's like on the inside. And I knew he wasn't a killer."

"Can I give you some advice?" he asked, after he'd

shoved his handkerchief back into his pocket and sat looking at me.

I pretended to admire the flash of the ring safely back on my hand. I had no intention of helping him through this.

"You did a good thing tonight, but your methods are way off base and your motivation is questionable. Women always fall for bad boys. And most bad boys aren't worth the trouble. I'm not just talking about Cooper. I have a feeling I know what kind of help you had." Turning even more grave, he said, "Sooner or later, associating with certain people will get you into trouble."

I gave him a smile. "I know what I'm doing, Detective."

"I'm not telling you this as a police officer," he said.

I raised my eyebrows. "As a friend, then?"

He summoned some of his Boy Scout mettle. "Now that you're finished with your investigation, I wonder—maybe you have some spare time? Like for a cup of coffee or something?"

I leaned over and gave him a kiss on the cheek. Then I got out of the car. I bent down in time to see him try to wipe the surprise off his face. "See you around, Detective Bloom."

I let the plate-glass door of the hospital swing shut behind me. The information desk wasn't open yet, and the lobby was deserted. I checked the overhead signs and headed for the elevators.

Maternity was on the second floor. I found a nurse at a desk doing paperwork. She smiled when I told her what I was looking for and gave me the short version, which was that I could wait a few minutes while Libby was settled in her room, or I could take a walk down to the nursery to see my new nephew.

Standing in front of the window were Rawlins and Emma.

Rawlins looked up at me with a big grin. "Hey, Aunt Nora. We're waiting to see the kid."

Emma had one arm draped around Rawlins's shoulders. In her other hand, she had a fistful of cigars. "Hey, Sis. You don't look half bad. I guess everything went well?"

"Better than expected," I reported. "And you?"

"Same here. You might want to talk to Mick, though."

"Is he okay?"

"Not scarred for life, but definitely rethinking any connection to our family."

"Where is he now?"

She pointed straight up. "His dad's upstairs. Why don't you take a walk? The baby won't be ready for a few more minutes."

I took Emma's directions and went to the third floor. Up there, the professional staff was already bustling around. I passed a busy nurses' station, but bypassed the waiting room that appeared to be full of snoozing relatives. Down the hall, sitting in two plastic chairs and playing cards, were a uniformed police officer and Aldo.

Aldo saw me and didn't say anything. Just pointed to the next room.

I peeked in the narrow window of the door. I could see a big man in the bed, sound asleep. At the window, looking out at the rising sun, stood Michael. He had his hands thrust in the back pockets of his jeans, and he looked like he'd been hit by a bus.

I hesitated, then eased inside the room.

He twisted around, and his face turned ten years younger. "You're okay."

I slipped into his embrace. "I'm more than okay."

"Your life of crime ended successfully?"

I kept my voice very soft and looked up at him. "Very well, thank you. And your mission?"

His grin broadened. "We had good results, too."

"Did you deliver a baby?"

"At the last minute we decided to let the professionals take over. Then those two Lamaze coaches showed up, and everything got too crazy for me. I stuck around long enough to hear the good news, then came up here."

We smiled at each other, then heard a distinct snore from the bed.

"Want to introduce me?" I asked, turning to look at the man in the bed. "Or shall we wait until he's awake?"

"This is the best way to meet him," Michael replied. "Trust me."

Michael's father had the same strong Italian features as his son—blunt nose, a full lower lip that looked forbidding in repose, and dark, eloquent brows. Michael had lazy eyelids, but I couldn't see if his father's were the same. Even punctured with IV needles, his arms looked powerful and his chest was deep.

"How's he doing?" I whispered.

"He's going to live," Michael said with a twinge of wry humor. "So I don't need to worry about inheriting anything right away."

"Right away?" I asked.

Michael reached out one hand and lightly smoothed his father's hair. "Yeah. I tried to talk him out of it, but he wasn't in a listening mood. I'll try again another time."

"So, you're speaking?"

Michael let his hand drop, and he shrugged. "He has this fantasy. He wants me to find him a 'sixty-nine Mustang, and we'll drive it cross-country to Venice Beach to look at girls in bikinis. I told him it would likely be the boys in bikinis now, but he thought I was joking."

I slid my arm around his waist. "Want to take a walk with me, instead?"

His smile reappeared. "Where to?"

"To see the newest Blackbird."

Quietly, we let ourselves out of the room and ambled down the hall, past Aldo and his card-playing partner.

When we were alone in the elevator, Michael said, "How about if I sell that old house to some people who want to start a school?"

"What kind of school?"

"I don't know. A charter school."

"Nothing weird? Something sensible and respectable?"

He nodded. "I'll ask."

Emma and Rawlins were making fools of themselves in front of a large window. On the other side of the glass, the youngest member of my family waved a small fist and scrunched up his face in a silent howl. Already, he had a beef with his relatives.

Rawlins handed Michael a cigar. Emma already had hers clamped in her teeth. She hadn't lit up yet, but I knew it wouldn't be long. She took Rawlins by the elbow. "C'mon, kid," she said to him, sending me a knowing glance. "Let's go see your mom."

With Michael behind me, I looked down at my newborn nephew. Lightly, Michael rested his chin on top of my head and put his arms around me.

"Isn't he darling?" I asked, hugging his arms.

"Damn cute," Michael agreed.

I gathered my courage and said, "I've been thinking."

"About?"

"Getting on with my life. Starting over," I said, hesitantly. Then, with more conviction, "I want to start a family. I want to have a baby."

"Hmm," Michael said. "Need some help with that?"

**Turn the page for an excerpt from**
**The next Blackbird Sisters Mystery**
**Coming from Signet in Spring 2004**

After my sister Libby gave birth to her fifth child, she decided to become a goddess.

"It's not hard," she advised me when I went into her bedroom to shake her awake one cold November morning. "You ought to try it, Nora."

"I'm too busy taking care of your family," I said, passing her the squirming body of her newly born son. "When you finish transforming yourself, could you make some peanut butter sandwiches for the kids?"

"I can't," she said, taking the child. "I've given up peanut butter as a sacrifice to Placida."

"Who?"

"My goddess within." Libby began unlacing the ties on one of her exquisite embroidered nightgowns in preparation of feeding her son his breakfast. "Placida is the deity of tranquility, sexual adventure and weight loss."

I sighed. "Libby, you had a baby just five weeks ago. And you can't expect to lose weight without getting out of bed once in a while. Giving up peanut butter is a good start, but if you quit watching all those episodes of *Trading Spaces* and get some exercise—"

"You don't understand the goddess process, Nora." Libby plumped the lacy pillows around her voluptuous figure and sat back with a beatific smile as the baby clamped onto her breast like a starving Yorkshire piglet. "You must open yourself to the possibilities so the goddess may flow from within you. It's a mental path to all kinds of fulfillment. Just last night I had an erotic dream about Dr. Phil."

I looked at my demented sister as she nursed her perfect baby with her beautiful skin glowing and her hair in a vixenish sort of tangle and her body all soft and glamorously flaunted as if ready to be ravaged at Versailles by a Bourbon king. After childbirth, women weren't supposed to look as if they'd been airbrushed by Playboy's most gifted photographer, but here was Libby looking divine while I felt as if I'd been beaten with a shovel.

I said, "If I strangled you with your own nursing bra right now, it would be justifiable homicide."

"I'm re-centering my life!" she cried. "Don't rush me! I must gather my cosmic resources, prioritize my most primal joys and learn to validate my sacred inner magic so I can evolve into the goddess of my mysterious potential. Such a powerful psychological makeover takes time."

"Well, the kitchen floor needs a makeover, too. How about using a mop while I'm out?"

She sat up and widened her eyes in pretty dismay. "Where are you going? Good heavens, you're not having clandestine morning sex with That Man, are you?"

I wouldn't dream of leaving Libby's five children alone in her custody for more than the few hours for any reason whatsoever, although clandestine sex might tempt me. Sixteen-year-old Rawlins had taken to suspiciously disappearing late at night with a group of friends who collectively had enough body piercings to start a surgical supply store. The thirteen-year-old twins, Harcourt and Hilton, were closeted in the basement making a Santa Claus movie that involved bloodcurdling screams every three minutes, and five-year-old Lucy had invented an imaginary friend who graffitied the living room walls with grape jelly when I wasn't vigilant. The baby, who still had not been bestowed with a name by his goddess mother after five weeks, couldn't bear to be anywhere but my arms except when he was trying to deplete his mother's milk supply.

To top everything off, Libby was lactating with more volume than a dairy cow so that one of my jobs was now bottling and freezing the overflow to contribute to a breast milk bank at a Philadelphia foster child agency. Which meant that there were even more children who depended on me while Libby lolled in postpartum splendor, dreaming of talk show hosts and cockamamie deities.

I had no time for anything, including clandestine sex.

"That Man," I said, "is fishing in Scotland."

She settled back against her pillows and muttered, "Yeah, sure."

I turned in the doorway. "What's that supposed to mean?"

Libby smoothed the fair hair on her baby's head. "Honestly, Nora, if you believe your mob boss boyfriend has gone fishing, I'm marching straight out to find a bridge to sell you."

"Oh, not that again."

"Do I need flipcharts to explain it? Michael Abruzzo is a dangerous man mixed up in so many shady businesses—"

"Name one."

"That new chain of gas stations," Libby said promptly. "Gas 'N' Grub? They're popping up all over the place."

"What's wrong with selling gasoline and sandwiches, besides the indigestion?"

"They're cash businesses, Nora. Even you must know what that means."

"He's making a living?" I said tartly, bringing up a sore subject since my parents blew the last of the Blackbird fortune and sailed off to a tax evader's paradise where they spend most of their time rehearsing for the weekly mambo contest.

"He's money laundering," Libby replied, covering her baby's ears lest he learn about high crime at such a tender age.

"Oh, for crying out loud—"

"The papers say he's under investigation."

"He's always under investigation. Because of his family, not himself."

"Well, this is a new one, and he's the star of the show. I heard it on the news last night. It's probably why he's fled the country."

"He hasn't fled! He's taking a vacation."

"Think about it, Nora. If you had ill-gotten gains, you'd want a place to pass the dirty money to an unsuspecting public in small batches. That's why he started Gas 'N' Grub. *Vanity Fair* had a big article about money laundering. Pizza shops, now, those are a gold mine for criminals."

"Michael is not a criminal."

Which I believed most of the time.

"He looks like a criminal," Libby declared. "A sexy criminal, I'll admit, with okay, a sort of fallen angel magnetism that some women find attractive, but—"

"I'm leaving now," I said before she could go into her riff about consorting with the devil. Somehow I wouldn't mind so much if I actually enjoyed a little consorting, but lately I'd been stuck refereeing her children. "I'll be back in two hours."

"Where are you going?"

"I told you. I'm covering the hunt breakfast for the newspaper. And Emma's riding, remember?"

Neither of us had quite gotten the hang of my employment yet. I'd spent my adult life being married to a doctor and devoting my time to good works and the Junior League, so I didn't have a respectable resume for job hunting when the family fortunes evaporated on tropical breezes. But an old family friend who owned a Philadelphia newspaper had found me a position as an assistant to the society columnist. The job required me to attend parties and report on clothes, guest lists and the details of so-called "high society" entertaining. It was work for which I was singularly suited, having been brought up in a tax bracket where the oxygen was very thin and party planning was an art form. I wasn't going to earn a Pulitzer any time soon, but the job helped me pay down the heart-stopping tax debt on Blackbird Farm.

This morning's assignment was the hunt breakfast at an exclusive fox hunting club just off the Main Line. And I needed to be there before sunrise.

Libby eyed me. "Are you going to talk to Emma?"

"I'm going to try."

"Maybe I should come along."

"I think I can address Emma's situation in a calm and rational manner on my own."

"Are you implying that childbirth has rendered me incapable of rationality?" Libby asked. "I'll have you know there are actually studies that prove motherhood makes you smarter. So you have something to look forward to."

My sister Libby has plans to make everyone's lives perfect. She decided that I only needed a few children of my own to reach a state of serenity, and she rarely missed an opportunity to remind me of the maternal rewards that lay just over my horizon.

"After five weeks in the household from hell," I said, "I'm having second thoughts about having a family of my own."

Libby appeared not to hear me. "I think I'll go along with you this morning."

"You're kidding, right?"

"We should present a united front. Yes, I'll definitely come. I have an invitation around here somewhere." She disconnected her son from his food source and began to burp him while she imagined the party. "It might be a nice re-entry into the world for me, too. All those handsome men on horseback!" The look in her eye reminded me of a pyromaniac lighting a match.

"Don't start, Libby."

"Don't start what?"

"Chasing unsuspecting men as if they were helpless rabbits doomed for the stewpot. You're in a hormonal fever right now. You're a danger to society. I'm not taking you with me. Besides, my car will be here in five minutes, and you'll never be ready."

"I'll follow you later," she said. "Run along."

"What about the baby?" The idea of Libby descending on an early morning party made me fear for the safety of my fellow guests. "And the rest of the kids?"

She waved me off. "I'll think of something. I want to see you in action. You're always stumbling into excitement, and Placida thrives on exciting things. See you there!"

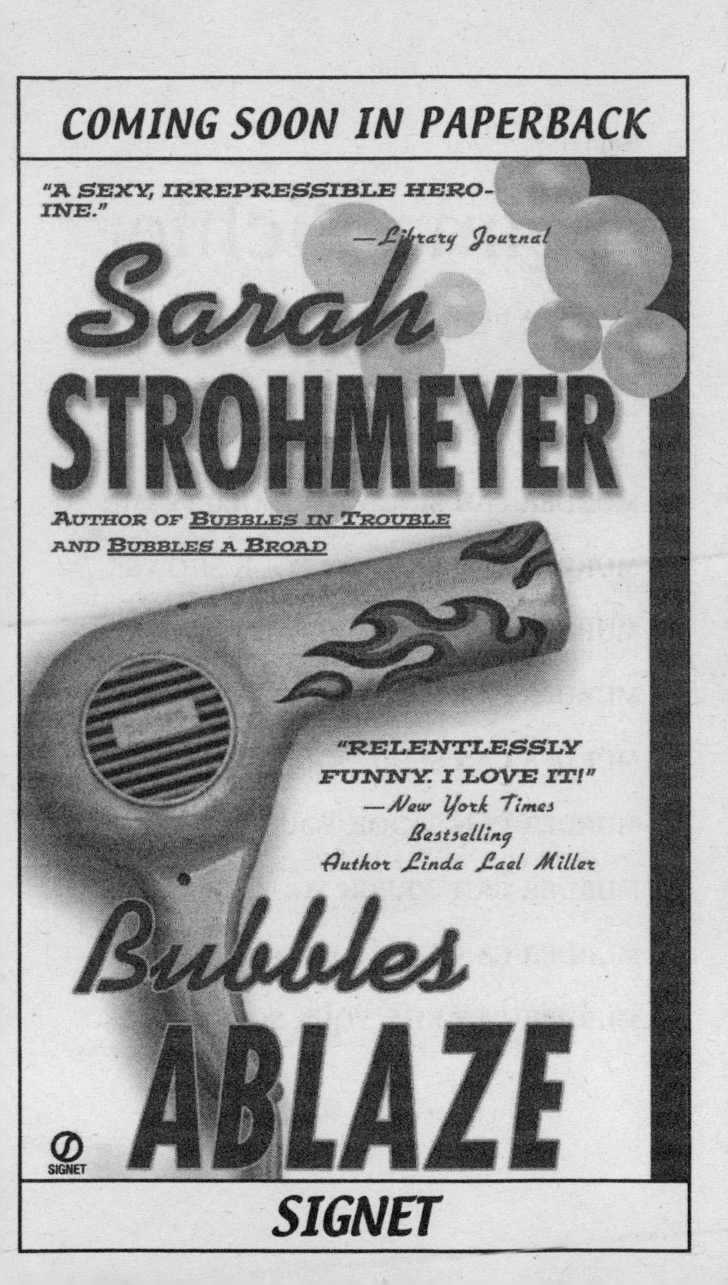
COMING SOON IN PAPERBACK
"A SEXY, IRREPRESSIBLE HEROINE."
—Library Journal
Sarah
STROHMEYER
AUTHOR OF BUBBLES IN TROUBLE
AND BUBBLES A BROAD
"RELENTLESSLY FUNNY. I LOVE IT!"
—New York Times Bestselling Author Linda Lael Miller
Bubbles
ABLAZE
SIGNET
SIGNET